The Player's Rebel

Copyright

Published by: Carxander Publishing
Minnesota

Opening Quote

A ripple in the calm, you keep me safe from harm. Somehow you still believe, you believe in me. Where it starts and ends, only time must know. Wherever you will be is where I wanna go. Every day, the sun comes up again. A little hope begins, and it starts with you 'cause you get me through it. And every day, I'm closer to the shore, I smile a little more. And because of your faith, I get closer now every day. 'Cause you set me free.

Everyday by Britney Spears

Chapter One

🍂 Harleigh 🍂

I let out an irritated sigh and close my eyes to the pounding headache forming just behind my socket. I feel like I have been in this too small room for days. Months. Years. I am not getting anywhere with the security officers surrounding me. Considering they allegedly work for a very smart man, they all seem superbly stupid. I'm only twenty and am seemingly a genius compared to these assholes.

"I already answered all of your questions," I say between gritted teeth.

"Well, Ms. Harlow. Your explanation doesn't make sense. You appeared on our cameras. Disappeared. Appeared again. How?" the older guy with the attitude problem says to me.

I shrug with just as much of an attitude. "Don't know. Maybe you need better cameras. Not like I was trying to hide. I was trying to get help. As I already said."

He crosses his arms over his chest. "Right. The running from the killer and all. Why didn't you stop at the guard who is stationed at the parking lot entrance?"

"I already told you," I growl with what I hope is a vicious glare. "Because they were right behind me, and your guard was the only one there. I was protecting him from getting shot."

"A modern day superhero," he scoffs.

My chest becomes even more tight. Anger or fear, though, I don't have a clue. I'm becoming exhausted. I already feel like I'm crashing. I slam my hands down on the table. "Look. You obviously can't help me. If you could, you'd have done it. The only good thing you've done is get me into the building where I'm safe from being kidnapped and likely murdered. I know this building belongs to Alex Lucinio. I know his brother is the leader of the Lucinio Mafia. And since my troubles are right up the Lucinio Mafia's alley, I need them. Not you. Them."

"Ms. Harlow, it would certainly help you out if you just told me what these problems are." His eyes narrow.

"You said yourself. You work for Lucinio Tech. Not Lucinio Mafia. I have nothing more to say to you." I cross my arms over my chest and focus my attention completely on the table in front of me.

He sighs in exasperation and throws up his hands as he shakes his head. "Fine." He walks out the door, leaving another younger dude in the room with me who hasn't said a word and is sitting in the corner.

I shake my head and roll my eyes, looking around the room. Everything about Lucinio Tech is shiny and new. It's all I've dreamed an office building for a huge Fortune 500 company would be. The wooden table in this room has no scratches. It looks like it's polished every single day. It even smells like brand new oak.

The walls are an off-white. The lights are warm and inviting. I bet if I looked close enough, everything would sparkle and shine. I could probably run my finger along the floor and wouldn't pick up a speck of dirt.

Truth be told I don't know if that makes me nervous or comforted. The attention to detail is a good thing. Especially considering the Lucinio Mafia kind of has to be detail-oriented. Also, because Lucino Tech is the leading security software company in the world. I wouldn't be surprised to find out they supply software to any alien planets that may or may not be in existence throughout the universe. According to everything I know about them, they're that good. Details in this family is mandatory.

Hopefully, they can help me.

I rub my temples to rid the memories of the last several hours. Days. The last several days. Weeks. Months. Years. It's been a nightmare come to life. My Hell. Like Nightmare on Elm Street has jumped off the screen and into reality. Only the man chasing me isn't someone who can manipulate my dreams and kill me in them.

No.

My own personal Freddy Krueger is a real life over six foot badass with a lot of tattoos and a very dangerous temper. Too bad I didn't know what his true motives were before tonight, though. I probably could have saved my father's life if I had.

The memory of his still warm and very lifeless body laying on the floor in the kitchen in his diner is still fresh at the forefront of my mind. The warm stickiness of his blood under my hands as I hid under a counter will not be likely to leave my brain anytime soon.

But I have to be strong for him. I have to be. I won't let his death be in vain. I know the Lucinio Mafia can help. Ever since they came into our diner and asked about a gang shaking us down for money every week, I knew they would be the only thing that could save us.

That *he* could.

The tall, hauntingly blue-eyed man I see in my dreams every single night.

Of course, I didn't know who he was when I gave into my libido and fell in bed with him. I've never done that before. Not once have I ever had a one night stand. I haven't exactly been with a ton of men, but I've never slept with them and then left the next morning either. I'm a relationship type of girl. I knew right away that he definitely was not relationship material. I left to save my heart from breaking when he inevitably walked away. Even though he was planning a few other dates.

But he haunts me. I can't stop thinking of him. When he came into the diner after what we did and left his card, I hid, only grabbing his card from the server he gave it to later on. After he left. I even worked up the nerve to let him know when that tattooed murderer came back, after leaving us alone for weeks.

I mentally shake my head. I can't think of him now. He might work for the same mafia I'm begging for help from, but he won't be able to help me. I need the top guy. At the very least, I need someone who can get me to him. I don't think *he* is that far up the food chain. Besides, *he* tried, and the fucker got to us anyway. My father is dead because of it.

Which is why I'm here. Alex Lucinio is my only hope. Without him, I'm as good as dead. Hopefully, the security assholes will at least call him. Maybe if they say they have someone here asking for Lucinio Mafia, he'll show up. I'm sure they don't get that every day.

I look up when the door opens again and breathe a sigh of relief when the man of the hour walks in. One of the Lucinio brothers. I don't know which one. They're twins. I'm so thankful, I let out an uncontrolled sob.

The Lucino brother doesn't say a word to the guard in the corner. He flicks his icy eyes to the door. Nothing more. The guard scurries up and closes the door behind him. The Lucinio brother takes hold of the chair. His demeanor is startlingly calm and insanely intimidating. The black t-shirt stretching across his torso shows off all the muscles rippling underneath it. His jeans, while loose fitting, don't leave any speculation to what he holds underneath. I'm convinced this guy's muscles have their very own muscles. A shiver runs down my spine. For the first time since I got here, I question my decision.

He spins the chair and straddles it, resting his forearms over the back of it. He levels me with that same piercing glare. His blue eyes show no mercy. "I hear you're asking for me."

The words I want to say stick in my throat. I'm just as terrified of him as the men I'm running from. Maybe more. "I…" I swallow hard. My hand slowly moves to my chest in hopes of relieving the pressure and ache suddenly filling it. "I… need… help." I say the words, but can barely hear them.

"I gathered. So tell me why." His voice is deep. Gravelly. No nonsense. He hasn't taken his eyes off of me.

I squirm under his stare. "U-um…" I hug myself and look down at the table. I need to get that confidence I had just a few minutes ago back. But it's evaporated. I'm close to hyperventilating.

"How about we start with how you got into my brother's building undetected until you started bashing in a window."

My eyes flick up to his, but I instantly look away. "So, you're Josh," I whisper.

"I'm the one you wanted, right? You kept asking for Lucino Mafia. Well, you got me. So talk."

I feel like curling into myself. Whatever adrenaline I had is gone. All I want to do is crawl under the table and wake up from the horrible night terror I'm having. "This was a mistake," I whisper. Josh, I know that's who I'm talking to now, is far more dangerous than anything I've seen. Even the gang I'm running from. He's cold. I can see that now. "I'll just leave." I start to stand.

"Sit," he growls.

My body obeys. I sit, unable to stop myself, and stare at him with wide eyes. "I -"

"Look. I already know you came up to the door screaming for help. When the guards didn't get there, you disappeared. They didn't see you again until you got to the third floor and appeared by the door with a brick trying to break the glass. I want to know how you got up there undetected, and then we'll have a conversation about why you need help, and why from me."

I chew on the inside of my lip and hug myself tighter. It takes me a while, but I give in. I take a deep breath. I know he won't let me out of this room until I talk. "I found a fire escape on the side of the parking garage. I had to climb a tree and shimmy across the branch to get to it, but I did. I climbed it until I got to the third floor. It was the only floor that had a small ledge I could get across. I almost fell a few times, but I got to the open cut out area and got in. From there, I wasn't trying to hide. I walked along the edge of the garage looking for the best way in. I found a brick by one of the columns and ran across the garage. I used the brick to smash the window and screamed for help."

"Why didn't you stop at the guard's booth at the entrance to the parking garage?"

"Because I was being chased, Mr. Lucinio. The guard was the only person there. I didn't want to put him in danger."

"Why didn't you wait at the front door for the guards? You had to know you screaming and pounding on the door would get their attention."

I nod and take another breath. "Because the people chasing me were too close. I saw them. I didn't think they'd get to the door before the ones chasing me got to me."

Josh watches me for a few moments before he nods. "Tell me why you were running."

I hug myself even tighter, if that's humanly possible, and sniffle. "The Ruthless Warriors." My voice cracks. I choke on a sob and swipe at my eyes.

"Where did the blood on your hands come from?" His voice has softened slightly, but I can still hear the hard edge.

"He killed my father!" I burst into tears. "R-right a-after my father s-said he wouldn't m-marry m-me off to his s-son!" I cover my eyes and sob into my hands. I hear the door open, but I'm too busy trying to calm down and quell the memories of my father's dull eyes open and staring at me; his face frozen in terror.

"Lance is on the cameras. Nick is trying to figure out where the fuck the glitch is. He just upgraded the security in this building and said there is no way she wouldn't have been seen," a male voice says low.

"Okay. Where's Dane?"

"Walking the perimeter with security. He's trying to figure out how she got to the third floor."

"A tree on one of the building sides. She climbed up and jumped to the fire escape. Shimmied across the third floor ledge."

"I'll let Dane know. The only trees around here are on the Northwest side of the building."

"Thanks, Cole."

"You got it." He must leave then because as I am wiping my eyes once more, I hear the door close again.

"So, you were going to be forced into an arranged marriage I'm assuming you didn't know about," Josh says to me. The hardness is gone, but the dark dominance is still there. I'm sure it's all natural and not an act.

It's obvious he's the leader for a reason. No one would dare challenge him.

I nod and use the sleeve of my long sleeve shirt to wipe my tears the best I can. "I was hiding. I heard the whole conversation." My voice cracks, heavy with emotion.

"Okay. Tell me about it. What was said?"

I finally take a chance to meet his eyes. "Please help me."

"I can't do that until I know what I'm up against. There's a difference between helping you and keeping you safe. I'm assuming, by what you've told me so far, you don't just want my help. You want me to keep you safe. So? Work with me. Tell me what I'm up against. I don't like guessing games. I don't like being caught off guard. Talk."

All I do is nod. "This gang," I begin. "They have been shaking us down for years. Every single week. They came in at the same time every Friday night. They asked for the same table in the back. And they always wanted me for their server. If I wasn't there, they wouldn't leave until someone called me or my father or something and made me come in." I shiver and cross my arms protectively over myself. "They'd leer at me. Sometimes, they'd touch me. But not just a friendly on the arm pat or something. They'd grab my ass."

"Who? Which one?"

"I'm not sure why that matters." I shrug. "But it was the older one. The one I found out was the leader. The others would grab my arms or legs. He was the only one who touched my ass."

Josh nods. A small smile creeps onto his lips. "Because he was exerting his dominance and claim over you. Even though you were meant for his son. As far as he is concerned, you belong to him and his family. It's important to know which one was grabbing you because it helps me to understand just how serious this arranged marriage is."

I inhale a slow, shaky breath. "Okay…" It takes a moment, but I force myself to continue. "We were supposed to see him that night when…" I trail off thinking of my gorgeous one-night stand's eyes. It causes me to lower mine. "When your people came in to talk to us about the shakedowns happening to local businesses in the area. We thought it was over. We were told we were under the protection of the Lucinio Mafia. That everyone in the area was. And that if we had a problem or he resurfaced, all we had to do was call."

"Which you did."

I nod again. "And it helped. We didn't see him again." I take another breath and close my eyes, swallowing hard. "Until tonight."

"Tell me what happened tonight," he says after a long pause, allowing me to compose myself in the process.

I open my eyes slowly because keeping them closed will only

make me see everything so much more vividly. Not like that isn't already happening. "We were closing." I shiver and sniffle. "I heard commotion in the kitchen. Sort of like someone fell and took pots and pans with them. Me and my father were the only ones there. I got scared. I thought something happened to him. He.. has… had… heart issues. He had two heart attacks a few years ago."

"Was that when the shakedowns started?"

I blink a few times and tilt my head. "Actually, yes." I tuck my hair behind my ear. "It was just before, I think. But after his surgery and during his recovery, they didn't show up."

"Probably because they'd made a deal with him."

I nod slowly. "I didn't know until tonight," I say quietly. "But they'd paid his bills. He knew he couldn't."

"And the payment was you."

"Yes. But he backed out of the deal. He said he'd pay them more money each week until the debt was paid. I saw them holding him over the grill. His face was close to it. I almost screamed, but I didn't. One of the people with him turned. I ducked under the prep table counter thing and hid. I listened to everything. How they were coming to collect. How he'd had enough time to say goodbye. How they gave him extra time with me. He refused. He kept saying he'd pay them extra. Anything they wanted. They slammed him against the grill." I cover my ears to drown out his animalistic scream; the sound of his skin sizzling.

"I understand. You can skip that part," Josh says soothingly.

I choke down another sob. "They told him it wasn't the deal. The deal was me. They paid off his bills, they got me. He said his son was waiting. My father kept refusing. They hit him. Threw him. He kept telling them they couldn't have me. That they'd have to go through him. They shot him. I don't know how I kept myself from screaming, but I did. His blood flowed under the table I'd closed myself into. The prep table has a door that can be closed. We can store stuff under there but never did. I'd never been so thankful for that decision because if we had, they would have found me. It was a miracle they didn't because when I felt his blood under my hands, I whimpered. They heard me and started looking for me. I listened and opened the door just a little. I saw them go out into the dining room."

"You ran."

I nod. "I saw my father's body. It was…" I look down and shake my head. "It was the stuff of nightmares," I whisper. "I ran. I tried to get help. No one listened to me. I knew in the neighborhood I was in, I wouldn't get anyone to help me. When I got to a better one, though, I thought someone would. But everyone was oblivious to me. They completely ignored me. I looked for a police officer and couldn't find one. I thought it was odd. You can always find a squad car in Chicago. I didn't have money for a cab. I left my purse at the restaurant. I thought I'd run far enough, but I didn't. I saw them chasing me. I ducked in and out of alley's and everything. Just when I thought I'd lost them, they'd find me again. I was exhausted by the time I got downtown, but I knew my only chance at that time was finding Lucinio Tech. Your guys said we were under your protection, but I didn't have my phone. I couldn't call."

"So, you came here."

"I came here hoping security would get me to you. I was pounding on the door and screaming for help. They found me again. I ran. I ran around the building hoping to find a guard or something. I did. At the parking garage. But he was alone, and the guys chasing me had guns. I saw the tree and quickly climbed up. I thought they wouldn't think to look for me there. And they didn't. They passed by. But I didn't dare come down. I heard them talking about how I couldn't go far. I was just a little girl. They said they'd circle around. So I shimmied across the branch to the fire escape I saw. I had to make a bit of a jump. I prayed I could do it. I quickly climbed up. I thought I would have to go all the way to the roof, but I saw a small ledge. It was only a few steps to the part that was cut out. Sort of like a window was going to go there, but wasn't put in."

"You pulled yourself through onto the third level of the parking garage."

"Yes. But as I was jumping over the ledge, I saw them coming around the corner. They were looking up, and one of them saw me. I fell onto the floor in the parking garage and ran for the door I saw. I picked up a brick on the way. I started screaming and smashing the window. I was terrified they'd climb up the fire escape before anyone got to me. I was looking for an escape when I saw security. I immediately dropped the brick and dropped to my knees. I put my hands behind my head and let them arrest me. I knew if I could at least get into the building, I had a shot at survival."

He chuckles, but it sounds more like a rumble. "I'm fucking impressed." He looks over his shoulder when the door to the room opens once more. A man steps through, and I'm frozen in place. "This is my second in command," Josh says, looking back at me.

I barely hear the words. I can't take my eyes off the powerful being in front of me. His eyes lock on mine, and I'm lost in their oceanic depths. The pounding of my heart must be able to be heard by them both. It's like a freight train to my ears.

"Gavin," I whisper. The entire world tilts on its axis. I very suddenly feel upside down. I grasp the edges of the table in hopes I won't fall off the Earth.

"Harleigh?" Gavin asks, shock snaking its way across his perfect face.

I fight it. I take deep breath after deep breath, but it doesn't help me. I feel numb. Sick to my stomach, even though the tiny butterflies only Gavin has ever brought out in me take flight and begin to flap their wings. I feel like I'm floating, flying, and falling all at the same time.

My vision darkens and grows fuzzy on the edges. I blink a few times, hoping to clear it, but it only makes it worse. The adrenaline that came with needing to escape has worn off. Coupled with the knowledge that the only man who has ever made me blush, the only man I've ever seen myself having a future with, is Lucino Mafia's second in command, my entire body has begun it's shut down.

The idea that I could have called him, I've memorized his number, to help me is something I can't quite grasp. I didn't know he was that far up the chain of command. Even though the leader of the Lucinio Mafia is sitting in front of me right now and knowing Gavin is part of it, I still never thought I'd see him again. Mafias are huge, right? I thought maybe he'd be somewhere else.

"I'm going to pass out," I whisper just as my world goes dark.

"Harleigh! Jesus fuck!" Gavin screaming my name is the last thing I hear before blackness overtakes me.

Chapter Two

☙ Gavin ❧

"Fuck! Harleigh, wake up! Wake up, honey." I lightly tap her cheek in an effort to get her to wake up. My heart is beating out of my chest. I pull her into my lap and hug her close to me. "Harleigh, come on, honey. Open those beautiful eyes for me."

Josh kneels next to me. "Take her home. She's out."

I'm hyperventilating. "Fuck, Josh. What the fuck do I do?"

He puts his hand against the artery along her neck. I know he's just trying to see if her too still body is taking in any oxygen, but seeing another man's hand on my girl is making the possessive fucker in me rear his ugly head.

I tamp it down because I know Josh is only helping; that Harleigh isn't technically mine. No matter how much I fucking want her to be. She's the one girl I've never been able to get out of my damn head. That includes the woman I married and am no longer with. Even if she hadn't been killed, I wouldn't be with her. Not after the amount of betrayal and deceit I found out about.

"She's breathing, Gav. Go home. I'll wrap up here. We'll be a while," Josh says.

I blink a couple of times and breathe deeply. I never cry. I'm not about to start now, though I'm having a hard time fighting the tears off. Fuck, this girl has done a number on me. I don't know the story behind what happened to her, at least not yet. I don't know if she's injured. I don't know what she went through. But I'm trusting my boss, my friend, my brother.

I stand with Harleigh in my arms and wait for Josh to open the door for me. I walk purposefully past Alex and several of his guards towards the exit at the front of the building. Alex's eyes widen. He's my best friend. He's one of the few who know anything about Harleigh and my feelings for her. What her walking out of my life then ghosting me until she needed help did to me.

Alex falls in step next to me. "You okay?"

"Fuck, I don't know, man. I have a war of emotions going on right now."

He walks with me out to one of the black SUV's we showed up in and opens the back door. "So, this is *the* Harleigh."

I can't help but chuckle a little bit. I'm sure his guards filled him in on who she is. Seeing me and how fucked up I am right now sealed it all for him. Two and two always equals four. Doesn't take a lot of brain power for him to put the pieces together.

"Yeah."

He pats my back and squeezes my shoulder as I climb into the backseat with her. "She'll be okay. If all I heard is true, the girl has to be fucking exhausted."

I hold her close and tight to my chest as Alex closes the door. I look at the driver, one of our guards. "Home," I command gruffly.

"Yes, Mr. Vandenberg." He puts the car in gear and pulls away from the curb.

I hug Harleigh tighter as the driver speeds towards our compound. I tangle my fingers in her dark brown, silky hair with one hand. The other is around her slim waist. And I do mean slim. I can feel her ribs. She's lost a lot of weight since I was with her. Whatever the fuck happened to her has caused enough stress to make her drop pounds that she didn't need to. On an already petite frame, she's definitely under what she should be.

I let out a breath and look her over as best as I can in the dark with only the streetlights we're passing by to briefly illuminate her. She's still beautiful. I can see the bags under her eyes, though. The slightly sunken cheekbones and pale skin. I don't know if the paleness has to do with her being out like a damn light in my arms, or if it has to do with whatever made her run to us, but it's worrisome. The girl in my arms right now, while still incredibly beautiful, is a far cry from who she was a few months ago.

I chuckle. A few months ago, when I met Harleigh, she knocked me on my ass. Literally. I was coming out of the bathroom at Jake's Diner, the diner her father owns and that she's worked at since she was just a kid. It was after a mission I was running with a couple of our guys. Nothing major, but it was a long fucking night. We were starving. We needed to take a bit of down time and feed ourselves before we went home. The diner had just opened. It was just after six in the morning.

Harleigh was coming out of the kitchen with a tray of food for a table of cops just starting their shift. I found out later that they were in there every morning they worked. The bathrooms were just past the kitchen. Harleigh, not expecting anyone to be in the hallway, came flying out the door. The diner was already pretty busy, even though they'd just opened a little over an hour before, so she was rushing to keep up.

The door flew open so quickly and unexpectedly that I had no time to react in my tired state before it hit me and sent me flailing backwards. I hit the ground before I even knew what happened. Harleigh's eyes fell onto mine, and that was it. For both of us. I was impressed as fuck that she didn't spill a drop of the food on her tray, but it was how fucking pretty she is that stopped the blood in my veins.

She still is the most gorgeous woman I've ever seen.

I was enamored with her. Fucking gone with just a look. I've never felt that way so quickly with anyone before. Including Marissa, my wife who was on her way to being my ex. Not my fault her treachery caught up to her. Or that her death didn't affect me at all. Coldhearted? I've been called far worse over the years.

In college, I was a player in every sense of the word. No one got more than one date. No one tied me down. Until Marissa. I was never really head over heels for the girl, but some dormant part of me felt an instant need to protect her. Mostly from herself and her self-destructive ways. I was with her for so long, it got to be almost a comfort in the chaos that was and still is my life. She was the one constant in my ever-changing world.

When I married her, I did it out of obligation. She'd been through so much shit with me, it was almost like I owed it to her. I hadn't been with anyone else. Neither had she. Or so I thought. When I came home to her, she was the one who always righted whatever the fuck happened in my world when I went to work. She centered me.

At least, sort of. As much as she could. I didn't know she was playing for both teams. Working with the enemy to take us down. It was only about a year ago when everything I'd suspected for the last few years of our relationship came out. All of the little things, like Damon or other guards coming to me and telling me she was trying to get them to fuck her, or security footage brought to me of her being sneaky as fuck, started to make complete sense.

My innocent wife, who was cut off by her family for pursuing her so-called dreams, wasn't so innocent. It's taken us the entire year since her death to uncover all of the shit she did. Marissa was a plant by Josh's and Alex's father, Matthew Lucinio, right from the beginning. As soon as he figured out Alex was dating and in love, he needed an in. Marissa was his in. He read her far better than I did and knew right away that she had a price. Fucker bought her off long ago.

But he played the game well. It wasn't until after we figured out that he was drugging Josh and brainwashing him into doing some shit he'd never in his life do, and after we took Matthew down, did the real fucking playtime begin. Matthew upped his payment to Marissa. Got her to tell him every fucking thing we were planning. We thought he was dead. Little did we know.

But Marissa did.

After we killed Matthew, or so we thought, Josh took his rightful place as the head of the Lucinio Mafia. He spent damn near four years growing us and gaining more alliances. So many that when Matthew clawed his way out of his goddamn grave, we were able to not only bring in the Crane Mafia, one of the largest in the world and family to us, but we had the United States Armed Forces on standby. Son of a bitch had no chance in hell, no matter what his cocky ass thought.

Unfortunately, Marissa was caught in the crossfire. She thought Matthew would beat us and take her away from the horrible life I gave her.

A life filled with money, a lavish as fuck home, vacations, anything her heart desired. I gave her everything and more. It still wasn't enough for her, though. It didn't compare to the promises Matthew filled her head with. Promises that would never have come to fruition.

A conclusion that she came to far too late. Before she could really ask for forgiveness, she was killed in an accident that also claimed the lives of Ethan and Jenny Crane, Ryan Crane's parents. Ryan is the leader of the Crane Mafia and just as much of a brother as those I'm close to in the Lucinio Mafia. Josh and Alex. Damon. Lance. Cole and Dane. We're all as close as family. Probably closer than that.

It wouldn't have mattered much anyway. As soon as I found out even a fraction of the things she'd done, I was finished with her. If she hadn't died, I would have divorced her. She wasn't the only one who came to life-changing conclusions far too late. She was barely cold by the time I went back to my old ways.

Asshole move? Probably. But I hadn't stuck my dick in her for far longer than I care to admit. I realized I didn't want a long-term relationship. I was never happy. I'd settled for what felt like normal. Calm to the bullshit. The longer she's in the ground, the more I understand that I never loved her. Which was okay, I guess, because she never gave a shit about anything more than what I could give her. Love me? Fucking hardly.

And then Harleigh appeared in my life. All of those mythical feelings that those in love say they get slammed into me with just one goddamn look from her and those amber eyes. Uncommon color for a very rare girl.

I knew she was special. Extraordinary even. Harleigh Harlow didn't just physically knock me on my ass. The girl blew through all of the walls I had no idea I'd built. It was more than just wanting her. I needed her. I was a hundred percent relentless in getting her phone number before we left that morning. She not only gave me her number, though. She told me what time she was off and when to pick her up. Where.

I showed up at her house with fucking bells on right on time. I wined and dined her. I gave her all of the effort I've never given another woman. Including Marissa. I pulled out all of the stops and actually enjoyed her company. I made plans for a second date and was surprised as hell when she told me to take her back to my place.

I didn't expect the best sex of my life that night. I didn't think she'd want to stay. I thought she'd fight me when I asked her to. Something I've never done. I take what I want and send the fuck of the night packing. Or I leave myself if I end up at their place, which is more often than not.

But she didn't fight me in the slightest. She curled up next to me like it was the most natural thing in the world. I went to sleep planning our fucking wedding in my messed up head. Yeah. I was that infatuated with her.

When I woke up the next morning, I thought she'd still be tucked into me. Protected in my arms. Wrapped around me. I was way fucking wrong. I don't know how she slipped out without me feeling or hearing her. I'm a light sleeper. It comes with the damn job. But she fucking did it.

No note.

No text.

Nothing.

Giving her the benefit of the doubt, and unwilling to admit that she did to me what I've done to countless women, I tried calling her. I left her messages. I texted her. I even showed up several times at Jake's Diner. She didn't respond to the messages I left for her there. She never called me back or responded to any texts.

It wasn't long after, though, that I thought I'd gotten kind of a break. There was a gang we'd heard about in the area of the diner. We went in and cleaned shit up fairly quickly. The gang was pretty ruthless. They wreaked havoc wherever they went and spent the rest of their time shaking down businesses in the area. Including Jake's Diner.

We thought we took care of them. We made sure they all knew they were under our protection. That if anyone tried to shake them down again, to tell us. We'd take care of it. If the gang showed back up and tried to take control again, to let us know.

It took quite a while, but they came back. We found out they were attached to another person we were after. Some asshole attached to fucking Matthew. Even from the grave, where he absolutely resides now; we made certain this time, that asshole is still trying to fuck with us. One of the motherfucker's associates thought he had a claim to Raleigh, Alex's soon-to-be wife.

Too bad for that associate. He's just as dead as Matthew now. Raleigh and Alex are getting their happily ever after. But Matthew still isn't done with us, apparently. We took out the douche who was messing with Raleigh and Alex. His brother happens to be the leader of the gang who was shaking down the businesses and tearing up the neighborhood. We thought we took care of them, but the leader resurfaced. It makes me curious to know if whatever happened to Harleigh tonight has to do with him. He's fallen off our radar. We know he's around. Just don't know where.

I shake my head to bring myself out of my thoughts when the driver pulls up to my house. Isn't the first time my mind has slipped into the past. Won't be the last. It's the only way I can learn from my mistakes and keep from making them again. It's one of the reasons I'm not only second in command in this mafia, but also have a reputation of being just as ruthless as Josh. Most people think I don't have a conscience. They might be correct. My world is very gray. I like it like that.

Keeping Harleigh in my arms, I get out of the SUV and kick the door shut behind me. When I get to my door, I shift her a little bit so I can open my door. After locking us both safely inside, I head straight for the stairs. I should bring her directly to a guest bedroom.

Of course I don't.

I'm an idiot and bring her to my bedroom. Because removing her scent the first damn time didn't take me long enough. I growl low and pull the bedspread back before laying her down. I sit down on the edge of the bed and sigh.

"Well, I can't leave you like that," I rumble low. Her clothes are torn and bloody. Fuck. She's got blood caked on her hands. "What the hell happened to you, Harleigh? And why did you run from me in the first damn place?"

I stand and rub my head. Keeping an eye on her, I head for my private master bathroom. I turn the water on in my jacuzzi tub, one of my personal indulgence I wanted installed when I had the place built. I make sure the water is soothingly hot, but not scalding, and then pour a stress relief bubble bath into it. A secret that if anyone found out and told, I'd have to kill them. I'd have no choice. A feared man who is high in command in one of the most powerful mafias this globe has ever seen can't be fond of fucking bubble baths. It would ruin my reputation. I'd never recover.

I chuckle a little as the bath fills and saunter back to my bedroom. I find a t-shirt and bring it back to the bathroom. I set it on the counter with a couple of towels. When the tub is full, I shut the water off and steel myself for everything about to happen.

I'm pissed off that Harleigh left. I still don't know all of the details of what happened to her, but I know that whatever it was, I could have helped her. Maybe I could have stopped it. I'm a cocky son of a bitch, but in this case, there's nothing cocky about the statement. I know I could have helped her. Even if she had taken off after our night together, she didn't have to ghost me. Granted, she did what she was told and called when the gang harassing them showed back up, but Christ. I scrub my hands over my face. Complete silence after that. Once again.

And she didn't even bother to contact me tonight. She specifically requested Lucinio Mafia. Not me. Talk about a blow to a man's ego. That right there will knock him down a step. Don't ask for him. Ask for who he works for. Like they can help, but he can't.

I let out a breath as I grab a cloth and wet it down with cold water. I walk to my bed and sit down. Harleigh groans just before I lay the cold cloth over her face with a wicked grin and low chuckle. Necessary? Probably could have just put it on her forehead.

But I can be pretty fucking vindictive when I want to be.

Chapter Three

🐾 Harleigh 🐾

"Mmm…," I groan quietly. My head is pounding. My eyes feel like they have sand in them. My mouth feels like the Sahara Desert. I'm surrounded by a familiar scent. Woodsy. A little spicy. Earthy and fresh.

But there's something else. Blood? Dirt? Grease. For sure grease. I was working. I remember that. I was closing. Something happened. Something… bad. I feel that. My heart is racing. But what was it? And why am I in a bed that's way too comfortable to be my own? That smells so… soothing?

I groan again and force myself to open my eyes.

Suddenly, something very cold hits my face. Something wet.

"Ah!" I scream. I sit bolt upright, ignoring every part of my body that protests. My head feels it's rolled off my shoulders. I feel like I'm hanging off the bottom of the Earth. "Ah!" I grip the wet thing on my face and throw it as I gasp for breath.

It's dark.

I grip the sheets underneath me. The only thing I can see right now is that I'm in a bed that isn't mine. It causes my breaths to come out in even quicker, short puffs of air. I tremble. Tears are freely flowing from my eyes. I don't have a clue when they started, but I can feel them streaming down my cheeks.

I blink rapidly because I don't need to be crying right now. I need to figure out where the hell I am because everything has come back to me.

My father.

Running.

The blood.

Lucinio Tech.

Josh Lucinio.

Gavin.

Gavin!

My eyes widen. I suck in hair and swipe my tears away with the backs of my hands. My face is probably covered in blood right now. My father's blood. I let out an involuntary sob and suck in more deep breaths.

After a few moments, I'm okay enough to allow my eyes to adjust to the darkness. I look around the room, but I can feel him before I see him. He's standing next to the bed. All six feet two inches of his solid muscle frame. I can just make out his silhouette, but I don't need to see anything more. Gavin Vandenberg has haunted my mind during the day and my dreams at night ever since I saw him.

I know his eyes are a beautiful blue that could cut diamonds with how sharp they are. I can feel them piercing me now. I know that underneath the clothes that stretch across his body are muscles any man would die for and an Adonis belt that any woman would have an unquenchable desire to lick. I should know because I did just that. I know that sexy V leads to a large and thick cock no soul on this Earth would be able to get enough of. And, oh my, does he know how to use it.

I swallow. Hard. Gavin was the best I ever had, not that there have been many. No one has compared to him. No one ever will. He knows what he's doing and does it well. Every part of him is large and hard, but it was how safe I felt with him that was the tipping point for me. I fell in love with him that night. I let him hold me after we'd had our fill of each other because I wanted to remember him just like that.

Before he'd inevitably send me on my way.

It was best for me to be the one to do it. Safer for me and my heart. Or so I thought. I left the damn thing on his pillow when I got up. And I never got it back. He owns it. Even though he isn't the type of guy to settle down. I know types like him. I see them all the time. Even if he was the type who wanted a relationship, he'd never want it with me. Gavin is a God. Compared to him, I'm nothing more than a peasant who has to beg for any scrap of attention he or anyone else wants to give me.

It doesn't stop the heat from pooling between my thighs, though. The wetness only Gavin has ever managed to give me. The instant warmth that only he's been able to create. The desire only he can satisfy.

I clear my throat in an effort to clear my mind and my body's reaction to him. "W-what are you doing here? What a-am I doing here?"

Gavin doesn't move. He stands with his legs comfortably apart; his arms crossed over his chest. "Oh, honey, I have a ton of fucking questions. And you'll be answering every single one of them," he rumbles dangerously. Dammit all for sending shivers throughout my entire body.

I hug myself. "Gav-"

"Nope. Not a damn word. I don't want to hear it. I'm fucking pissed, Harleigh. And I'm doing every damn thing I can to tamp it down, so I can help you like I know you need to be. I don't know what the hell happened tonight. I didn't get a chance to get the story before you passed out and my boss told me to get you someplace safe."

"I -"

Gavin continues on as if I didn't say a word. "So, you're going to clean up. There's blood and dirt all over you. I'm praying to every fucking God in existance that it's not yours. And that in itself is stirring up the war I have going on inside me. Part of me wants to take you in my arms and take care of you. The other part wants to throw you out and tell you to deal with it all on your own since you walked out on the one person in this world who could have kept you from this ever happening to you."

"I'm sorry, Gavin. I -"

"Congratulations, Harleigh. If the goal was to break an unbreakable heart, you did a hell of a job." He turns and walks towards his bedroom door, leaving me staring after him with my mouth half open.

"W-what?" I ask. *Unbreakable heart? I broke it? What is happening?*

"Tub is full. Water is hot. T-shirt is on the counter. Couple towels are out for you. I'll try to find you some clothes that will fit. Maybe one of my sisters have something." He closes the door to the room behind him, bathing me in darkness once more. The only light in the room is coming from an open door at the far corner of the room. Probably the bathroom.

I jump out of the bed to follow him, suddenly terrified of being anywhere without him near. I still don't know where I am, and that scares me more than the anger I felt radiating off of him. I reach the door and wrench it open only to be met with more darkness in the hallway. My heart leaps into my throat.

"Gavin!" I practically scream out of fear. Tears prick my eyes again.

"Get your ass in the bathtub!" he calls from somewhere in the house.

My head snaps towards his voice, and I run towards it. I reach a set of stairs and step down them as quickly as I can. "Gavin?" I call shakily again. I hate the fear in my voice, but I'm not ashamed of it. I'm too afraid to be.

He appears at the bottom of the stairs and flips on a light. He glares at me. "You don't like listening, do you?" he growls.

I stop in my tracks, but I can feel myself trembling. I hug myself. "I d-don't know where I am. I'm…" I take a deep breath. "I'm scared, Gavin," I whisper.

His glare turns a little more vicious. "Really? Don't know where you are?" He crosses his arms over his chest again. "Nothing about my house looks familiar to you, huh? Slipped out when it was too dark to make anything out?"

I flinch and look down, realizing all at once where I am. I probably knew, but I still haven't fully come to yet. And I'm terrified of the men who were chasing me. Not that they are here, but that they could get to me if he's not near. "I-I'm sorry. I panicked." I choke back the sob and glance at him once more before turning and making my way back up the stairs.

There is nothing familiar about the man glaring after me right now. The Gavin I remember was hard, but only in body. This Gavin is dangerous. Probably more than all of the Ruthless Warriors combined.

It makes me question my sanity. I should be terrified of him, but I'm not. I feel like a walking conundrum. I didn't want to reach out, but I feel like he can keep me safe from the Warriors. I feel a little like a hypocrite, but I can't seem to help it. It's like I'm torn in two.

Maybe the problem is that I don't know much of what the Lucinio Mafia does. I don't know if they hurt or help people. Or if they expect something in return for the help they give. I've heard rumors of legit mafias, but I always thought it was a myth. Something they tell everyone to keep the police off their backs.

I silently shake myself out of my thoughts. They aren't helping. Maybe, once I've gotten some rest, I could ask Gavin more about his job and the mafia he has dedicated himself to. Maybe he will even let me explain why I never called after I went to him for help after our explosive night together. Surely, he knows that I did what I had to do to keep my father safe. Not that the outcome was any good since they came back anyway. He can't be mad that I called him to get his boss to help us. That's what he told us to do.

"Harleigh!" he barks. I jump, jarred from my thoughts, and turn to him as I reach the landing at the top of the stairs. "The light to my bedroom is on the wall to the left of the door." Something familiar flickers across his face, something that shows me the kind Gavin he hides just under the angry exterior. He covers it quickly, though, and I hug myself tighter. "You're safe here. You're in a compound filled with mafia. There's more fucking guards around here than there are cops in Chicago." He says nothing more as he turns and disappears around a corner, but his words ease my fears. At least a little.

I sniffle again as I enter his bedroom. His scent is all over this house, but it's strongest here. I make my way to the bathroom and quickly undress. I slip into the bath, but I don't allow myself to relish in the relaxing heat or aroma coming from it. I quickly clean the dirt, grime, and blood off me and out of my hair. I drain the tub and dry off. I put the t-shirt on and find my panties in my discarded clothing, but they are sweaty and just as dirty as everything else, so I pick them up and carry them with me as I make my way back downstairs.

"Gavin?" I call quietly. He doesn't answer. I bite my lip and listen for him as I walk around the house.

I never really had a chance to look at it before, but it's truly a gorgeous house. It's modern, but masculine. Elegant yet fun. The trim is wood. The walls are warm. There are accent walls in each room that give the entire decor something extra.

When I find him, it's near the back of his house. There is a door halfway open. Gavin is sitting in a leather chair behind a large black desk that looks to be some kind of wood but is shiny. Like it's polished daily. The entire house smells new. Like the walls were just painted; the frame freshly built.

And then there's *him*. Gavin. His scent. The subtle reminders of him throughout the entire house. There's no questioning who the King of Castle Vandenberg is. It's the man sitting behind the powerful looking desk pouring over paperwork with a tight black shirt stretched tightly over his perfect body.

"What do you want, Harleigh?" Gavin asks me without looking up from whatever he's doing. At least his voice isn't so harsh right now.

"Um… my clothes… I was wondering if I could wash them." I cross my legs, suddenly very aware that I'm not wearing panties. Even angry, Gavin does things to my body that I'd be ashamed of if they didn't feel so damn good.

"Put them down. I'll take care of them. Go to bed. I have shit to do."

I bite my lip. "I thought you wanted to talk…?"

He lets out a deep sigh before looking up at me. "I do, Harleigh. But I also need to calm the fuck down. You walked out on me after the best fucking night of my life. I've never felt a connection like that with anyone, so when I woke up and you were gone and then didn't answer any of my calls or texts, it stung. Have I done shit like that? Yes. But it was with girls I didn't have a connection with and knew they didn't with me either. Girls I knew wanted one thing and one thing only. You weren't like that. I figured you leaving was me paying penance for all my fucking sins, but what hurt the most?" His glare is penetrating. "When you called me for help. Then ghosted me again. All you gave a shit about was what I could do for you. Just like all the others before you. It tore me up, Harleigh. Not as much as you not calling me for help tonight, but it stung."

I shake my head as tears sting my eyes. "I'm sorry, Gavin. I am. I didn't know who you were at first… I swear."

"Just go to bed." He looks down at his paperwork again. "I have shit to do. You can take my bed. I'll sleep down here."

My eyes widen. "Gavin, I can't -"

"Harleigh!" he snaps and pins those glacier cold eyes on me once more. "Drop the clothes. Go to bed. No fucking negotiation."

My body obeys his command because he leaves no other option. I drop the clothes on the floor and scurry back to the relative safety of his bedroom. I close the door behind me and crawl under the covers.

I'm not sure what's more torturous. Being in *his* bed surrounded by *his* scent without him, or the only man I've ever truly felt something for hating me like he obviously does. Can I really blame him? I'm the one who left. I fucked up. Not him.

I allow the tears to fall freely as I clutch his pillow and curl up. I left because I didn't want to get my heart broken. I didn't realize it already was. I thought ignoring his calls would save me the inevitable pain I'd feel when he found someone better than me. A man like him could do so much better than someone like me. I'm not even old enough to drink yet. Compared to the women I'm sure he's been with, I'm hardly more than a girl.

When he came in that day a couple of months ago after I fled from his bed, I knew he was looking for me. I hid, but I could see him scanning the diner for me. He'd done it a few times after I'd left, but I hid each time.

That day was different, though. He looked… fierce, yet worried. Extremely. I almost went to him when he asked for me but didn't. I saw him give the server his card. I had her give it to me after he left, though I didn't need it. I'd saved all of his texts and voicemails. I read them and listened to them often.

I always berated myself after he left that day. I don't know why I always hid from him. I could have just ignored him, but deep down I knew. I knew that if I spoke to him, I would give in. I wouldn't be able to stop myself from jumping him. I've never had the kind of connection with anyone like I did with him. I felt like my soul was calling out to his.

Truth is, as much as I wanted it, it also terrified me. Not just in that moment, but when I let myself think about the what ifs. If I let myself imagine what would have happened if I answered one of his calls or texts. All I could think about was him one day leaving me for someone better. Prettier. My insecurities would rise up, and I would almost throw my phone away from myself in an effort to keep that future hurt at bay. Childish? Maybe. Stupid? Probably.

It might have been a mistake, but it was my mistake to make. And as I'm discovering now… a mistake that may have cost me a future with the man of my dreams. The anger that I could feel pouring off of Gavin did nothing to mask the hurt I could see in his eyes. Hurt that I caused. Just the thought makes my heart clench, and I burrow further into his blankets.

When the guy from the Ruthless Warriors came in a little while after Gavin said we were under the Lucinio Mafia's protection, I was truly terrified. Fear led me to call him. They threatened my father. They told him that payment was due. My father gave them everything in the register to appease them.

I guess, given what I know now, though, it was just to buy time. After I told Gavin they'd shown back up, though, they disappeared again. I thought he'd taken care of them. When they showed back up tonight, or last night, I don't even know anymore, after closing, I realized that no matter what kind of protection the neighborhood had wouldn't have saved us.

Looking back on my behavior, I can understand why Gavin is so angry. I ignored all of his advances. I called him when I needed him. Used him and his connections. Then dropped him again. It wasn't my intention, but I'd be stupid not to understand that's what he would think. I had no idea who he was at first, though. I didn't know his connection to the Lucinio Mafia. I just thought he was a really hot guy who had an interest, however brief, in me.

I didn't know what he did until he came in and told us that we, and other area businesses, were under the protection of Lucinio Mafia. Truthfully, that may have scared me. A lot. Who in their right mind would get involved with someone in the mafia? No matter how good he is in bed or how much he rocked my world, getting involved with someone in the mafia is insanely dangerous. I might not have been able to afford to go to college, but even I know better.

I told myself fear was the reason I didn't contact him again until we needed help, but it was a lie. It was my own selfishness and stupidity. I didn't realize my actions to protect myself hurt him, though. I thought he just didn't like the fact that I took matters into my own hands and walked away before he could do it to me. But looking in his eyes and seeing all of the pain he tries to hide breaks my heart.

The very heart I tried to protect.

I need to be more open with him. I need to tell him all of this. Maybe then he'll understand my side. Maybe we can work on him giving me a second chance. Not like I deserve it. I know now just how wrong I was. Just how poorly I handled all of this.

Clutching Gavin's pillow to my chest, I cry a little harder because I feel like my entire life is over; that it's all my fault. I hurt him. I hurt myself. But mostly? I can't help but wonder if my actions killed my father. What if I'd called Gavin back? Answered a text? What if I hadn't hidden from him? Would my father still be alive if I'd acted more mature?

My mind tells me that what's done is done. Life isn't fair or just. The events leading up to right now prove that. Things are going to happen that don't make sense and suck. There's nothing that can be done.

But my heart…

My heart knows how false that is. It's telling me that I could have chosen a different path. I could have answered a call or text. I could have chosen to not hide. If I'd only not ignored my head and not run from Gavin, maybe things would have been different.

Maybe if I'd listened to my heart, my father might still be alive.

Chapter Four

☙ Gavin ☙

I jump and groan at the loud banging at my door as my eyes fly open. My heart races as I sit up. I'm still in the same jeans and t-shirt I was last night. And I'm sleeping on my fucking couch. I growl low and glare at my ceiling.

Harleigh.

She's lying in *my* bed upstairs. In *my* t-shirt. Snuggled into *my* blankets. Clutching *my* pillow. How do I know that? Because I checked on her last night after I calmed down enough to look at her without wanting to throw her in the lake.

I sigh and scrub my hands down my face before rubbing my tired eyes as I get up and head for my door. I pull it open and glare at Alex, Josh, Damon, and Cole. Lance is behind them all with his head in his laptop, and Dane is on the phone.

"It's five in the fucking morning," I grumble. "Who could you possibly be talking to at this hour?"

Josh raises an eyebrow. "Long night?"

"Nope. I'm this prickly all the time." I step aside. "Be quiet. I don't want Harleigh to wake up."

"Did she give you a nice confession last night? Did you forgive her of all her sins?" Alex grins as he walks by me, but I glare. My best friend is one of the biggest assholes I know. I'm sure it's why we get along so well. I'm just as big of one. Probably more.

I close the door behind them when they are all inside. "I gave her a bath and put her to bed. Then I fell asleep on my couch to thoughts of drowning her in the damn lake outside."

Josh furrows his brows. "I'm confused. Isn't this the same chick you've been pining over? The one who caused you to lay off women and take out your aggressions on the poor souls I bring to you for a sacrifice so you won't murder me in my sleep?" He's grinning like a dickhead.

I know he's fucking with me, but he's not that far off. Ever since Harleigh walked out on me, I have been unnecessarily violent when we bring in bad guys. Not that I wasn't before. The guys in this room have teased me quite a bit over the years about having no moral compass. The past couple of months, though, I'm pretty sure they might be right.

One night.

That's all it took for her to fuck me up.

One goddamn night.

Harleigh was the best lay I've ever had, but it was more than that. So, so much more. They say when true love hits, it hits hard and fast. Love at first sight and all that shit. I've been around long enough to see it happen with my own eyes, but I never believed for a second I'd be on the other end of it. That I'd be the one who fell to my knees with just one look. One kiss. One touch. I knew the second I saw her that she was it for me.

Even though I'm pissed off that she walked, I still ache for her. It took all of my strength, and some I didn't know I even had, for me to walk out of my bedroom last night after I checked on her. I wanted to crawl in next to her. Hug her. I know she needs it. I still don't know all that happened to her last night. I hadn't talked to Josh or any of the other guys after I got her home.

All I know is she went through something that made her run. Something that made her seek us out. It had to be bad because she had blood all over her. She was exhausted enough after the adrenaline dump she went through that she passed out as soon as she knew she was safe. Before I went into that room, I saw the cameras. I saw who she was running from.

Gregory Franklin. Back from whatever dark hole he crawled out of. Not that I knew he wouldn't show his face again. We did kill his brother when he went after Raleigh. Fucker underestimated who he was messing with. It was his own fault for believing the words that came out of Matthew Lucinio's mouth. Shouldn't have believed him when he said Josh was a weak leader and we weren't all that big.

He also shouldn't have thought Raleigh was Matthew's property. That Matthew could just promise her hand in marriage like Raleigh didn't have a choice. I can't help but shake my head at the thought. Killing Matthew should have ended it all. But he had his hands in more shit than we ever dreamed. We might be rid of him, but we're still dealing with repercussions.

Gregory Franklin is one of them. After we got rid of his brother, he disappeared. Not that we weren't looking for him. We've been diligently searching for his hiding places, but he hasn't been seen.

Until last night.

He was all over Alex's security cameras. When I walked into the room Harleigh was in at Lucinio Tech, I'd intended to tell Josh we knew who was chasing the girl and how she got in without being seen. All I saw on the cameras, though, was a still image Nick and Lance paused for me to look at. The image of Gregory. I hadn't seen the girl.

From there, they told me how the girl got up to the third level without being seen. There were several places the cameras aren't able to cover. While they swivel, they don't hit all areas. Nick West, Josh's and Alex's half brother, and fuck wasn't that a kick to the gut when we discovered that secret, is the one who deals with all security for all Crane and Lucinio buildings. He was pretty pissed off when he figured out that some cameras weren't working and Alex's security didn't bother to say anything.

I'm sure there will be hell to pay, if there wasn't already. We all take security very seriously, but given what happened to Raleigh, Alex has become pretty fucking vicious about it. No one blames him in the slightest.

I wait for everyone to settle before I sit and put my feet up on my coffee table. "So?" I say, looking at Josh. "What happened last night? I came in to tell you we know who was chasing her and the reason we didn't see her while she was running around the building. I have no fucking idea what the hell happened."

Josh leans back. "So, you know it was Gregory Franklin chasing her. Leader of the Ruthless Warriors."

I nod and move my hand in a 'gimme' gesture. "Catch me up because I know very little. Far more questions than answers."

Josh glances towards the ceiling before leaning forward. He rests his elbows on his knees and lowers his voice. "Her dad made a deal."

The growl that escapes my throat is from deep within. I don't need to ask the question I'm about to, but I do it anyway. "What... deal...?" I hiss but don't move an inch.

"Her dad had a heart condition," Josh begins. "He knew he'd need a little help to keep his restaurant alive. The Ruthless Warriors were already shaking down those businesses. Quietly. They weren't on our radar yet. They made a deal with him. His daughter and they'd pay off his medical bills and everything related to the restaurant to keep it going while he was out. They went to collect last night. She hid while they killed her father. She saw and heard the entire thing and stayed hidden while they looked for her. She took off when they left the kitchen. I sent a team to the restaurant. It's burned to the ground. I know there's more to the story, but I'm positive she doesn't know what it is."

"That's not all," Dane says, finally hanging up his phone.

"Of course, it isn't," I grumble. I pinch the bridge of my nose.

"Word on the street is these guys are into some bad shit. No one knows a lot about them, but they're into trafficking guns. It's possible they've pissed off the fucking cartel." Dane tosses his phone onto the table as he glares. "I don't need the cartel in my backyard. We need to finish them. Now."

"Why?" Damon asks with a shrug. "Let the cartel have them."

"See, I'd love to just hand them off to the cartel," Dane growls as he turns his glare onto Damon. "But there's a problem."

Dane's viciousness doesn't bother Damon in the slightest. "What's the problem? I don't see one. They take care of them for us."

Lance chuckles and pats Damon's knee. "The cartel won't just stop at them. They like territory just as much as the next fucker."

"They wouldn't come after us, though," Damon says with a raised eyebrow. "I mean, come on. The forces we have? We're untouchable. They know that better than anyone."

Josh leans back. "I don't want a war with the cartel. They might know we can beat them, but they're cocky motherfuckers. They'd come after us just because they can. It would be a bloody fucking mess over the city of Chicago. Dane doesn't need that, and neither do we. No."

"Then we team up with them," I say.

"Are you insane?" Dane nearly chokes.

I shrug and look at him deadpan. "You have a better idea?"

"Yes! Leave the fucking cartel out of it completely!" Dane's voice raises.

I shoot him a glare of my own that silences him immediately. He might take no shit from anyone, just like the rest of us, but there aren't many people in this world who have the balls to keep talking after I shoot them a look like that. Josh might be one of the few, but Dane sure as hell knows better.

"Seriously. I'm not fucking kidding. Do not wake that girl up," I growl low and in warning. "I'm not in the mood. I slept less than two hours last night and have no damn clue what I'm going to do with her."

"I don't think you have much choice, buddy," Alex chuckles with a grin. "She's being chased by a gang that we know has no conscience. We have to protect her."

I narrow my eyes. "Then she can stay with you."

Alex shakes his head as someone knocks on the door. He stands with an even wider grin. "Pretty sure she wouldn't enjoy herself with all the fucking Raleigh and I do."

"Fucking hell, you're an asshole." I can't help but laugh with everyone else, though, as my best friend answers the door.

Moments later, Alex leads Alec Cassidy, or Ace as his motorcycle crew, the Viper's Venom, know him as. Alec is the club's President and Josh's best friend. Alec is tall, intimidating as fuck, and covered in tattoos. I highly doubt anyone would fuck with him even if he weren't a dangerous as fuck leader of a pretty damn vicious motorcycle crew.

"I hear you guys are looking for the Ruthless Warriors," Alec says as he sits on the arm of the couch next to Alex.

I look at him, my eyebrow quirked. "How did you know that?"

"Got my sources." Alec shrugs and looks down at Josh. "They're a new motorcycle crew. Fucked up motherfuckers. They've been around for a few years. I've had a couple of run-ins with them. I get rid of them for a little while, then they show back up like fucking fleas."

"They're a motorcycle crew?" Josh says, surprise evident as he looks at Lance.

Lance blinks a few times in shock before looking back down at his laptop. "Nothing here would have ever led me to that. But I haven't gotten that far. It's only been a couple of hours. I haven't done a lot of research with them because we already took them out."

"Or so we thought," Damon says. "Even after we figured out who his brother was, he didn't show back up. Not until last night."

I take a breath and let out a growl as I rub my eyes. "I'm fucking tired. What's the plan?" I drop my head back on the cushion on my chair.

Josh stands with a yawn. "I think we're all tired. The plan. I promised Harleigh we'd keep her safe. She came to us for help."

"Then she can stay with you," I say very seriously.

"No," Josh says simply. "She's staying with you. I have enough shit to deal with. Playing bodyguard is not in the cards for me. Call Jessa. She's about Harleigh's size. She'll get clothes for her. We all need to get some sleep. No way we're getting anywhere when no one can think. We've all been awake for more than twenty-four hours." He looks at Alec. "Can you send Lance the info you have on these guys?"

"You got it," Alec says as he stands. He looks down at me with a grin. "If you want to get rid of her, I'm sure some of my guys wouldn't mind the eye candy."

I glare, even though I know he's kidding. "You and your guys can stay the fuck away from her."

Alec laughs. "Well, you know where to send her when you get sick of her."

"Get the fuck out," I rumble. I'm not at all in the mood for jokes. "All of you. I need to either sleep or go for a damn swim before I starting ripping off heads for the fuck of it."

"This is different from any other day how, exactly?" Alex asks as he stands with everyone else.

I chuckle and shake my head. "Point taken. I'm a sadistic motherfucker. Now, everyone out. I know what happened. It's all I care about right now. The rest just needs to wait until I can get my fucking head on right. I'm between wanting to drown her and wanting to hold her and never let her go."

Alex smiles as everyone else files out of my house. He waits until we're alone before he crosses his arms over his chest. "You realize I was in your shoes not that long ago."

I chuckle as I stand slowly. "Yeah. I know." I stretch and glance towards my stairs before I look back at him. "I'm still thrown from her walking out."

He raises an eyebrow. "Because she walked out? Or because you've never had anyone do it to you?"

"Both. But if you want honesty out of me, it's because she only contacted me when she needed help. When I gave it to her, she was gone again. And then last night. Why didn't she call me? Why didn't she have them contact me?"

"I could answer that, but I think you can do it yourself. And then talk to her. You've said yourself. She's the girl of your dreams. You've told me how many times that no one has ever hit you with that much of a connection? Not even Marissa." He reaches out and squeezes my shoulder. "Go take a swim. Clear your damn mind."

I stand in the middle of my living room long after Alex is gone before I finally decide he's right. I need to clear my mind. I need to take a swim. I glance at my stairs once more and decide to forego swim trunks. I'm too tired to walk up the stairs. Some slightly unfrozen part of me wants to allow her to sleep. She needs it.

So, instead of walking upstairs and grabbing swim trunks, I go outside to my private pool. We all have pools that are enclosed and private, blocking us from any onlookers who might be on the lake. Most would just see an aesthetically pleasing brick wall if they look up. No one has to know the reason we've done that is more for safety than privacy. Don't need anyone shooting my dick off from the lake or anywhere else.

On the way out, I stop by the laundry room. I strip my jeans, t-shirt, and underwear off. I throw them in the washer and start it, then take Harleigh's clothes out of the dryer. It's not lost on me as I fold them that the clothes are her work clothes. A pair of black jeans and a purple t-shirt with the Jake's Diner logo on it. I can't help but notice that her panties are worn and a little torn. Her bra has seen better days.

I knew from our night together that Harleigh doesn't have a lot. The diner doesn't make much. Her father makes enough to cover their bills, including the mortgage for their rundown house, but she gets paid very, very little if anything at all. She wanted to find another job, but after her father got sick, she didn't want to leave him to work the diner himself.

I didn't know it was this bad, though. The outfit she wore when I picked her up looked fairly new. And her sexy black, lace bra and matching panties certainly didn't look ratty or beat up. Not like this. I know in my heart that she just wanted to give a good impression of herself to a complete stranger. But my head tells me it's one more thing to be pissed off at. She didn't lead on that she was in a position where even her undergarments need replacing. One more thing I could have fucking helped her with if she'd stayed.

I leave the clothes on top of the dryer after I fold them and walk outside to the pool. Stark naked, I dive in and stay under the water as long as my lungs will allow. When I finally resurface, I start laps. I swim back and forth across the pool and let all of my aggression and anger melt off me, but it takes quite a while for my mind to clear enough to actually think.

I know very well I'm being hypocritical. I've done exactly what she's done to many women before her. The difference, though, is that the women I was with knew the score. They knew there wouldn't be a second time. They knew there was no connection for me, and that I was using them just as much as they were me. When they made contact, or tried to, even though it wasn't often, I didn't return texts or phone calls. I always said it wasn't my fault they wanted more than what I told them I'd give them.

At least I was honest.

When I met Harleigh, I actually took her on a fucking date. I've never done that. I've picked women up, had my way, moved on. With her, I never had the 'this is a one time deal' conversation. I told her that the next date we went on would be to a restaurant she'd always wanted to try but never could. Some five-star restaurant run by a Michelin chef. Don't remember which one, and I'm not sure I want to. I won't step foot in it anyway without her.

The girl watched them kill her father. That's something that hurts me to know. Knowing that she had to go through that. She had to have been terrified when she ran, but she did it anyway. She saved herself last night. I have to be proud of that.

But as I continue to lose myself in laps in an attempt to exhaust my body, the war inside my mind rages on.

Chapter Five

❦ Harleigh ❦

I blink awake slowly and yawn. My eyes feel puffy. Like I cried myself to sleep or something. I can't help but chuckle a little because I know I did. It's kind of hard not to. My father was killed right in front of me. I ran with his blood all over me from people who wanted me for their own nefarious purposes.

And then I find out that Gavin Vandenberg, the literal object of every fantasy I've ever had before and after I knew he existed, is not only the second in command of a giant and ruthless mafia, but is also hurt that I walked out on him. Granted, I did it because I really didn't think a man like him would want anything to do with me after that one night, but I shouldn't have just left. I should have been an adult and had that conversation.

Now, not only am I completely alone in the world, but I'm pretty sure I've lost the only man I've ever had any kind of connection with, sexual or otherwise, who made me feel. Gavin gave my heart a reason to beat. When I left, it was hard, but I had the memories of the best night of my life. I figured while I was suffering, he was off giving another girl the best night of her life. Maybe he was, but I didn't know I actually hurt him.

I never wanted that. I only wanted to protect my heart. It's easy to fall for a man like him and get hurt.

I know I need to talk to him. About so much stuff. Including about what happened to my father. I'm sure he already knows. My sleep was fitful because all I could see was my father. All I could hear were his screams. Seeing and hearing everything that happened on repeat while now knowing I upset him with my actions, talking to Gavin needs to be my number one priority.

After spending a little time in the bathroom, and noticing the toothbrush Gavin set out for me with a note saying it's for me, I start to feel a little more human. I don't see my clothing anywhere, though. I didn't really expect him to have it folded neatly on a chair or anything. I'm pretty certain he probably left it on the floor in his office where I dropped it. I wouldn't be upset with him at all if he did.

I hug myself and walk quietly down the stairs. It's still early. Gavin isn't in his bed. If he's sleeping somewhere in the house, I don't want to wake him. Though, he was really upset. I wouldn't be at all surprised if he didn't sleep for a second.

I wander the way I remember his office was and see the door is closed. Respecting his privacy, I don't attempt to open it or knock. I remember there was a couch in there. He might be sleeping on it. I didn't see him anywhere else.

I turn and shuffle as quietly as possible towards the kitchen. This house is so massive, I'm glad it has an open floor plan when it comes to the living room and kitchen area. I'd probably never be able to find it otherwise.

I meander into the kitchen and let my hands fall to my sides. I see he has a water and ice maker right on the door of his fridge, but I don't know where he keeps his glasses. I don't want to snoop. Thankfully, there's a coffee cup on the counter that looks as if it was just washed. It's sitting on a towel upside down, like it's drying. I bite my lip, then decide to use that for water. I don't think he'll be angry with me for that. I really don't want to upset him more.

After getting the ice water, I decide that his patio looks really inviting. It's private and enclosed. I didn't see too much more than that through the kitchen window, but I don't really need to. I need fresh air.

And if he's sleeping, he won't have to worry about me accidentally waking him up by being too noisy.

I blink against the bright sunlight, but the air is fresh and crisp. It's a stark contrast to the slums, where I live. The air isn't fresh there at all. It smells like drugs, smog, and death. Nothing close to here. A person can't sit on their deck in my neighborhood. We often don't sit near walls if those walls are on the side of the street. A stray bullet from a driveby might strike us. Gavin's neighborhood is so incredibly quiet. Serene.

Taking a sip of my water, I close my eyes and relish in the cool breeze hitting my skin and cold fluid snaking its way down my throat. But the peaceful feeling is quickly shattered. My eyes fly open when I hear something like splashing behind me. I spin. My water sloshes over the rim of the cup, landing on my chest and making me squeak.

My eyes widen when I see Gavin slowly walking up the stairs of the pool I wasn't aware he had until right now. His almost demonic glare makes me want to flee back into the relative safety of his house, but I'm rooted to the spot I stand. I feel my lips part. My throat, which I just literally wetted, is dry once more.

Gavin is completely naked.

The morning sun makes his wet skin look like it's glistening. His muscles ripple with each step he takes. He looks like he was cut from the hardest stone. I think he might look more ripped than when we were together. His abs are just as chiseled as his arms and legs. When he reaches for the towel on the patio chair a few feet from the pool's edge, his defined muscles flex and tense. As he dries his hair, his movements enchant me. His intense gaze doesn't leave me for a second. It all looks so natural and mouthwatering that I forget completely I'm not watching a porn video starring Gavin Vandenberg.

His dick.

Holy… shit… his dick. It's thick. Long. And standing straight out, like it's at attention. It flexes and bobs with each and every fluid movement he makes. Each and every delicious and dirty thing he did to me with it is at the forefront of my mind. I lick my lips. I can't tear my eyes away, even though staring is so incredibly rude.

Gavin drops the towel over his shoulders after drying off and raises an eyebrow. "Get your fill?" the thirty-six-year-old object of my dreams asks.

41

I try to form words, but none come. Just one. "Wow," I whisper.

Gavin chuckles low. I'm sure it would sound dangerous to anyone else, especially with those eyes looking as if they are capable of cutting holes into titanium. He's still holding the edges of the towel over his shoulders, making his already defined muscles even more so. His eyes travel up and down my body. I shiver. Instant heat pools between my thighs. I'd whimper, but I'm positive he'd hear it.

"Your clothes are on the dryer." He gestures with his head towards the house but makes no move to cover himself. "Laundry room is off the kitchen."

I force myself to turn around and run back inside the house. I search for the laundry room and lock myself in it, gasping for breath as I lean my head against the door. My racing heart begins to calm, but I feel like the world is on fire. With such few words, he managed to set me ablaze. Then doused the inferno completely with the ice in his sexy, blue eyes.

I quickly grab my clothes and dart up to the sanctuary of his bedroom. The hope is that I can calm myself enough while I get dressed to have a normal conversation with the man, but I know as soon as I walk into the room that won't be happening. His scent is far too intoxicating to allow me that small privilege.

I throw a mini tantrum and send my clothes flying onto the chair near the window. I lay down on the bed and glare up at the ceiling. Despite the small fact that Gavin is part of a dangerous mafia, he's also way too attractive for someone like me. He has the word 'player' written all over him. He's not one to settle down. It's obvious.

So, why can't I stop thinking of him? Why is he the only one who can make me feel the way I do? Why couldn't I take my eyes off him outside? And why do I want him so badly now that it makes me ache?

Not that he made it easy for me. Swimming naked in his pool knowing I'm here and could see him? It's probably routine or something. He probably wasn't even thinking about me being here and possibly seeing him. And I'd believe that... if he hadn't stood in front of me totally naked and watched me the entire time he was drying off, making absolutely no motion to cover himself or keep me from seeing all he has to offer. It makes me feel like he might really not be as angry at me as he comes off. Maybe there's still a chance for us after all.

I groan and close my eyes, rubbing my thighs together to relieve the pressure, but it doesn't work. I can see nothing but Gavin coming out of the pool naked as the day he was born. His muscles flexing; his gorgeous cock dangling standing at attention. It may not have been for me, but I'll gladly let myself believe it was.

The ache grows and spreads until I can feel myself getting wetter. I glance at the door and let my hand wander down my body as I shift and sit up a little bit. Seeing it's securely closed, I slide a finger through my own wetness, imagining it's Gavin.

"Oh…," I moan quietly as I bite my lip. I circle my clit with my finger and arch into it, letting my head fall back against the headboard. It's not the first time I've touched myself. I'm not innocent in that way. And it's not the first time I've imagined Gavin getting me off. No one I've ever been with has been able to make me come.

Just him.

I've never been able to make myself come either. Not until after my night with him. All I have to do is think of him. Pull up images of him in my mind's eye where he's forever seared. Ever since that night, it's been like my body is attuned to him.

I press down on my clit and let my eyes close. It's easier to conjure up images of Gavin while in his bedroom and surrounded by his scent. I slide my middle finger inside myself and arch off the bed. I thrust to the pace I'm rubbing myself and moan almost silently. The last thing I want is for him to hear me getting myself off, but I'm so pent up just being surrounded by him, I need this.

I've been on a couple of dates since Gavin, but neither of them made me feel like Gavin did. That connection I feel with Gavin was non-existent for the other two. For anyone I've ever been with. No matter how hard I've tried to move on and forget him, I just can't. Not contacting him was so incredibly stupid of me. I know that now, but the damage has been done. I'm not sure I'll ever be able to fix it, no matter how hard I try to explain myself to him. I know I have to try.

Just thinking of the heat and the passion I shared with him that night sends my rising pleasure to new heights. "Oh, Gavin," I moan as I ride my fingers. I stroke my clit faster thinking of his dick proudly on display. I imagine him dropping to his knees in front of me and plunging his tongue into my pussy. Letting me ride it until I come all over it.

I'm so entranced in the pleasure and my thoughts that I'm feeling that I don't realize how much louder I have been moaning as I get closer and closer to the edge. Just as I'm about to jump off into my pleasure abyss, a rough hand grips my wrist and yanks my hand away from my pussy with a rumbling growl. My eyes fly open.

"If you're going to get off using me for inspiration, you're damn well going to do it the right way," Gavin growls. He doesn't hesitate in spreading my legs wider. His magical tongue that I've missed so much replaces my fingers and dives into my pussy.

"Ah!" My eyes roll back, and I shout. "Gavin!"

He lets go of my wrist as he grips my hips. He pulls me into his mouth. I grip the sheets and uncontrollably thrust against his tongue. He grips me tighter and doesn't allow me to move as he dominates my pussy like only he knows how to.

He growls low, sending vibrations through my pussy. I tremble. My pussy pulses erratically. I spear his hair with one hand. "Gavin," I moan. "I'm gonna… come…" I writhe under him.

"Not a chance in hell," he growls right before he pulls away from me.

I whine. "Wh-what?" I look up at him, panting.

He gives me a devilish smile as he licks his lips. With his thumb, he wipes the corner of his mouth. "You think I'm going to let you come that easily?"

His tone sends shivers down my spine. My stomach clenches. But it's him stroking his beautiful cock as he slowly leans over me that makes my entire body erupt in tingles. I watch him with wide eyes. The release is so close, yet so far away. He leans on his elbow. His dick rests against the part of me aching for him the most. It makes me tremble for him even more.

His thumb, the one he used to wipe my essence off the corner of his mouth, runs over my bottom lip before he slides it into my mouth. I gasp. My sweet and tangy taste mixed with the uniqueness of his skin, clean with a little bit of the woodsy earthiness I'm sure is his cologne, hits my taste buds. I swipe my tongue around it then suck like I would if it was his dick. I keep my eyes on his.

He slowly removes his thumb after thrusting it a couple of times. I release it with a pop and relish a little in the deep groan that falls from his lips. He lets his hand make its way slowly down my body, leaving goosebumps in its wake. He squeezes both of my breasts and tugs on each nipple, making me whimper and arch into him.

"Sh-shouldn't we t-talk first…?" I whisper breathlessly.

His hand moves between my legs as he leans down. "If talking is what you want to do, then I'm not doing something right." He nips my neck and scrapes his teeth over it, then licks it and kisses it to soothe the delectable pain. He fists his dick and slides his tip through my wetness.

"Oh! Oooh…," I moan. I grip his shoulders and scramble to get closer. "Gavin…"

"Do you do that a lot?" he rumbles against my neck. "Do you finger yourself and pretend it's me?" He pushes his dick against my clit.

"Fuck, Gavin!" I arch into him again and again as he rubs himself over my clit.

He kisses across my throat, nipping along the way as he rubs his dick against me faster, driving me to near madness. "Tell me you fuck yourself and think of me."

"Oh God, yes!" I get closer and closer to that desire the more he moves against me.

"Say it," he commands. "Tell me how much you think of me just so you can get yourself off."

I can barely comprehend his words. All I can do is moan, tremble, and writhe against him. I grip his shoulders. "My God… so, so good. I'm… gonna… "

Gavin's chuckle is dangerous, but I don't understand the implications until he stops, once more ripping my orgasm out of my grasp. "No way." He sits between my legs. "Not until I say. And I don't."

I'm close to tears as I pant. My release slowly gets further and further away. If this is punishment for what I did, it's too cruel. I'm just about to say as much when he slams into me, hard and deep, giving me no warning.

"Ah!" I scream. I'd arch into him, but he's holding me too tightly for me to move in the slightest. I'm completely his to do with what he will. And as much as I hate to admit it, I love every second of it. The way his cock stretches my pussy. The way I feel every bump and ridge as he thrusts hard and deep.

"Tell me. Say it. Say this is what you think about when you're playing with yourself," he growls as he thrusts, punishingly.

"Gavin!"

"Tell me you pretend your finger is my dick." He rolls his hips and slams into me as he pulls me into each thrust.

I grasp for anything I can because if I don't I'm going to rocket into another dimension. He's not being gentle. Not in the slightest. It's nothing like before, yet he's still the best I've ever had, and far more.

My pussy clenches down like a vice around his dick. "Ah!" I scream again as I careen towards cloud nine.

"You think I'm going to let you come without an answer to my question?" Gavin stops thrusting and slaps my ass.

This time, I do cry, but not because of the sting. Because he's torturing me. "Gavin, please!"

"You might want to think about answering me if you want that release you're begging me for." His eyes pierce my soul.

"Yes!" I scream. "Yes! I do! Okay?" Both wanting him to give me that orgasm I need so desperately and exhausted from the teasing and edging, I sit up, but I don't get far.

Gavin pushes me down. Without pulling out, he shifts and pins my wrists above my head. "Did I say I was done with you?"

I heave out a breath. "No, but I can't handle any more, Gavin! Let me come! Enough torture!"

He gives me a wicked grin. "You think I've even begun to torture you?" He starts thrusting hard and deep again. Not fast. Hard enough, though, so I'll feel it for days. He holds my wrists tightly with one hand and grips my ass with the other. He squeezes as he lifts, angling me so he slides even deeper. "I haven't even started."

I arch into him. His cock slides over the place only he's ever been able to find. That spot deep within my pussy that brings me higher and higher. With each and every thrust, I get closer and closer to the point of no return. Even if he stopped right now, I wouldn't be able to hold back.

Pushing up against his hand as he thrusts, my hips jerk into him, meeting his thrusts. "Gavin!" My pussy spasms as I come harder than I've ever come in my life. I soak his dick and my thighs.

He doesn't stop. "Holy fuck," he moans against my neck. Like a man possessed, he thrusts faster. He pants against my neck and rolls his hips.

As he fucks me through my orgasm, I realize all at once just what he meant when he said he hasn't even begun. I feel him thicken inside me, but I already know he'll chase my next release before he gives into his.

Still reeling from the mind-blowing climax, my thighs tremble. My stomach is still clenched. My pussy is gripping him hard. But it doesn't deter him. If anything, it spurs him on. He twists his hips side to side, hitting me in all the right spots and making me quake underneath him.

My body hums for him. Sings. Screams. He knows just what to do, the strings to play, the chords to hit, to make me beg for him. All of him. I can't speak, but I do all I can to convey to him what I need. Which is everything he has.

"Oh...," I moan and buck into his thrusts. I clench around his dick with each thrust, making him impossibly harder and thicker.

"Christ, Harleigh. What the fuck are you doing to me?" he asks hardly more than a whisper.

He reaches between us and starts rubbing my clit just as furiously as he's thrusting. He buries his face in my hair. I don't think he meant for me to hear his question with how low he spoke it. The words are simple, but they're everything I need to give me a little hope that I can fix what I broke.

Without meaning to, I come again, just as intensely as the first time. With a roar, a stark contrast to my quiet mewls, Gavin comes deep inside me. He thrusts us both through until we're spent and exhausted. Gavin pulls out and collapses on his back next to me. It takes me a few more moments to come down, but when I do, Gavin is already asleep. I pull the covers over us and curl up on my side facing him but giving him space.

I'm sure he didn't mean to, but his actions have given me a little more hope. Gavin told me our first night together that even though he's had a vasectomy, he's never been with any woman without a condom. Even his wife, who he told me died a little while ago. He said he never completely trusted her, and that she was adamant about not having kids, forcing him to wear a condom anyway.

Our first time together, he wore one. This time, though it was the heat of the moment, Gavin didn't use one or even bother to reach for one. I'm oddly comfortable enough with him that it doesn't bother me, but the fact that he didn't even attempt to grab one makes me feel a little more faith that I might have a future with him after all.

It's that thought that has my heart settling as I drift off.

Chapter Six

❦ Gavin ❦

It takes me a minute of blinking myself awake to realize that the vibration I hear in my head isn't actually my brain. It takes another full minute for me to realize that the weight against my left side isn't me suddenly paralyzed.

What the fuck is Harleigh doing curled up against my side draped around me? Why the hell am I holding her so damn close? And why are we naked? Did I drink too much? I glance at the clock on my nightstand and see it's late afternoon.

"What the fuck did I do?" I grumble. I don't have much time to dwell on every mistake I've apparently made in the past twenty-four hours, though, because the insistent vibration that is my phone is going off again.

I untangle myself gently from Harleigh, even though I should just push her off. It would serve her right. She's managed to make me question my entire fucking life choices without even saying a damn word. I'm pissed off at her. Then I'm not. Then I want nothing more than to be between her legs. I groan at the memory of doing just that. Right after she moaned my name and sent me off the fucking ledge.

I sit up on the edge of my bed and scrub my hands over my face. After coming out of the pool and seeing her, I decided right away to give

49

her a little taste of the turmoil she put me through. She had me once. She can stare all she likes, but she's not getting anything more than a memory. Just like she did to me.

But when I walked upstairs to grab some clothes and heard her moaning, getting louder and louder, and then my name falling from her lips, I couldn't help but crack the door open to see what the hell she was doing. I already knew, but I couldn't believe it. And it pissed me off even more. Who gets off in someone else's bed? Not only that, but to use me to get herself off after everything she did? Who does that? I couldn't believe her audacity.

Above and beyond all of that, instead of just talking to me, she ran off. Again. I might have had something to do with it this time. The shock of seeing me naked in front of her probably threw her off a little. But to run to my bedroom and get herself off to thoughts of me in my bed? I don't know whether to be angry or turned on as hell. Obviously, the being turned on thing won out earlier, but I refuse to let it happen again.

I glance at her as I grab my phone when it starts vibrating once more and stand. I hate that she looks so pretty and peaceful as she sleeps. I hate even more that I like the way she looks in my bed. Like it's right where she belongs. The fact that I feel like she does makes me let out another growl as I walk out of my bedroom.

"What?" I snap into the receiver. I lean against the wall across from my bedroom and glare at the door after I close it.

"Don't tell me you're still in a piss poor mood," Josh says. I can tell he's smirking.

"I'd be lying."

"And we know you hate that. Well, I have something that might make you feel better."

I raise an eyebrow and perk up a little. "An assignment? Tell me it's something big."

"Oh, it's big. I need to set up a few things here with Harleigh and her protection while we're gone, but I need you to go to Texas. Today. I'll bring you to the airport. I want to run by Jake's Diner again."

I sigh. I haven't told her about that. I intended to. I still should. "Okay. I'll bring her to Jess. She can help babysit Jackson while Jessa works on that huge project. Jess might even invite the girls."

"For now. Until I figure it out. I hate to pull you off this, but this shit in Texas is big. Brystone Springs. We might need to pull in Ryan on this one. From the little information I do have, there's a detective down there who thinks the entire city is corrupt. He said he was exaggerating a little bit, but he knows there's a lot of shit going on that's above his paygrade."

"What's his name?"

"Colton De Lise. I have some information for you. You can read it on the plane. Catch yourself up. If you think you need me, let me know. If you don't, I trust you to handle the situation. But I have a bad feeling about this. I think this is bigger than he thinks. I had Lance pull some shit. It's in the folder."

"Okay. What about Harleigh's mess?"

"It's still priority. We're just working this right now, too."

"You know that's not what I meant."

"I know exactly what you meant. But I'm not answering that for you, Gav. You need to figure that part of it out for yourself. I'll do my part and keep her safe while we resolve this bullshit with the fucking Franklin brother. But everything else? I don't have the answers for you, man."

"Come on. Not even a little brotherly advice?" I grin a little.

Josh laughs. "My brotherly advice? Figure out your heart. The rest will fall into place."

I shake my head. "Fuck you. I'm calling Lyric."

"Whose advice will be exactly what I just said. Only with a little more pep and a lot more bluntness. All wrapped in a pretty little Brit package. Granted, she might fly up here just to kick Harleigh's ass. Get your shit together. You'll be gone for a little while."

I laugh because I can actually see Josh's ex-girlfriend doing just that. Lyric Sharpe is all kinds of viciousness wrapped in an adorable package. She might live in Florida and be in a happy relationship with a couple guys who are pretty incredible, but she's still very protective of those of us up here who are close to her. We're the family she never had. Besides her brother and a couple others, we're all she's had for years. Even after her and Josh split. Very amicably. They just both felt they were better friends. But piss that girl off, and she'll tear the world apart to get her revenge.

One of my favorite things about her is that protectiveness in her. I still laugh thinking about the time when one of her husbands called me and asked why he had to rush after her to stop her from getting on a plane to kick, in his words, some little bitches ass for breaking her brother's heart. The girl has a lot of heart, but can definitely pack a punch.

Not to say she doesn't already know about Harleigh. I have told her. She's not happy with her either, but I think she understands a little bit more than she lets me believe. And since I'm torn between being pissed off on one hand and wanting to just make all of the pain go away on the other, Josh's point about Lyric telling me exactly what he did isn't that far off.

I pinch the bridge of my nose and close my eyes. "Give me twenty. Meet me at Jason's and Jessa's. I'll have my stuff."

"And Gavin? I know you're pissed off and battling right now, but we're not abandoning her. So, don't just leave her sleeping at your fucking house." Josh hangs up before I can come up with a snappy retort. Probably wise.

I hang up and walk back into my bedroom. I toss my phone onto the bed without breaking stride and slap Harleigh's naked ass, which is on full display since she's kicked off the covers and is laying on her stomach. Harleigh jumps and makes a sexy as hell squeaking noise as she curls into herself and looks up at me in total shock.

I turn away from her and walk to my closet. She can't see it, but I'm grinning from ear to ear. "Get up," I rumble. "I need to go. Which means I need to figure out what to do with you."

"What?" she asks, obviously confused.

"Get up!"

I get dressed and throw a couple more pairs of jeans and some shirts into a large gym bag. I grab a few other necessities to last me a few days and stride to my bathroom to grab my body wash and a few other things I'll need.

"I said I need to go to work," I call. "So, get up. Get dressed. Move."

When I come out of the bathroom, Harleigh has moved to her knees on my bed. She's blinking like she's trying to wake up, but I don't have the time to wait for her. This assignment will give me time to think about what I want right now without her clouding all of my thoughts and judgment with her pretty lavender scent.

"What's happening? Is it about my father? The diner? I need to go there." Whatever thought just crashed into her beautiful mind just made her go pale. It makes me furrow my brows and want to take her in my arms to make whatever she's thinking disappear.

My chest actually tightens, as if I can feel her pain. I watch her leap out of the bed and quickly throw her clothes on. I shake my head a little as I try to keep up. We've gone from needing to go to the diner to panicking.

"Harleigh?" I ask.

She looks at me like a deer in the headlights. Like she doesn't even know who I am. She's near hyperventilating. "I -" She sniffles and quickly finishes getting dressed. Then, she runs past me like she's being chased.

I reach out and stop her, pulling her against me. "What the hell is happening?"

"Let go! I have to go! Oh my God, how could I have been so stupid and immature?" She pushes against me, but I don't let her go.

"Harleigh!"

She stops pushing and looks up at me, fighting for breath. "I have… to -"

"Stop!" I command and pull her closer. I force her ear against my heart and breathe steadily for her, even though she's scaring the ever living fuck out of me. I sway with her. "Harleigh, please talk to me. I'm begging you. I may be pissed off about everything else, but I can help you with whatever the hell this is. Just talk to me."

"I'm so incredibly stupid, Gavin," she mumbles into my chest after taking several breaths to calm herself. I just stay quiet and hug her tighter because I do actually care about her. Fuck knows why. "I didn't think at all about the employees at the diner this morning. The openers get there at three in the morning. All I've been able to think about is myself. Me getting away from the killers. Me being here with you and wanting to apologize. Me and my reaction to seeing you coming out of the pool. Me, me, me. Never them and how they would feel walking into a bloodbath. And then me not showing up. I'm either going to be labeled as missing or a murderer, but I should have been there. I've been so selfish."

"First of all, getting away isn't fucking selfish. And second, when you woke up, you were still processing all that happened. That's not selfish. And third, my coming out of the pool like that didn't help you out with that desire or what you did to alleviate it at all. I'll admit to my role in that. I wasn't at all an innocent party." I glance at the clock. "This isn't how I want to leave this, Harleigh, but something important has come up, and we need to go. I have a plane to catch, and I need to get you someplace safe."

"But -"

I shake my head and take her hand, pulling her with me. "I know you don't have any idea how mafias work. I'm sure you think I'm being an asshole right now, and maybe I am, but I do need to go." I lead her down the stairs and through my house. I lock my door behind us then tug her with me again. My strides are long. My grip is tight. "Jessa is Ryan Crane's sister-in-law. Ryan is a leader of another mafia we work with. He's like family."

"Gavin, I have to go talk to the employees!" She yanks her wrist back, but I simply hold it tighter. "They had to have found my father by now!"

Jessa's and Jason's house is only a few doors down from mine. It's why I chose theirs to take her to. By the time we've reached her front lawn, my patience snaps. "Harleigh, for fuck's sake! Are you fucking incapable of trusting me? Is that why you ran the first fucking time? I made plans with you for a second and third date! You fucking sat there and acted like you were excited about it!" I drag her the rest of the way to the door. I angrily bang my fist against the door before turning back to her. "All of the employees who worked there were called. We handled everything. As for the diner? It was burned to the ground. We aren't the ones who did it."

"Hey, Gavin," Jessa says as she opens the door. She looks between me and Harleigh.

"I know I haven't called you to tell you what the fuck's happening, honey, but I'm needed in Texas." I watch as she nibbles her lip and looks up at me. I lean down and kiss her cheek, giving her a one-armed hug and still holding Harleigh's hand in a vice grip. "This is Harleigh," I whisper.

Jessa's eyes widen. "Oh… Oh!"

I pull Harleigh forward. "Harleigh needs clothing. How much do you know about what happened last night? Did Josh call you?"

She shakes her head. "I got a text from him saying you were coming by with someone who needed help and he'd explain when he got here. But don't you worry about that. I know you are in a hurry. He can fill me in."

I look down at Harleigh just as Josh pulls into the driveway. "You'll be safe here. I need to leave." I drop her now slack wrist as she nods at me, wide eyed. She trembles as she hugs herself.

Truthfully, I could explain more to her, but I don't want to. I want to get away because I'm fighting the urge to kiss her senseless again. I don't want to just give in and say all is forgiven. I don't even know if I want that. If I do, I need to go into this with clear air between us, and a clear mind. I don't have time right now to do either of those things.

And honestly, I'm not even sure I want to think about her at all. I don't trust her with my heart. I don't trust her to stay when she doesn't need me anymore. I shake my head as I turn away. Focusing on something else away from her can only help me.

"Gavin, wait!" Jessa calls after me.

I take a deep breath and close my eyes when I get to the SUV. I open them slowly and hand Josh my bag. He puts it into the back of the SUV as I turn towards her. "Yeah?"

"Have you… talked at all?" Jessa asks when she reaches us.

I let out a breath. "No, Jess. I'm far too fucked up over that girl to talk. The most I have been able to figure out on my own is that she thinks I'm a player. I also get the feeling that even though she has given a feeble apology, she doesn't feel like she did anything wrong. And right now, I don't want to hear any of her excuses. I don't think I could trust a word she says. I'm so fucking conflicted and mind-fucked because of her. I'm pissed off one second and fucking her the next. Then, I'm pissed off that I gave in and fucked her, which pisses me off more at myself and her all over again."

Jessa chews her lip like she wants to say something but doesn't. Instead, she hugs me. "So? What do I do with her?" she asks Josh when she pulls away.

He glances up at Harleigh, who's looking at her feet. She looks so sad and lost that, once again, I'm fighting myself to go to her and comfort her. I scrub my hands over my face and close the hatch on the SUV.

"A gang we're after that's connected to the fucker who went after Raleigh is after Harleigh," Josh begins. "We know he's the leader of the gang, and she was sold by her father to them to pay off his debt. Harleigh was supposed to marry the leader's son. She had no idea until last night. Apparently he refused to hand her over. Said he would pay more cash. That they couldn't have her. She hid while they killed her dad, then ran when they looked for her."

I lean against the SUV and fold my arms over my chest as it tightens. The possessive feeling I have for her is something completely new. I've felt it before for people like Jessa, but it's more of a protective possessiveness. My family. With her, she's mine, even though she really isn't. Tell that to my traitorous fucking heart.

"Poor thing," Jessa whispers as she glances sadly at her.

"Or she's acting," I rumble with a glare. Even I know that's not true and feel a little bad about the words that came from my mouth.

"Gavin," Josh growls low and in warning. "Get in the fucking vehicle. Fuck." He turns back to Jessa. "I need you to keep her occupied. Ryan will be over after his meeting to talk to you. I should be back by then. Have her watch Jackson so you can work."

I don't typically back down to anyone, but I do Josh. I know what he's capable of. I push off the SUV and head to the passenger side of the vehicle as Josh tells her what he needs her to do. When he's finished, he wraps Jessa in his arms and hugs her tightly before letting her go. He slides in the driver's side and pulls out of the driveway while Jessa makes her way back to Harleigh.

"I need to get the fuck out of here," I mumble.

"What the hell was that? I mean, no doubt you're an asshole, but I've never known you to act or say anything like what you just did."

I close my eyes and let out a frustrated growl as my head falls back against the seat. "I know."

"So, talk to me. I know I'm not Alex, but I still think we're close enough to hash this shit out."

I chuckle but keep my eyes closed. "I'm just as close to you. You know that."

"I'm fucking with you."

I smile and shake my head. "Okay. I'll tell you. I'm struggling. I want to forgive and forget, but I can't get past what she did. I'm possessive as hell over her. I don't want anyone else touching her. But then I start thinking I don't give a shit what she does with her life. I don't want her anywhere near me. If she thinks I'm not a good choice for her and doesn't want to give me a chance to break her preconceived notions of me…" I shrug. "So be it, I guess. But I can't ignore my feelings for her. I connected with her on a level I've never felt before. I settled for Marissa because we'd been through so much. I guess I just figured it was time to put a ring on her finger." I scrub my hands down my face. "Fuck, I don't know."

"I know it hurt to find her gone."

I sigh and watch the Chicago traffic. "Yeah. It did. She knew the score from the moment we met. I was honest with her. I told her I liked her. I did things with her I've never done. I did it all. Wined and dined. Made plans. I opened up about Marissa. But what's more? I made love to her that night." I look over at him. "When the fuck have you ever known me to do that?"

Josh chuckles. "Well, there was a big chunk of my life you were more in the background, but before and after? I've never known you to be the tender loving kind."

"I'm not. Not even close." I lean my elbow against the window and prop my head up on my hand. "I feel like I've been in love with her my whole life, Josh. Yet, I'm so pissed off, that I can't even talk to her. I don't even think it's because she left the first time. It's because she ghosted me and then called me when she needed me. Then just… fucking ghosted me again. Then she turns up at Lucinio Tech? Father dead? Screaming for the leader of Lucinio Mafia?" I pinch the bridge of my nose as Josh turns into the private entrance to the airport.

"Speaking as someone who dealt with a fuck of a lot, trauma does things to you. She watched her dad die. I'm pretty sure all she was thinking of was that we might not be the good guys, but we sure as hell cleaned up the neighborhood that diner was in. We showed up when she needed us. She might end up owing us, but the price has to be better than what they wanted. I think you need to give her a break, Gav. At the very least, talk to her. Find out what was going through her head. People don't make smart decisions when they're afraid. You know that better than anyone. You've seen just as much shit as I have. I know you weren't in that room until the very end, but she was terrified. She was afraid of the gang. Me."

"Even if I do talk to her, Josh, what's to say she won't do the same thing when we get her out of this fucking mess? What's to say she won't just disappear again? I don't trust that she'll stay. As dramatic as it sounds, I don't trust her with my heart."

"No one said you had to give it to her. But she's been through hell. Literally. It's not every day that your father is killed right in front of you. Not everyone is stoked to be involved with the mafia. You never know. Maybe finding out you were part of a huge mafia scared her."

I chuckle. "Funny. She runs straight to the lead guy of something that scares her?"

Josh sighs. "Gavin. Come on, man." He stops next to his private jet and looks at me. "Lesser of two evils, right? If you were running your own mafia or gang or whatever and made enemies with me, what would you do? Run to Ryan Crane, knowing he's on my side? Or run straight into the arms of the devil himself?"

I laugh. "The devil himself. He's less fucking dangerous than you are, but combine you with Ryan? No thank you."

"So? See my point? Are you going to sit there and use that excuse on me? Or are you at least going to talk to her?"

I look at the plane as the staff stands near the stairs, waiting on orders. "What would you do if the girl of your dreams did this to you? What if you were in my shoes? You meet her. You talk. You have an intense connection. You spend hours talking before moving things to the bedroom. You wake up and find her gone. No note no nothing. I thought something happened to her, Josh. Until I saw her at the diner ducking into the kitchen as soon as she saw me." I look over at him again. "I'll be honest and tell you that I didn't tell her that night what I do for a living, but when she found out and called me for help? I thought we would at least talk, and that I'd be able to find out her true feelings. If she didn't want me, okay. It would fucking suck for me, but at least I'd know. I didn't even get that, though."

"Gavin, I get it. I do."

I sigh as I open the door. I walk to the back of the SUV. Josh follows. I grab my bag and put the strap over my shoulder. "I just don't know what to do. I've never been so fucking conflicted. Not like this."

"And I think that's where a lot of this is coming from. The back and forth. You want my advice? You need this. Get your mind right. Forget about all of this and focus on something entirely different. And then, when you're ready, talk to her. Because talking to her when you're not ready to listen isn't going to get you anywhere and will only make you more miserable." He holds up a folder. I take it with a half-smile. "Call me if you need me sooner than a week from now."

"You got it, boss." I grin and wink. I know he hates being called boss.

"Get the fuck out of here." He glares, but he's smiling.

I smile wider as I head for the plane but end up pausing and turning back to him. "Take care of her, okay?"

"You don't need to worry about her. I got her. This is the best thing for you right now. You need to figure out what you want. Then take it from there."

I nod and turn back to the plane. The staff finishes grabbing the gear Josh packed and is sending with me. I hand my bag to the flight attendant. "Live rounds in there."

"We got it, Mr. Vandenberg." She smiles and takes my bag. She puts it with the rest of the gear as I climb the stairs.

I settle in my seat and open the folder to start reading up on the information gathered so far on this new job. By the time we take off, I can feel myself relaxing. Josh was right. I needed this.

Chapter Seven

❦ Harleigh ❦

(Three Days Later)

"I thought you might like some tea," someone says quietly from the door of my prison. I glance at the door from the oversized chair I'm curled up in. Arianna. The Queen of Castle de Crane.

I turn back to the window and stare absently outside. "Thank you," I say quietly. I hug my knees to my chest.

Arianna makes her way into the room and sets a steaming hot mug of a delicious smelling tea in front of me. "It's lavender with lemon. My personal favorite for many reasons. Mostly, though, it's relaxing and soothing." She sits on the arm of the other chair. "Are you doing okay? You didn't come down for breakfast or lunch."

I sniffle as tears sting my eyes. "Have you ever seen the movie *Mean Girls*?"

She tilts her head. "Yes… Why?"

I look at her. I'll be honest in saying that she hasn't really been cold towards me. Not like everyone else. But she also hasn't been really talkative. Most of the time, she's not even around. And if she is, she's not around me. I'm either alone in a giant house I can't leave, or one of the other girls is around being snarky towards me.

I sigh. "You really want me to be honest?"

She smiles a little. "Honesty is a big thing here."

"Okay. Pure honesty coming your way. I hate it here. I feel like I'm being held prisoner. I can't go to see the diner. Even if it's just ashes. I haven't been allowed to do anything about getting my father's…" My voice cracks. "My father's anything in order. I don't know how much debt he had. I don't know what to do about our little house. There's still a mortgage on it. I don't know if he had life insurance to help me pay off his debts, like the restaurant and house. I don't even know if he had any insurance on the diner. Or how to pay the employees. They are who I am the most worried for. Their livelihood. Some are barely scraping by and depended so much on their tips to feed their kids. But that's not all. I have all of this worry and anxiety going on and no one to help or open up to."

"I -"

I hold up a hand. "Please. I don't mean to be rude, but please. I need to finish or you won't understand."

She folds her hands in her lap and nods. "Okay."

I take a deep breath. "I know I made my bed. I know I messed up so badly with Gavin. Given he hasn't answered any of my texts or calls, I'm pretty sure he hates me. And I deserve it. I do. I got scared. I thought I'd just be another notch on his belt. That everything he was saying to me were things he said to everyone. I took those words and our night together and kept the memories locked away. I tried to forget him and move on. But then I found out he was mafia, and that was something he didn't tell me."

"It was something you needed to process," Arianna says quietly.

I nod. "And I did. I really did. But by the time I realized that no one that I tried to replace him with measured up to him, even if he was mafia, the damage was done. I'm not a stupid person. I know what I did. I didn't feel like I could go back. Not after that. And then everything with my dad happened." I look down in order to compose myself. "I still have no idea what you all do here. And it's quite obvious I'm not part of the inner circle of all your family. I don't expect to be, but I didn't expect all of the hostility. They all hate me."

"Oof… that's a lot. You have a ton on your mind."

"You're telling me," I mumble and wave a hand down myself. "And as selfish as this sounds, I'm not even wearing my own clothing."

"I can help a little. If you'll let me."

I look up at her and sniffle. "Are you going to tell me to suck it up?"

She chuckles and shakes her head. "No. I'd never do that. We all have, in our own ways, been in your shoes. What I can do, though, is tell you that, while I will not speak for him, Gavin is very busy. I would never tell you that's definitely why he hasn't responded to you, but I do know that he's been constantly on the move. I don't know the details, but I do know that whatever it is, it's dangerous. It needs his full attention." She glances towards the backyard before turning back to me. "As for the others, we're all very protective of our own. We only have a few facts to go on. We know that you're in need of help. We know what happened with you and Gavin. We know you only got in touch with him because you needed something from him. Other than that? We don't know you. I can speak for the others on this, though. No one is intentionally trying to be mean to you. We all have our opinions on what you did, and we've been handling it the best we can. Something we all have in common is that we all wear our hearts on our sleeves. Gavin is like a brother to us. So we're all rather protective of him."

I hug myself. "I know… It's just the hostility is very, very evident. I didn't expect to be welcomed with open arms, but I'm already going through so much." I shake my head. "I sound like a whiny child who wants to fit in with the cool kids."

"I can also do one more thing. Josh was pulled into something big. Ryan has been working on things going on with you here. Maybe talking to him would help?"

"I'd like that," I say quietly. "I just want to know what's happening." I rest my head on my arms and hug my knees to myself tighter. "I don't know what to do. I don't know what I'm supposed to do."

Arianna stands. "Well, I think Ryan can help you with that." She waits for me to stand and follow her. After a few moments of hesitation, I do.

I keep my arms locked around myself as Arianna leads me through the house and out to the pool area. Ryan is standing in the pool with his young boy. He's flying him like an airplane high above his head and dipping him low enough to skid him gently across the water. The boy, Christopher, if I remember right, is squealing and laughing. Ryan is making propeller noises and everything. It's quite adorable and makes me smile. Such a large man being so gentle with his son reminds me of my own father. At least the happier times with him.

Ryan looks up at me and Arianna and winks. He flies Christopher out of the pool and walks towards us. Christopher, still laughing, sees Arianna and reaches for her eagerly, seemingly forgetting all about his dad. Arianna laughs as she picks him up.

Ryan looks at me as he grabs a towel. "See this shit? He only loves me when mama isn't around. She enters the room, and it's all over for dad."

Arianna laughs. "That's so not even true." She playfully swats Ryan's arm. "Harleigh has some questions. With Josh pulled away and Gavin gone, she's sort of been left out of things she really shouldn't be."

Ryan nods; the smile falls from his lips as Arianna takes their son inside. Ryan starts to dry off, turning his intense eyes on me. He's so tall and darkly intimidating that I take an inadvertent step back. He's not quite as scary as Josh, but he still has that aura about him. I take a deep breath, though, because he hasn't given any reason to fear him. He's been nothing but kind, though he hasn't said a lot. He's been quite obviously busy.

"Take a seat." He gestures to the pool chair behind me and sits in the one near him. His voice is deep, but has a kindness about it that I haven't heard from anyone. Even his wife, though she was being kind, still had a bit of an edge to her.

I do as I'm told and sit, clearing my throat. "My head is spinning."

"I don't doubt that. You've been left in the dark. I assure you I didn't intend to. I have a tendency to throw myself into work. Arianna says I obsess over it. I say it's what makes me so damn good at what I do."

"And what do you do?" I blurt out. I put a hand over my mouth with wide eyes. "I'm sorry. That... I shouldn't have asked. That was rude."

He chuckles. "I'm not ashamed of it." He leans back in the chair. "Was Josh able to tell you anything before he left?"

I shrug a little and sigh as I cross my arms over myself. "He told me that he'd gone to the location of the diner and talked to someone investigating it. It's arson. It was definitely started by someone. And an accelerant was used. I was upset. I didn't really think about asking him what he does. I just know from the news and stuff that you run a legit mafia. I recently learned Josh runs his own legit mafia. From what I've found out, you both do a lot of good in Chicago and around the world."

I can feel his eyes on me. After a few moments he chuckles again. "You have your doubts."

I look at him a moment before turning back to focus on the clear water in the pool. "When I think mafia, I think crime. Drugs. Guns. Violence. Mayhem. I think danger. When Gavin came in and told the server that we were under Lucinio Mafia's protection, I didn't know what to think. I don't know how exactly it works. I thought we'd owe them somehow. Like we owed Ruthless Warriors. They told us that same thing, you know. We had to pay for their protection against other gangs. I didn't know how it would work with Lucinio Mafia. I still don't really know the price I'll need to pay for going to Josh for help."

"Okay. Well, let me ease your mind a little bit. Legit mafias don't run like the mafias you see on TV or in your history books. We weren't always legit. I turned us legit when I took over many years ago. Josh is still working at it. He's legit, but he's still finding deep corruption and illegal shit from when his father ran it. Legit mafias aren't into the drug trade or gun smuggling. We aren't into human trafficking or prostitution rings. Our companies are what keeps us afloat, and we have a lot of them. According to the IRS, I'm a billionaire who runs several successful companies all over the world. I pay my taxes like a good boy. So does Josh. I get audited regularly, just like any other billionaire in this country."

"But you have to be into some things that aren't on the up and up. If you weren't, you wouldn't know about what's going on in my little part of the world."

He nods. "You're right. I'm not saying I'm an angel. I'm far from it. Josh isn't either. Gavin isn't squeaky clean. He's second in command to one of the most powerful men in the world. We all have blood on our hands. But it's dirty blood. Think about the people who killed your father. About the people who bought you. People like that are slippery as fuck to the cops. They have to build a case. Get search warrants. They have to try them in court and win their case in order to get them put away for maybe twenty years, if they're lucky. But those guys get out on parole in half that time. Depending on the crime, maybe they only get five years. They're out in three. I don't have the red tape. I go in and don't have a rulebook to play by. I give the cops the busts and the cases on a silver platter, but those really bad guys? The ones who will slip through the long arm of the criminal justice system?" He shrugs with a dark chuckle.

"Those are who you kill…"

"We aren't a danger to people like you, Harleigh. I can't say all legit mafias are like us. They aren't. But me and Josh? Our entire goal in life is to make this world better. It's a never-ending fucking battle. But we do it because we want our kids to grow up in a safer world. No one likes to hear about another shooting on the news. No one likes to hear about another gang driveby. No one likes hearing about a gang terrorizing a neighborhood. Or another girl has gone missing and is suspected to have been sold to the cartel's human trafficking ring. We don't have our hands in everything. I don't like to hear about school shootings, but that isn't my territory. That's the police. Now, if the corruption within the department is so blatantly obvious and they're doing shit to cover their asses, well, that's where we come in. Most of the time, it goes all the way to the top. We help the Department of Justice or the FBI to fix it. Sometimes, there's something very sinister going on behind the corruption. Another mafia. A gang. The cartel. The cops can only do so much. We can do more."

"How, though? If they know what you do…"

"Well, it's complicated. Sometimes, we have to pay people off. But most of the time, cops look the other way for the greater good. One of my brothers is the leader of the Drug and Gang Task Force. My other brother is his Sergeant. I work with them on a lot of shit. They get the big busts and recognition. I stay behind the scenes and take out those they won't be able to prosecute. The lead guys I was telling you about. The bad guys who can pay people off to stay quiet. No case, no conviction. It's a lot of bullshit, but it happens every day. My job is to help them stop it. I have allies all over the world. Military. Law Enforcement. Other mafias. Governments. Josh has that same level of respect because he works with me. I've built up my reputation over the years. The fact that I get to help him now is my reward for all of my sacrifices."

I nod. "I think I understand."

"The Lucinio Mafia would never make you pay them for their protection. That isn't how we work. We don't go in, clean up a neighborhood, and expect the residents and business owners to pay us to be there. We have enough money rolling in from our companies. We don't need to make more money off your back. When we say you're under our protection, we mean that. If someone fucks with you, tell us. We'll deal with it. That's our job. It's what we're around for. Make sense?"

I breathe out a sigh of relief because that does actually ease a lot of my worry. Knowing I won't have to pay them somehow for what they're doing for me goes a long way in making me feel they really aren't dangerous. At least to me.

I nod. "Makes sense."

"What else is on your mind? I can sense that's not everything."

I chuckle. "Well, other than Gavin and feeling like I'm never going to get a second chance to make things right with him? The other worries have to do with the diner." I look down. "My father. The Ruthless Warriors." I shake my head. "All of my back and forth anger at him for doing what he did, and the overwhelming sadness that he's gone."

"Beginning with Gavin. All I will say is that he's pissed off. Is it warranted? If it were me, I'd be pissed off, too. I know Gavin. He's a lot like me. He throws himself to work. Ironically, it helps everything else make sense. I also know that he's busy as hell right now. And I know what's going on is taking all of his focus and attention. You need to talk. But not now. As for the diner and your father. What would you like to know?"

I shift and turn so I'm facing him. "The employees. I'm so worried about them. Some of them depend on that job. Others are just students who are looking for extra money, but those that depend on it are without income." I sniffle. "One of the servers who works there is like a grandmother to all of us. She takes care of her ailing husband, but sometimes they don't have enough money after their bills for food. What is she going to do? How can I help? Did my dad have insurance money on the diner? I'd give every penny of it to them. And then the house. Life insurance. I know it might be selfish, but did he leave me anything to help in the event he's gone? I'm not worried about a place to live. I could probably live with one of the people I work with or couch surf, but did he leave anything to help pay off any debt he has that the Ruthless Warriors didn't pay off?" I wipe my eyes when the tears silently trickle down my cheeks. "I don't even know how to figure this out. I don't know if he has paperwork anywhere. I know nothing, and it makes me feel so helpless. I should have asked him to show me. Teach me more. Something so I can help the employees."

"Okay -"

"And again. Selfish. But I'm wearing other people's clothes. Other people's underwear. I already feel like I'm having some sort of bizarre out of body experience, but to not even have my own clothes? And then my dad. He sold me!" I become more and more agitated. "Who does that? Why? Why would he do that? Did he ever love me? Did they force him?"

"Harleigh." Ryan reaches over and puts a hand on my arm. "Trust me, sweetheart. I know where the anger comes from. It was something that threw you. And I don't have any of those answers for you. What I can say is that I can help with everything else. The diner. The employees. Even the clothes." He squeezes my arm as I breathe deeply. "Diner first. It doesn't matter if he does or doesn't have insurance. The investigators ruled it arson. You won't get insurance unless they can prove that the person who started it wasn't paid by your dad to do it. They will eventually get around to proving it was a murder cover-up and pay out, but there's a lot of red tape. I'll put Robby on it. He's my tech guy. He can tell us if your dad had insurance, and if you're listed on the policy. That's another battle."

I let out a frustrated breath. "Great."

He squeezes my arm again and lets out a breath. "It's complicated. Long battle. But we'll get through it. Okay?"

I look at him afraid to hope that I won't have to do it alone. "Really?"

"Yes. Really. As for the property insurance for the house, again, that's another battle. I'll put Robby on that. In the meantime, Robby can easily find all of your dad's debt. I'll take care of it."

"Like a loan," I whisper.

"No. No, Harleigh. Not like a loan. I'm going to sound like an asshole, but two-hundred thousand dollars in debt, as an estimate, is nothing to me. I make that in a day."

I chuckle a little. "That was more cocky than asshole."

"I'm accused of being cocky every day." Ryan grins. I laugh. "Anyway. The insurance, when you do get it, is yours. I don't want it. You can use it however you want to. Regarding the employees, all I need is contact information. If you can't get it or don't know it all off the top of your head, Robby has his ways. Wouldn't be the first time the kid has hacked into the IRS."

My eyes widen, and I choke on my own spit. "What?" I squeak out.

Ryan just grins and winks. "Not for me. At least not regarding my shit. He's found employment records for me and may or may not have fucked up a few people's lives using the IRS. To his credit, though..." He trails off and lets me finish the sentence.

I can't help but giggle. "Bad guys."

"Very bad guys. My point, though, is we'll take care of the employees. We'll get them new jobs. The one you consider a grandmother doesn't need to be working. I'll happily help her retire. Even move her to a retirement community in Florida, if she wants."

My heart squeezes at the kindness he's showing. "Why are you doing this?"

"Because it's what we do, Harleigh. This is a legit mafia. Is there dark shit that goes on in the background? Yes. Will it ever harm you? Not if you're a good person." He smiles as he stands and stretches. "As for those clothes, I know it can't be comfortable for you."

"It's not that I'm not grateful... I just... feel a little like an alien or something."

"Well, I can't say I'd want to wear another man's underwear, so I understand. I wanted to survey your neighborhood anyway. I can grab clothes. Essentials. Sentimental things if you want. I have a couple of my guys meeting me there later. Mainly because we want to see if they went looking for you there and left any kind of hint as to where they're hiding."

I nod slowly. I know I can't go with, but I am a little more confident that, with his help and that of those he works with, I might be able to get my life on track.

Chapter Eight

☙ Gavin ☙

(Three Weeks Later)

I stare through my scope on my rifle waiting for the command to take my shot. The situation in Brystone Springs blew up into something I never expected. For the size of the town, the level of corruption is beyond my level of comprehension. I've never seen anything like this, and I've been in the game for a long time.

"You realize what we're about to do?" Josh's deep whisper comes over my earpiece.

"Yep. We're about to start a fucking war," I respond.

"You know I don't often second guess myself, but I'm damn well doing it now." He chuckles. "Fucking hell."

"We don't have a choice," Ryan whispers. "We need to stop the trafficking train. It might have trickled to that other cop, but it starts here."

"Are you absolutely positive this guy isn't attached to the cartel?" Josh asks. "We don't need that shit. I have enough on my plate."

"Positive," Ryan answers. "He's the leader of the Mexican Armadas. Take him out, I can take his factions a lot easier. You know I've been looking for this motherfucker for a while."

"Christ," Josh rumbles. "I trust you. But if you get me stuck in a war, I'm coming for you, you asshole."

Ryan laughs. "Wife is in her bedroom. Upstairs. North corner. She just got into bed and shut out the light."

"That's our cue," Luke Massena, Ryan's second in command, says.

"Take your shot, Vandenberg. And don't fucking miss," Alex says to me with chuckle.

I grin. "You mean don't shoot him in the ass like I did that one dude when I was fucking fourteen and training?"

There are quiet laughs before Josh silences everyone. "I remember that day," he says. "If you can shoot this guy in the ass, I'll be impressed."

I smile wider. "Considering he's sitting on it on that expensive leather couch, it might be an impossible challenge." I tilt my head a little bit. "Might be fun to fuck with him, though." I lower my gun and let out a breath before I shoot. "Well, look at that," I say with an even wider grin when I hit my mark. "I still got it."

Everyone quietly laughs as our target jumps up and grabs his ass, then sinks to his knees when the pain hits. He looks out the window. I know he can't see any of us, but he looks right in my direction. I take my second shot and revel in the blood and brains splattering against the wall behind him.

"Direct hit," Josh says. "Clean up crew. Go. Gavin, with me."

I stand and move my gun so it's across my back. I brush myself off and meet Josh near the house. "Do we have a place for the wife?"

"We're helping her disappear. She's going back home to France. She should be ready to go."

"We got company," Ryan rumbles. "Get her out. Hurry up. You only have a couple of minutes. We'll keep them off your back, but it's about to get loud and wake a lot of people up."

"Fuck," I whisper. Josh and I follow the cleanup crew into the house and sprint up the stairs to the bedroom the wife is in. I knock on the door.

Josh takes out his phone. "De Lise," he says after a few seconds. "Keep the cops off me. We're finishing up."

He hangs up as the wife opens the door, thankfully dressed and ready to go. She looks up at me. "I'm ready," she says tearfully. "Is he gone?" Save for the bruised cheek and black eye, the almost sixty year old woman is truly beautiful. Even though she's been in America for years, her French accent is thick. She's rather tall, like a model, just not as unhealthily tiny as one.

"He'll never bother you again," I say as I take her hand and lead her out. Just as we reach the front door, the promised noise starts.

"Oh God!" the woman screams. She tugs on my hand, as if she's trying to pull me back to the safety of the house, and drags us both into Josh.

"Get down!" he commands as he shoves her to the ground.

"Fuck!" I yank my hand away from her just before I end up on top of her. Crouching, I pull my rifle into my hands. "Where are those shots coming from?" I yell into my earpiece.

"We have them cornered! Get her the fuck out!" Luke barks. "You're clear!"

Josh tugs her to her feet and pulls her behind him. I keep my gun ready and follow him, covering them both. Gunshots ring out and echo in the quiet night air, but Josh keeps pulling her with him, his gun and eyes scanning for any threats, just like mine.

"Down!" I yell. Josh doesn't hesitate, trusting I see something he doesn't. I shoot, hitting my target between the eyes and immediately scan for other threats. "Move!"

Josh pulls the screaming woman with him until we get to one of our SUV's. Covering them both, Josh pushes her into the back seat and climbs in behind her. I close the door behind them both and jump into the passenger side.

"Get us the hell out of here," Josh rumbles. The driver takes off. "We have the falcon," he says into the radio. "De Lise has the cops. Don't dally. Meet you at the airport."

Everyone falls silent as we catch our breath. The guard driving turns up the police scanner we have in the vehicle. I keep my eyes open because we never know when a threat is going to catch up with us.

"They called out a shots fired call," the guard says. "Four squads answered."

"De Lise will deal with it," Josh says.

Colton De Lise is the detective that called us in. The day after we showed up, three weeks ago, one of his so-called friends tried to poison him. Didn't work well for him at all. Colton got sick, but we caught it in time. The fucker he worked with got everything he deserved and more. We found out he was the leader of a huge betting ring that involved a lot of disgusting shit. Everything from how long it takes for a man to die after he's bitten by a venomous snake or spider all the way to selling young virgins to men who covet their virginity. And then selling them to a human trafficking ring when they've gotten what they want.

It took us a little while, but we were able to find the leader of the human trafficking ring. Lucky for us, his wife gave us the in we needed. Her husband knew we were in town and let it slip to her. She sought us out and helped us set him up for his downfall. He thought he was about to meet some big buyer tonight. We knew he'd call in backup, but we didn't expect it to be so early. The meeting was set for three in the morning. It's just after ten at night right now. We thought we gave ourselves enough time to get in and get out. I guess he's a little smarter than we thought.

"We're Code Four here," Colton says over the scanner. "All squads on the way to the shots fired call can back off. My team has it under control."

"10-4," the dispatcher says. "Shots fired call is Code Four. Squads responding can call off."

A chorus of '10-4s' go out over the radio. A squad in front of us shuts off his lights and sirens as he slows down. Instead of continuing straight, he turns and drives down another road.

"Nine-nine-three will take that neighbor dispute on Donahue."

"10-4, nine-nine-three. I'll put you on the dispute."

"Nine-seventy-six will go with nine-ninety-three," a deep male voice says.

"10-4," dispatch responds. "Nine-seven-six on dispute on Donahue."

I let out a relieved sigh as we get further from the scene and closer to the edge of town. My tension lessens even more when our people start clearing the scene after all threats have been dealt with. Ryan's people will be there a bit longer cleaning up, but I feel a lot better knowing we didn't lose anyone. We've lost guys over the years. None of us take it well. We compartmentalize, but we all fall apart in our own way later on when we're able to decompress. Losing someone is never easy.

When we pull onto the highway on the way to the airport, I allow my mind to drift. At least a little bit. I'm still highly vigilant as we drive, but my thoughts aren't on the asshole we took out in Brystone Springs.

They're on Harleigh.

She's texted me every single day since I left Chicago. At first, I was too busy to respond. I forgot about the call or text by the time I fell into bed, often sometime early in the morning. The next day was filled with just as much work as my nights. By the time I realized I hadn't responded to her in the slightest, that sadistic asshole part of me shrugged it off and kept it up. I ignored her calls but listened to the voicemails and didn't respond to her texts, even though I read them. Not that she'd know that. As far as she's concerned, I've ghosted her just like she did me.

I thought she'd stop texting and calling, but I have to give her credit where it's deserved. She called every single morning and left a voicemail that just told me she's thinking of me and to have a good day. I'm not going to pretend the gesture didn't warm my heart a little.

Her texts broke me, though. One of them said Ryan went to her house. It was burned to the ground just like the diner. She felt lost, but what hurt me is that she also felt alone. She's mentioned in the texts that no one is really all that kind to her, and that she understands why, but it makes her feel even more alone. I almost responded to the one where she said she feels like it would be better for everyone if she just left and took her chances, but she sent another after and said that she doesn't think she'd be able to do that. She might feel alone, but at least she's safe.

It's quite obvious that she's beyond heartbroken, and there is a part of me that feels for her. She lost her father, her entire world, in a matter of forty-eight hours. Truthfully, of everyone surrounding her right now, Raleigh should be the one who is the most sympathetic. She woke up in an entirely different place surrounded by men who were absolutely doing all they could to be intimidating. She had nothing. Knew no one. And we were all suspicious of her for a period of time because of who her father was.

Turns out Matthew Lucinio wasn't her father at all. He adopted her when she was a baby because her real parents couldn't take care of her. But Matthew never did anything without a bigger picture plan. He intended to marry her off to Edward Franklin in order to merge businesses and God only knows what else. We found out Raleigh's real parents were Damon's.

Our Damon's. The same Damon who has been part of our circle for as long as we all can remember.

While I can understand at least a little why the girls are less accepting of her than any of the others, I'm honestly baffled why they aren't supporting her by now. One thing I can say about our family is the girls are very nurturing and protective of each other. They all have a pretty good track record of rallying around one another. It's both sweet and pretty damn scary to watch. Which is why I'm confused at her feeling lonely. I'd ask what the hell is going on, but it's been far too busy, and I'm exhausted. I guess I'll figure it out when I get home.

"Will you be able to take down the rest of his gang now? Without him?" the woman asks quietly, pulling me from my thoughts.

"We won't be," Josh tells her. "But there is another crew that will be. They're just waiting on the command from their boss."

"That's not you?" she asks.

"No, ma'am. I work with other mafias. The leader of one of my allies will be going after them. By the end of the night, there won't be anything left of the gang."

She falls silent once more. I glance over my shoulder. "Why did you decide to come to us?" I ask. It's a question that's been on my mind.

She chuckles, but I can hear the misery and sadness. "I probably could have handled the beatings. But it was when I found a girl in the shed out back with our gardening tools chained to the floor that really got me. I didn't feel I had much recourse to the other stuff he does. I went to the police. He just bought his way out of trouble and gave me a few broken ribs and a nose for his troubles. He let it slip that you were here. I knew that you would be able to help. I knew no one else would get sold into his human trafficking ring, which I knew nothing about until I found the girl. I thought it was just drugs and guns with him. Lord knows I've seen my fair share of deals go on outside that house. Though, I was never supposed to."

"And why are you so afraid now that you're asking us to get you to France?" I ask.

"I don't know his connections." She shrugs a little. "Who's to say another gang won't come for me? At least this way, I have a chance."

"No one will get to you," Josh assures her. "We have connections all over. And we protect those that give us information that leads to the downfall of prolific people. We'll keep you safe."

His words seem to give her some measure of comfort, because I watch as she damn near deflates. She closes her eyes and leans her head back against the seat with a soft, tentative smile. A sense of hope.

🍒🍒🍒

Several hours and a very long plane ride later, Josh and I walk into Ryan's house with him and Luke trailing after us. Ryan's brother, Nick, walks in behind us all. He yawns and stretches, then smiles when his wife, Dani jumps in his arms. We're all dead on our feet, but he catches her without stumbling.

Luke's husband, Robbie, smiles as he hugs him tightly. "Missed you. You okay?" he asks.

"I'm good, baby. Just tired as fuck," Luke says as he buries his face in Robbie's neck.

Arianna wipes her eyes as Ryan folds her in his arms. "I'm okay, beautiful," he rumbles. "Just a scratch."

"I don't care," she whispers as she sniffles. "It could have been worse."

"Aww, come on now," Luke says, reaching over to rub her back. "You know I'd never let anything happen to him."

I chuckle, but I understand why Arianna is so upset. A stray bullet from the gunfight grazed Ryan's arm. It really is just a scratch. It didn't break more than a couple layers of skin. It was just enough to make him bleed. But Arianna is right. It could have been worse.

The rest of the family hugs and kisses us all, but my eyes keep falling on the one person in the room not joining in on the welcome home celebration. The one person hugging herself and very obviously trying not to cry. If everyone here knows about Ryan's minor injury, then they know about my near death experience. The bullet that sailed so closely to my cheek, I could feel the fucking heat as it whizzed by.

Which means *she* knows.

It's not the first time it's happened. Not long ago, Josh had one sail over his head. Whenever we end up in gunfights, there's always a danger of some kind. Bullets sail by us all the time. What makes the situations so significant and scary is that we didn't know where they came from. We were lucky as hell that the shooter wasn't a better shot.

I drop a kiss to Breetana's head and assure her that I'm okay before I make my way in the direction I saw Harleigh disappear. I check each room, all of the doors are open, but she's not in any of them. When I get to the den, though it's dark, the sun is just starting to color the sky as it rises, I see the slightest movement.

I move quietly through the den and see her standing near the wall that encloses the pool area. Her head just barely reaches above the five foot wall. She's hugging herself tightly, something she does that breaks my defenses against her a little more each time I see her do it. It signifies a loneliness that I'm starting to realize goes bone deep within her. It's almost like she's never been hugged or something.

I take a breath and open the sliding door as quietly as possible, closing it gently behind me. The sound of her quiet sobs being carried to my ears gently with the breeze takes my breath away. She sounds beyond melancholy. Like she's being crushed under the weight of the world. Her shoulders move up and down with the cries she's desperately trying to keep at bay.

"Harleigh," I say quietly as I stop behind her.

She jumps and instantly starts wiping her eyes. "I'm s-sorry. I th- thought you died!" She breaks down in sobs once more.

I pull her in my arms because, while I have no idea where she came up with that conclusion, I can't stand to see her cry. "Shh... I'm not dead. Why would you think that?"

She clutches my shirt as she cries and takes several deep breaths to calm down. "Th-they s-said..." She trails off as she sobs and tries to breathe.

"Harleigh, shh... You need to breathe," I whisper in her ear and hug her tighter. I sway gently with her and wait for her to calm down enough to talk. "Talk to me. Tell me why you thought I was dead. Was it because I wasn't responding to you?"

She nods and then shakes her head. Then, she pushes away from me. "I don't know! They were talking a few days ago about how you were involved in a shootout. And how a sniper or something almost got the jump on you. They weren't sure if anything happened or not. And then when I walked in the room, everyone just went quiet!" She looks up at me. "I know I hurt you, Gavin. And it's something I'll never forgive myself for. And I know how protective everyone here is of each other. It's the reason that I didn't feel like I even had the right to ask them what happened and how you were. But I called you! I called you so many times. I kept telling myself you were busy. So, I gave up and just kept calling and leaving messages every day and texting every day hoping that you or someone would say anything to me!"

"I didn't know you -"

"I was begging for any scrap of information from you or anyone you were with. I was begging someone would answer your phone. I -"

"Harleigh, stop!" I yank her back against my chest and wrap back around her. "I had my reasons for not responding, and I won't lie to you and tell you that I'd go back and change anything about my decision to not. But had you said something, anything, regarding what you just said, I would have responded. Or at the very least, made certain someone told you. Christ, I'm not that much of an asshole." I tangle my fingers in her hair. It's scary as hell that I feel like she's where she belongs. Despite everything, this feels right.

"I'm sorry."

"We need to talk. But I'm so fucking tired, Harleigh. I need to sleep." I hug her tighter when she tries to pull away. "I can see you haven't slept well. Which means you need it just as much as I do. So, we're both going home. Right now. We'll talk when we wake up, but I'm not in the right frame of mind, and neither are you."

Without giving her a chance to respond, I take her hand and lead her back to my house. Every time she tries to speak, I silence her, telling her I don't want to talk. When we get to my bedroom, I quickly strip down to boxers, barely able to keep my eyes open, and wait for her to put something on to sleep in. When she reaches the bed I've already fallen into, I wrap her in my arms and snuggle her as close to me as possible.

I tell myself that I'm just showing her kindness. That I'm comforting her and letting her know that I'm okay. But if I'm being honest with myself, going to sleep with her in my arms is everything I need to help me feel centered again. As I drift off to sleep, a very startling thought hits me with the force of a rocket that I'm too tired to fight.

I missed her.

Chapter Nine

☙ Harleigh ❧

"Mmm…," I murmur as I slowly blink my eyes open. I smile hesitantly at the weight of Gavin hugging me closely and tightly to him. The room is dark, but the sun peeking through the sides looks to be nearly down. I glance at the clock and see it's nearly dinner time.

Maybe I'll make him dinner. That could start the conversation. I decide resolutely to make something for us to eat. Talking is always done better if there's food involved. It's something my father always said to me. I gently slip Gavin's arm from around me and instantly miss the warmth and feeling of safety. Feelings I shouldn't feel. I don't even know if he'll accept my apology.

"If you're planning on sneaking out on me again… I'm gonna be pissed," Gavin grumbles into the pillow. "The punishment is going to be severe. I don't know what yet, but I'll damn well figure it out. Then again… it's not like you can go far."

I look back at him with wide eyes. His eyes are still closed. Just those words send heat directly to my core and make me ache for him.

Not fair.

Not fair at all.

I bite my lip and wrap my arms around myself. "I was going to make dinner," I say quietly.

A slow smile spreads across his lips. "Are you a good cook?"

I smile softly and shrug slightly. "I'm not terrible."

"Do I have time to take a shower? I fell right into bed. Didn't get a chance to get the dirt and grime off me from last night's battle. At least I thought to remove the dirty clothes."

I let out a quiet breath and let my eyes trail over his ridges and muscles. To anyone watching, they'd think I'm checking him out. Truthfully, I kind of am. For injuries. To make sure he's whole. I hug myself tighter as I slowly stand.

"You have time," I say just above a whisper.

I quickly grab the shorts I was wearing last night and head for the door before he can see me cry. Thoughts of him being hurt, or worse, cloud my mind. Once I'm outside of the bedroom, the tears escape. I pull the shorts on under his t-shirt and hurry down the stairs to the kitchen.

In order to distract myself from all of the thoughts that don't make sense screaming through my head, I immediately set to work on dinner. Pan fried chicken. It's my specialty. We used my recipe at the diner, changing the one my father made up and used for years. I have my heart set on it and am ecstatic when I find all of the ingredients I need. Except for two, but I really don't need thyme or rosemary.

I find some canola oil and a pan. As I heat up the oil, I set to work on the breading for the chicken breasts. After I finish and check the oil, I pound out the chicken to thin it. At least a little. No one likes dry chicken, and that's what happens if it's too thick. I could finish it in the oven, but I don't think it's as good.

I smile softly as I put the chicken in the oil. "Perfect." I nod as it starts to sizzle. I search the fridge for anything I can make as a side. I like mashed potatoes, but I didn't see any potatoes.

I smile a little wider when I see that I can make a nice salad and some asparagus. I take everything out and start chopping things for the salad while the asparagus slowly cooks in butter water. By the time I'm done with the salad, everything else is just finishing.

I take out the chicken to let it rest and start dishing everything else up. I smile when I'm done, proud at what I put out, but suddenly, a loud wailing sounds throughout the house. All at once, I smell smoke.

"Oh my God!" I scream as I whirl around. The grease in the pan is smoking. Thinking swiftly, I shut off the burner I forgot to shut off and move the pan to the back of the stove, where it's cool, just as the grease catches on fire. "Aah!" I scream, jumping back. I frantically look around for a lid to the pan, but can't find one. I lunge for the sink and turn on the water. I cup the water in my hands trying to remain calm.

"Don't you dare," Gavin growls in my ear, suddenly appearing behind me. He shuts off the water and grips my wrists. He pulls them apart and lets the water drop from my cupped palms, then pushes me away from the stink and flaming pan. "Never throw water on a grease fire. Didn't you learn that at the diner?" He finds a lid and puts it over the pan, smothering the flames as I gasp for air.

"Holy shit. I panicked. I could have made that so much worse!" I cover my mouth and nose with my hands to slow my erratic breathing. "I could have caused a huge fire!"

"Could have. Didn't." He throws some kind of powder over the flames.

I watch with relief as they go out, but clutch my chest. "Oh my God."

Gavin grabs a chair and, with incredible balance, climbs on it and reaches for the smoke detector. He shuts it off. He jumps down and opens the sliding glass door leading to the patio. "Bring dinner outside. We'll let it air out in here. I just need to make sure this is doused completely."

I just nod and grab the plates. I hurry outside and put them on the table. I quickly walk back in and grab the drinks I made as he takes a couple of towels and picks up the pan. I open the screen for him and close it behind him as he sets the pan on the ground, keeping the lid on.

"I'm so sorry," I whisper as I watch him. I immediately wrap myself in my arms to stop the trembling. I look down. "I forgot to turn the grease off after I took out the chicken. I didn't even smell the smoke. I was too busy trying to make sure the plates were perfect."

Gavin wraps me in his arms. I nearly melt into him. "Shh… It's okay. Remind me to tell you about the time I nearly burned my bedroom down when I was in high school." He sways with me, and the move is so soothing and relaxing, I want to cry. I keep hugging myself, afraid that if I hug him, he'll stop holding me like this.

After a few moments, the trembles subside. Gavin lets go of me slowly and helps me into a chair. "It's probably cold now," I grumble looking down at the dinner I was so proud of but now resent.

"It looks delicious." He puts his hand close to the food. "And it still feels warm." He nods to the glass with the drink in it. "What's that?"

"Oh." I brighten a little and sit up straighter. "It's a really good summer drink, but I love it all year long. It's strawberry and watermelon blended with a little lime juice and some club soda. It's really refreshing. I used your last bottle of club soda, though. I'm sorry."

He chuckles. "It's fine. I don't have a lot in the house. Never know when I'll get called away. My assumption is one of the girls went shopping for a few things so I didn't starve when I got back. I never would have. We all take care of each other, but they go above and beyond sometimes. I never have to worry about spoiled food no matter how long I'm gone." He takes a bite of the chicken as I watch. His eyes widen. "Fucking hell. That's really good." He looks down at the plate. "How does something that looks so plain pack that much of a flavor punch? Jesus Christ."

I giggle softly. "I don't know if you really like it, or if you're trying to humor me after the kitchen fiasco, but thank you."

We both dig into the food as we fall silent. He's right. The chicken is really good, just not as it usually is. It doesn't quite have the subtle kick the seasoning of the thyme and rosemary give it, but at least I didn't burn down Gavin's house. That's a plus.

I keep my eyes on my plate, trying not to take in his shirtless physique. He looks amazing. Very well taken care of, but I suppose he has to be in tip top shape, considering what he does. All of the men who work with the Crane or Lucinio Mafia are all hard ridges and lickable lines. Every one of them look like they've been chiseled from stone or carved from ice or something. Badasses with a glacier exterior.

And what is it with men and gray sweatpants? It's completely unfair how good they look. Gray sweatpants should be outlawed. Why don't they look as good in white? Or black? Or red? Why gray? And why every freaking shade of gray? Why can a person see the outline of everything they have to offer underneath, but they can't see the same thing in another color? Even if the package they're sporting is huge?

"Are you finished?" Gavin asks.

I blink, snapping myself out of my thoughts, and shake my head slightly. It's only then I realize I've eaten just over half of the meal, but I'm not hungry anymore at all. "Yeah, I think so." I force a smile as I look up at him. "I'll clean up." I start to stand, but Gavin beats me to it. I look at him.

"You cooked."

"And almost burned down the kitchen."

He grins. "Yeah, I probably shouldn't let you in there again." He takes the plates and laughs on his way in.

I can't help but laugh quietly, even though I know that we need to talk, and it won't be pretty. I wrap my arms around myself and focus all of my attention on the table. When we were sleeping, I had a fantastic dream. One I would love to come true. One where we were okay. Happy. I wish I could have just stayed asleep. Maybe we'll get to the point we were in my dream. Or maybe he'll tell me to fuck off.

"Why do you do that?" Gavin asks.

I jolt as he sits back down across from me, and I give him a blank look. I really don't know what he's talking about. "Do… what…?"

He studies me. It makes me hug myself even tighter under his scrutiny. He nods towards me. "That. You hug yourself. A lot. You did it most of the night I first took you out. And you do it a lot with or without me around. You did it last night when I found you by Ryan's pool. You're doing it now. Why?"

I look down at my arms and let them fall shakily from my body. "I… guess I don't really even realize I'm doing it most of the time." I bite my lip and fold my hands in my lap. "My dad… I love him… loved him…?" I shrug a little. "I don't really even know what to say."

"You love him. He's dead, but he still lives in your heart."

I smile softly but don't meet his eyes. "I love my father… but he was never that affectionate. When my mom died… the rare hugs became pretty much non-existent. I guess whenever I wanted comfort, I just took to hugging myself. It became second nature. I didn't even realize I was doing it then."

He leans forwards and rests his elbows on the table. "I promised you a talk. But I'm starting. You're listening. Understand?"

I nod and keep my eyes down. "I understand."

"Good." He leans back in his chair. I can feel his eyes turn colder. He crosses his arms over his chest. I wilt under the intensity. "When I woke up and you were gone, it was a shock to the system. I actually joked around about it because I'm usually the one who skips out after the sex and doesn't respond to the girl I was with. But there's a huge fucking difference between me and you."

I look up at him and swallow. "What?" I ask hesitantly.

"I've never not been upfront about my intentions. When I go into it, I tell them it's one night. Nothing more. I won't contact them. I won't give them more. If I don't feel a connection for someone, I'm not going to waste my time or theirs. It's not fair to me. It's certainly not fair for them. I might have a reputation as a player, but it's never been flaunted for the media. Just like me being Josh's second in command has never been something the media gives a shit about. I'm in the background. My personal life is in the background. I might be everything you think I am, but it's one hell of an assumption on your part. Just because I'm attractive and confident doesn't mean anything. For all you know, I could have never had sex with anyone in my entire life."

I nod and fight the urge to hug myself. "I'm sorry." There's nothing else I can say.

"But that isn't what hurt, Harleigh. Yeah, I played it off to everyone for a while. The one who ghosts everyone else and disappears into the night never to be seen again, had some hot girl do it to him. Funny. Ha. Ha. Everyone laugh it up. I'm not fucking immune to how ironic and humorous that is. But what really got me was when you called me for help. I know you did exactly what I told you to do. And I treated it as business as usual when we went in there. We took care of the issue, but you still wouldn't return any call or text. So, you called me when you needed me. Used me. But couldn't be bothered to return one text or phone call. Just answering one text message telling me you weren't interested and to fuck off would have sufficed."

"I -"

He holds up a hand, successfully silencing me without words. "But you didn't even stop there. You knew I could help you. That I'd be right there for you. I told you that in one of the texts and even when we talked, so I know even if you didn't read the texts, you knew that. Still, instead of contacting me that night, you ran. I get that. I know fear fucks a person up, and I'm glad you got out. I'm glad you thought to run to Lucinio Tech. But why not call me? Why not ask for me instead of Josh? Did it suck for me that you only wanted me for what I could do for you? Fuck yes. But I didn't care. As long as I knew you were safe, Harleigh, I didn't care. That was the only thing that mattered to me. I could live without answers about why you took off a lot easier than I could knowing something happened to you. It took me a long time to realize I wasn't pissed off. At least not anymore. I was hurt. Hurt that you fucking didn't come to me. That I wasn't the one you called when you needed help. It's not like you were against using me to get what you wanted before. You didn't want me, but you could have at least given me that one courtesy and come to me to keep you safe." He leans forward once more and rests his arms on the table. The move makes his muscles bulge. "Your turn."

I nod slowly and take a deep breath. I close my eyes for a moment and open them as I let out a breath and begin. "I left because I didn't think you were serious about wanting someone like me. I know you were telling me that you'd love to take me on a boat ride on the lake and just spend the day with me out there. I know you said you'd take me to *The Diary of Anne Frank* play that I really wanted to see but couldn't afford. And I know you said you'd take me to that upscale restaurant I always wanted to try. And my heart heard you and believed you." I look at him, but I'm barely able to hold his gaze. "I was scared. The night was so incredible. I've never been made to feel like that by anyone. And I'm not just talking about past boyfriends or sexual partners. You made me feel like no one ever has. It scared me because I fell in love with you. And my head told me how stupid I was for thinking someone so far out of my league could ever love me back. Especially that quickly."

"But I did," he says quietly. "I felt that same connection. That's why when I woke up and you weren't there, I was so blindsided."

I stand and give into the need to hug myself for the support I'm going to need. I walk slowly towards the edge of the pool. He doesn't follow, but I know his eyes are. I turn and let out a frustrated sigh.

"I thought you were playing me. Okay? I thought you were going to just build me up to break me down. I come from a horrible part of town. And that first night, you brought me to dinner at a fancy restaurant. You let me order anything I wanted. You let me pick the movie. And then you held my hand while we walked by the harbor. I'm used to dates at McDonald's and a movie at home! Not... all of what you did. And then this house!" I gesture to it.

He furrows his brows, giving me an incredulous look. "That's your excuse? You ran because I treated you like a woman should be treated, and then you got overwhelmed by my house? Are you kidding me?"

"No! Do you not see?" I look at him in exasperation.

He stands. "No! I don't! Everything you've said so far sounds like an excuse! Oh, holy shit! He treated me kindly? Took me on an incredible date? Made plans to see me again? Fuck, I must run!"

I fight myself from throwing a tantrum at him not understanding. "Are you really going to make me spell it out for you? Am I not being clear enough?"

"Yes, Harleigh! I am going to make you spell it out. Because I don't fucking understand how any of that would make you just flat out not respond at all to me! Especially if you were in love with me!"

"Oh my God, Gavin! Look at you! And then look at me! You are so far above my league! I was so scared that I'd get attached to you, and you'd get sick of me! Just like everyone else! Just like my father!"

"What in the ever living fuck? You didn't even know about what he did until how long afterwards? Come on!"

"You don't know what I've gone through in my life!" I scream at him. "You don't know what it was like for me growing up! I didn't have it all, but at least I had my mom! And then I lost her, and it was like my father completely forgot I existed! And then when he remembered me, he was always so kind and caring! But then, just like he always did, I was just an employee! Some ghost of my mother that he lived with who haunted him like she did! After he got sick, I thought maybe he'd realize just how much I loved him and the things I did for him and sacrificed for him. I thought things would change!" I wipe angry tears from my eyes. "And don't worry. I know what you're thinking. Poor girl with daddy issues. Never felt any love or affection. Thinks she can get away with all of what she did just because she's heartbroken over a man who doesn't deserve her sympathy."

"There you go again. You have no fucking idea what I'm thinking right now!" Gavin yells.

But his anger fuels mine. "Don't I? I can see it written all over you! I know my fears don't matter to you. I'm sorry for what I did to you.

I've apologized a thousand times! I didn't know how you felt. I was too stupid to have an adult conversation about it. And when I was ready to, so much time had gone by that I chickened out. And then you came in, and I find out you're part of some big and powerful mafia. And that scared me all over again! I had no idea that you toe the line of light and dark! I didn't know all of the things you do to better this world! And I was, again, too stupid to ask!" My eyes widen when Gavin moves suddenly. I jump and have the immediate urge to run, but I know I wouldn't get far. He's far too fast.

"Call yourself stupid again," he growls, inches from my lips as he grips my upper arms tight enough to leave a bruise. His blue eyes look like they're on fire. "I fucking dare you. Do it."

"I…"

His grip tightens. His eyes flash. "Start talking to me like an adult and leave the childish name-calling fucking out of it."

I stare at him in open-mouthed shock. My heart is racing out of control. But not from fear. That feeling passed just as quickly as it came. No. This. This is a primal response to the man in front of me who is so incredibly powerful and strong I'm sure he could break me in half if he wanted to.

And the scariest thing? I'd fall at his feet and let him.

Chapter Ten

𝕭 Gavin 𝕭

I let go of Harleigh and breathe deeply. I take a couple of steps back and run my fingers through my hair. "It's completely fucking offensive to me that you would fear me just by finding out I'm in the mafia. I understand why, but it's information that I would have told you. Was I wrong to not tell you straight out? No. No. Because that's not information you just tell everyone. You, though? I would have told you. If I'd woken up to you in my arms where you goddamn well belong, I would have told you. I would have answered whatever questions you had. And if you needed time, I would have fucking given it to you."

"All I can say is how sorry I am Gavin. And ask you to give us a chance and move on."

"What if I did? Huh? What if I stood here and said, okay, the past is the past, and let's move on. How can I trust you? How do I trust that you'll stick by me and not run at the first sign of trouble? How do I know you won't say you were scared of the mafia shit? Even though you were happy to call us in to save your ass from your fathers mess. Why should I take a chance on you now? You never did for me."

She growls. "That's what I'm trying to tell you! You refuse to listen! Why the hell did you even say we need to talk if you won't even listen to me?" She marches past me, but I, once again, grab her arms. This time, though, she fights my grip. "Let go! I'll figure it out on my own! I don't need you or anyone else! I'm so fucking sorry I bothered you with my petty bullshit!"

The ball of anger in my stomach grows into a raging inferno. "Again, Harleigh? Again with the fucking running away?" Keeping my grip firm, I pull her into the house. "Let me show you what happens to people who run away right into the danger we're fucking trying to protect them from!"

"Aah!" She tries to yank her arm away from me. This time, I let her. She falls back onto the chair in my living room.

I put both hands on the arms of the chair as I lean down. I choke down the anger and lean in. "You want to know the shit I deal with on a daily basis?"

I push away from her and grab a file from a drawer in the end table next to her. I open it and toss it on her lap. She gasps at the image and squeezes her eyes shut. The image is of a young man bloodied and beaten to a pulp. A kid.

She makes a strangled sound and tries to shove the folder away from her as she starts sobbing. "What -"

"What is that?" I cage her in once more. "Open your eyes. Look at it," I seethe.

She shakes her head. "No! No... I can't..." She reaches up to her eyes and vigorously wipes at them.

I roughly tangle my fingers in her hair and push her head down, not enough to hurt her, but enough so she knows I'm not fucking around with how serious this situation is. "Look at it!" I command. Her eyes snap open, and she fights to get away. I let go of her hair and stand in front of her. "That kid was only fourteen. Fourteen, Harleigh! Full of fucking life and an attitude to match. His parents begged us to protect him while they put measures in place to get out of the country. They pissed off the wrong people. This kid constantly snuck out. We caught him every single time. Except once. The one time he was able to get out was on my watch."

"Oh God," she whispers as she coughs, trying to stop the tears.

I feel the damn things prick my eyes, but I won't fucking cry. "He didn't take the situation seriously. Didn't think they'd touch him. A kid. I woke up the next morning and felt like I'd been hit by a damn train at a hundred miles an hour. He drugged my drink. Fuck if I know where he got it, but he fucking roofied me. That's what he looked like when the cops found him. Our contact called us in. Knew we were looking for him. That we were supposed to protect him!"

She shoves the folders off her lap and covers her ears. "Stop! Just stop!"

I kneel in front of her and grip her wrists. "Is that how you want to fucking end up? Because that's what's going to happen if you go after that motherfucker yourself!"

"Why would you show me that?" she screams at me as she trembles.

"Because nothing I fucking say is getting through to you!" I yell right back.

"Am I not already fucked up enough for y-"

I don't let her finish the sentence. I lean in and kiss her. Hard. Punishingly. So fucking dominantly that I scare myself, but I don't back off. I deepen it. I nip her lip and scrape my teeth over her tongue before I tangle mine with hers in a dance only I know. She fights to keep up, letting out little whimpers and moans.

I push her back against the chair and kiss her harder. My chest tightens because I know what I'm doing is probably hurting her, but I can't force myself to stop. Thankfully, she doesn't seem to want me to. She grips my arm with one hand and pulls my hair with the other. I grip her hips and dig my fingers into her. I groan. She tugs again, making me groan once more.

Her fingers scratch up my arm and dig into my shoulder. She lets out the sexiest sound I've ever heard, and my cock jumps. It's like she's singing a song just for it. A song only it understands. The beast that only she's ever managed to find roars to life inside me.

And it's that feeling that makes me pull back, leaving us both gasping for air. I quickly get to my feet and pace. Maybe I'm the caged animal. Part of me wants to demand she stay right where she is while I go for a run. Or to Alex's. Anywhere but fucking here. Around her.

But that would be running away. It's something I just yelled at her for doing. What kind of hypocrite would I be if I did the same damn thing? I suppose the difference is I'd come back as soon as I calmed down, but she probably wouldn't still be here.

I scrub my hands down my face and turn around to look at her. "I can't lose you."

"I get it! Okay?" She buries her face in her hands as she cries. "I get it. Don't leave or I'll end up like that. Never be safe again. Stay with the man who can protect me, even though he doesn't understand how I feel about him and considers me his job." She stands up.

"It's not just about a fucking job to me!" I shake my head and let my arms fall to my sides. I drop to the couch and rest my elbows on my knees. I scrub my hands over my face and take a deep breath. I look up at her. "Sit down, Harleigh. We need to go through this all. Piece by piece. Because we're having a serious communication breakdown, baby. We need to talk. Properly. No shouting. No yelling. Just talking. Openly and honestly. Or we're just going to continue going around in circles."

I watch as she wraps her arms around herself again. "How do we start?"

I sigh because I can't stand seeing her do that. It's a blindingly obvious sign of how alone she feels. So, I hold out a hand. "Come here, Harleigh. Please. It breaks my heart seeing you do that."

She looks at my hand like it might bite her but eventually takes it and lets me pull her to my side. I wrap an arm around her and pull her close to me as I lean back. I run a hand up and down her arm.

"I feel like you hate me," she says quietly.

"I don't. I don't, Harleigh. And that's not where this needs to start. We need to start from the beginning. We had a really good night. Made plans for other nights. You told me you ran because it was overwhelming. Not what you're used to. I don't buy any of that, Harleigh. And don't say it's the mafia part either, because this was before you found that out. So, tell me why you ran."

She sniffles and curls so into herself, I'm not sure she'll ever manage to get out of the ball she's in. But at least she's staying against me. So, I keep running my hand up and down her arm and hugging her close.

"Because I don't feel like I measure up," she whispers.

"What does that mean? Did I not make you feel special that night? Did I make you feel like I was above you somehow?" I keep my voice as low and calm as I can because I actually feel like we're getting somewhere. The problem is I feel like she's about to break me even more.

"No... You made me feel like a million dollars. That's what I meant when I said no one has ever made me feel like that before. You made me feel incredible. Like the only woman in the world. The only person in your life who mattered." She rests her chin on her knees as she holds them as close to her body as she can.

"Harleigh, sweetheart, I don't understand. I'm trying, but I don't."

She closes her eyes. I hug her closer and reach up to wipe a tear sliding down her cheek. She lets out a breath. "I don't... feel... like I'm the kind of person you'd be happy with...," she whispers.

Of everything I thought would come out of her mouth, that wasn't it. "Where would you ever get an idea like that?"

"Look at me," she says softly. "I have bigger hips. My thighs aren't perfect. My boobs aren't perky. Not like the other girls around here."

I blink a few times before the words rolling around in my head actually formulate a coherent sentence. "You... I... Harleigh, holy fuck. Do you honestly think you aren't pretty enough for me?" I look at her incredulously. She says nothing but gives me a barely perceptible nod. "Honey, look at me." I cup her cheek and gently turn her face so she's looking me directly in my eyes.

"I just felt like you'd wake up and see me for who I really am. And regret everything. I couldn't take the heartbreak," she whispers.

I keep one arm tightly around her. The other hand finds itself tangled in her hair. "You're the most beautiful woman I've ever seen," I say with as much conviction as I can because it's fucking true. "I've never in my life felt a..." I trail off with a smile. "You told me your favorite movie might be childish to some, but not to you. It's Hotel Transylvania."

Her eyes widen a little. "You remembered?"

"I remember everything you've ever said. I never saw that movie, but I watched it that night after you left. And I watched it every fucking night after for days. In the movie, they talked about zinging when they met their true love. Well, I fucking felt that. I couldn't look away. I was captivated by you. I still am."

She keeps her questioning eyes on me for a long while, but I don't flinch. I want her to see everything I feel. Not only do I need her to see it, but she needs it just as much. I'll stay here all night just like this if that's what she wants.

She starts to relax. She lets her knees go and allows me to pull her even closer. She rests her head on my shoulder, but her arms are still locked around herself. "I really believe you."

"You really should. I mean every word." A harder question next. I let my head fall against the back of the couch. "Why didn't you respond when I texted or called? And why did you hide when I came into the diner?"

She's quiet for so long that I have to look down at her to make sure she didn't fall asleep or something. I squeeze her arm. She lets out another breath. "At first, it was because I thought I was doing the right thing for myself. I thought I was protecting my heart. That if I didn't respond and avoided you, you'd eventually stop calling and texting and coming into the diner. What I didn't expect was the emptiness I felt when you actually did. I kept all your texts and voicemails. I could hear the hurt, but I really didn't know what to do with it. I talked myself out of calling you back and telling you how I was a complete fool because by that time, I knew you were angry. I could hear the emotion and hurt in your voice change to something else. Not quite hate, but bordering on it. I guess by that time, I knew I'd messed up. The damage was done. So, when you came in that day and told us that we were under the protection of the Lucinio Mafia, I hid for a different reason. I couldn't stand to face you after I hurt you. And… I… couldn't bear to face your anger."

"Okay. I can understand that. Especially adding in that you already felt like I was out of your league. All of that could have been completely resolved, though, if you'd just talked to me. I would have gladly told you exactly how I feel about you. And I would have spent as many hours or years as you needed to make you believe just how gorgeous you are."

"I know that now…"

"But you didn't then."

She hugs herself tighter, and I'd give anything for her to hug me like that instead. I'd never force her, but I'm convinced she needs some kind of permission or something from me. Like a sign that I won't be upset with her for using me for comfort.

As soon as I realize and understand what she needs in this moment, I hold out my hand. An invitation, however slight. She shakily takes it after staring at it for a few moments. I gently drag it across my waist. She shifts positions so she's pressed against my side and lets out another relieved breath as her fingers curl in my waistband. She closes her eyes and rests her cheek against my chest. I tuck her into my side as close as I can and rest my hand on her ribcage just underneath the round mound I've come to memorize.

Not that it took me long. I see her every night in my dreams. She's seared in my brain and won't be going anywhere anytime soon. I wouldn't want her to. I didn't have a lot of time to think over the past few weeks, but when I did, there was one thing that kept a strong presence. I don't just want her. I need her. There's no one else for me. There hasn't been since I got a taste of her.

I clear my throat. "You said you were afraid of me when you found out about the mafia. I call bullshit because you weren't afraid when you called me for help."

I feel her deflate, but she does grip my waistband harder. I take that as a good sign. "At first I was. I knew nothing about the mafia. And I know that I could have talked to you about it, but again..."

"You didn't know that then," I finish for her as I rest my cheek against her head.

"I really thought that by that time, I'd ruined everything."

"But I texted you and called you after that, Harleigh. I said I had no idea what happened to us, but I wanted to figure it out because I really liked you."

She nods slowly and lets out a sigh. "I know. But I needed to think. I didn't know what you did. I was waiting for the Lucinio Mafia to come after us just like the Ruthless Warriors did. But when you didn't, I guess I was a little shocked... I started looking into Lucinio Mafia and found out a little bit of stuff, but I kept letting my head get in the way. My heart said you were really one of the good guys. I just didn't listen to it... I was trying to be logical. Like, even though you hadn't come after us for something, it didn't mean you still wouldn't. Everything I found just kept saying that you were a legit mafia. And I believed it, but I knew that it couldn't all be roses..." She shrugs slightly. "There's no way you would have been able to clean up the area the diner was in by doing everything by the book. But again, once I got to the point that I wanted to contact you, I felt like too much time had gone by."

"I felt like you'd used me. Got what you wanted from me, and that was it."

"I think deep down, I knew you felt like that. I didn't know how to fix it, and it made me feel so… naive? Like, not only was I not even in the same universe as you, but now I wasn't even in the same playing field intelligence wise. Here you are. You're this amazing person who went to a really good school and works for a very powerful man. And then here I am. Uneducated and so young and… I can't say innocent. I'm really not. So…" She sighs at not being able to think of the word.

"I'd say innocent. You know nothing of this world. All you really knew then is what you learned online and in history books. Mafias are filled with thugs who hurt people to rise to the top. Get into gunfights in the middle of the city."

"Exactly. But after I finally got out of my head and was going to suck it up and be an adult, the…" She trails off and takes a breath. "The night… happened."

"Right. That night. Why didn't you contact me?"

"I dropped my phone somewhere. I think maybe when I was hiding. Or before. Something. I'm not sure. I heard pots and pans crashing. I thought something happened to my father. I ran to the kitchen. I saw the leader guy there and some others. They were yelling at him. I knew that he'd done something with them. Some kind of deal. He never told me, but it wasn't long after he went back to the diner after his heart attacks that they started showing up and collecting money. I didn't know the extent of what he got into. I'm still struggling with it. But when I ran, I was thinking about you. I knew Lucinio Mafia would help. But I went straight for the leader because…" She lets out a shuddering breath. "I don't want you to be upset with me…"

My heart squeezes in my chest. I can't help hugging her tighter. "I can promise to try."

Another long pause goes by before I feel her take a deep breath. "I understand if you never trust me again after… well, after everything. But the reason I asked specifically for Josh is because after you got rid of them, they came back. I didn't know that you were second in command to him. All I knew was that they came back after you said they were gone, and they got to my father. I was upset. Angry." She sniffles. "I thought you'd taken care of them. I trusted that you did. When they came back, I guess I just… thought that maybe you weren't high enough in the ranks to make sure they were gone for good. I know that makes me sound so horrible, and

I'm so sorry. Truthfully, I also think I wanted to protect you somehow. I thought it was too big for you. I didn't want to lose you completely. Even if you never spoke to me again, or I never saw you again, At least I'd know that you were safe. I hoped, anyway. I hoped with the leader of the mafia involved, that you'd be protected."

There's a part of me that wants to laugh. Another part that wants to scream. But the part overcoming each of those reactions is the feeling those words bring to me. She wanted to protect me? I see the other women around here feel that way and even take actions to do just that with their significant others, but I've never had that kind of relationship. I've always been the guy protecting everyone else.

"Now that this is all out, I don't want anything else between us. No secrets. No fears. No running. Talk to me, Harleigh. If you really want to give this thing between us a real shot, then there can't be all of this bullshit between us. If you're feeling down on yourself, I don't mind at all being the one who convinces you just how beautiful you are. How worth it you are. Now that I understand where all of this shit stemmed from, I want to move on from it."

She looks up at me with the most adorable hopeful glimmer in her eyes. "Really? You... you'll give us another chance?"

I kiss her forehead. "I want to. We can take things slow, if that's what you need, but you are all I want, honey. You're all I've ever wanted. I know I told you that I've only ever given women one date, if that. Many didn't get that far. But I wasn't just fucking with you or your emotions when I told you how different it was with you."

She nods and snuggles herself closer. I revel in the feel of her relaxing completely against me, still reeling from the fact that protecting me was at the forefront of her mind. Even while running for her life, she was thinking of me. It both shatters my heart and puts it back together. It's true. Innocent.

Love.

Now that I know this feeling, I'm never letting it go.

Chapter Eleven

 Harleigh

(One Week Later)

"What does that have to do with anything?" I hear Gavin growl into his phone. I stop outside his office with a glass of ice cold strawberry lemonade not wanting to interrupt him. He sees me, though, and waves me in while he paces back and forth as he talks on his phone. "Fuck me. You have to be kidding." Gavin looks at me as he runs his fingers through his dark hair. "No. No. Fucking no. I'll tell him myself. This is a colossal fuck up of proportions you can't possibly understand." He hangs up his phone.

"Why do I just feel like something bad happened?" I ask quietly but with wide eyes. Gavin is radiating anger and something I've never seen before. Something a lot darker.

He crosses the room to me, softening immediately. He gently takes my hand and his drink and leads me towards his desk. He sets the drink down and leans on the edge of it, pulling me close. I inhale his scent to calm my sudden nerves and focus on the way he fills out his jeans and black t-shirt. I wrap my arms around him, letting him pull me tight and close to him.

"We found Gregory Franklin last night."

My heart beats faster. I hug him tighter. "He got away," I whisper.

"Not just got away. Our guys were supposed to be watching him. Doing surveillance. Seeing how many guys he has, so we know how to go in and take him out. It's a tried and true method. We've done it for years. Except this time, one of our guys was made."

I sigh as my knees buckle. I sink more against him. It's a good thing he's a strong man. Otherwise, I'd be on the ground. "I can't do this anymore." Tears sting my eyes, and I feel instantly selfish and weak.

Gavin tightens his arms around me even more. "I know, baby. But this is our top priority. We'll get him. We always get our man." He rests his chin on top of my head.

Over the past week, Gavin and the mafia have been working hard to catch the gang members of the Ruthless Warriors. Each time they get close, though, he slips away. We were all really hopeful this time because they managed to get surveillance on him before he disappeared. It wasn't just them following up on a tip and him already being gone. I was actually excited that this would all end soon.

I gently pull away from Gavin and slowly walk to the couch in his office. I wipe away a tear and sit down, hugging myself. Gavin watches me until I sit. Then, he pushes off his desk and walks to the couch. He sits next to me and pulls me into his lap.

Another thing that's happened over the last week is Gavin and I have been working hard on our relationship. We're going slow, and taking our time getting to know each other on a deeper and more personal level. Whenever I hug myself, Gavin is right by my side holding me close. I'd almost forgotten what such a simple action from another person feels like, but with him, it feels so different. Real. Like his soul is hugging mine.

"I know how hard this is, Lei. But it takes time."

I smile at his nickname for me as I lay my head on his shoulder. No one has ever had a nickname for me. Not even my mom. "It's not that. I mean, it kind of is, but it's not all of it."

"Then talk to me. Isn't that what we promised each other when we first started this?"

I take a breath and inhale his scent as I bury my face in his neck. He hugs me tighter. "When I said that I can't do this anymore… I immediately felt selfish for thinking of myself. And weak. That was the worst part. I feel like I don't even have the strength to keep going with this.

Yet, as you've told me, every other woman here has gone through so much. And they're all so strong. So different from me. It makes me start to understand why they don't like me."

"Baby, enough." He kisses my temple. "They're hostile towards you because of how things went down when I first brought you here. Those girls are all like my little sisters. They're all protective in their own way. Of me. Of every other person here. Of each other. They don't know the entire story behind us, but they do know I was hurt. Even when I refused to show it, they saw." He soothingly runs his fingers through my hair. "It also has to do with you not understanding the danger you were in at first. Ryan may have understood your need to have at least something of yours. Clothes. Whatever. And I did, too. They didn't see why you couldn't shop for yourself online or something."

I sniffle and blush a deep shade of red. "How? That costs money… I left with nothing."

"I know that. So does Josh and Ryan. But we aren't going to blab to everyone that you had nothing. I mean, Jessa was able to go home and get some of her things when things went down with her. Bree and Nicole. Same thing. Arianna had a lot of stuff at Ryan's already when everything happened with her. But it wouldn't have mattered because he would have given her anything she needed him to. Dani had her own stuff. Raleigh is the only one who came here with nothing like you did, but we all knew that. Josh bought her everything she needed as soon as we realized she wasn't out to get us. It was very different with you."

"It doesn't make me feel any less awful about where my thoughts went. I have nothing to my name. We lived paycheck to paycheck. Everyone thinks business owners have such a great life, but that's not true. Most of our money went to paying everyone and back into the diner. The rest went to bills. When they started taking money, we started falling behind. We were barely able to pay the mortgage. All of my pay went to utilities. And food? We ate at the diner." I shake my head as I sit up.

Gavin, though, isn't having it. He pulls me right back against him. "Are you ashamed? Because that's the feeling I'm getting here."

My heart stutters before beating regularly again, just much faster. Am I? Am I ashamed of where I came from? I never have been before. I've always been proud of surviving despite my circumstances. Am I embarrassed by it now that I'm here in this complex surrounded by lavish homes and people who seemingly have all they want and need in life?

"Well, that thought makes me feel worse. I've never been ashamed of where I came from."

"Then, maybe that's not it, baby. I'm just throwing things out there."

I sigh and shift so I'm between his legs with my back to his chest. I wrap my arms around his as he kisses my neck. "I'm not ashamed. At least, I don't think I am. I feel bad because I can't stand on my own two feet without help. I don't have a job. Everyone else does. I don't have anything... Just you. I don't feel like I'm contributing to anything or anyone. I'm just... here. A ghost of myself and who I used to be."

"Well, now, I don't think that's true. I'd say you're pretty fucking amazing. Still that vibrant, sweet girl with a fiery attitude that I fell in love with." He nuzzles my neck, but his words stop my heart.

Did he just drop the L word? I can't have heard that right.

I swallow hard and look back at him. I don't need to see my hopeful look reflected in his eyes. I can feel it. "Did you just say..."

He grins. "Say what?"

My eyes widen when I realize he's messing with me. I swat his chest lightly. "Gavin!"

He laughs. "Come on," he says seriously, but still with that dangerous, sexy grin. "You had to know that. I was in love with you the second you knocked me on my ass."

My mouth drops. "I did not! You -"

He silences me with a searing kiss. His fingers tangle in my hair and meet the nape of my neck. He squeezes a little bit as he pulls me closer. I love when he does that. When he takes control. I relinquish it because I like that I feel like I can trust him enough. That I don't feel like I need to be the strong one around him. I feel like he has me. That I can break if I need to.

And all at once, I realize it. The feeling that I knew all along.

"I'm in love with you, too," I whisper when he pulls away.

He smiles. His kiss is softer, but just as intense. His tongue slips into my mouth and meets mine in a passionate dance. He sucks on my lower lip when he pulls slowly away from the kiss that is ending far too soon. He tugs my hair slightly.

"There's something going on in that beautiful mind of yours." He searches my eyes, and I can see the moment he figures it out. Which is good because I'm having trouble articulating it. "You're at war with yourself about your feelings about your dad." He kisses me softly again. "We've talked about this. It's okay to be pissed off and still feel some kind of love towards him."

That makes me sigh, and I slump against him. "But that's the problem. I'm having trouble because I can't process the feelings. I don't know how to. I just feel like there are two sides to me who are arguing and bickering about it, and I don't know what to do."

"You could start by talking about it. You tend to clam up when the conversation turns to your dad. Maybe now that we've gotten over the tentative stepping around each other and admitted that there's more to this than a slow dance, you can trust me a little more."

I kiss his jaw and lean forward in his lap. I'm quiet as I formulate my words. They're a lot. "I don't know where to start."

"How about from the beginning?"

I stand slowly and walk slowly around the room before my eyes fall on the glass I brought him. "I don't want to sound whiny and bratty...," I say as I grab the glass.

"First of all, I don't think that. I think you need to stop thinking that I'll think the worst of you and be open and honest with me. That's the only way this is going to work with us, baby." He shifts and puts his arms on the back of the couch as he watches me.

I take the glass to him, but keep it clutched in my hands. Something for them to do instead of wrapping themselves around me. Gavin leans forward and gently takes the glass. He guides me down so I'm sitting on the table in front of him as he takes a drink. He puts the glass down next to me and takes my hands in his, resting his forearms on my thighs. He says nothing, though. He just waits me out.

I let out a breath after a few moments. "From the beginning. Okay. I can do that." I smile softly.

"Good girl."

"It wasn't always bad for us. Not until my mom died. She was the glue that held everything together. After she died, he got sick. I was only ten. I couldn't do much. By the time I could actually legally work, the diner had gone pretty downhill. We still had a lot of business, but the morale sucked. It wasn't clean. I went in there like a little boss lady." I smile softly at the memory. "I was only fourteen then. I couldn't work a lot, but I went there after school. I did my homework there. Ate there. And bossed people around. I think everyone just thought it was adorable. But then everyone noticed how much that low morale went up. The diner was clean. More business was coming in. And we were actually doing pretty well. For a couple of years, at least."

Gavin squeezes my hands. "Then he got really sick."

I nod slowly. "Everyone pulled together for him, though. We all kept the diner going. We were like a little family. They all made sure I still went to school and did my homework. Everyone made sure we were both fed while he recovered. He came back and just started doing paperwork at first. But I overheard one night that things weren't that great. He was talking to the manager who had been running things in his absence. It didn't seem to me like business was getting worse, but there was money missing. I was never there at closing. So I had no idea what was really going on. The manager, though, told him that we were being shaken down. His words. He mentioned the Ruthless Warriors."

"How long ago was that?"

"Four years, I think? But they started coming just before he got sick. I'd never seen them, but when I talked to my dad later, he told me. It was why I wasn't allowed to close. They made me go home before. But after I talked with him, they stopped shaking us down. I was old enough to stay and close, and he let me. I expected I'd see them."

"But you didn't."

I shake my head. "No. At least not shaking us down. Not then. They came in, though. I didn't know who they were at first, but they always sat at the same table. They always ordered the same thing. I'd seen them before, but never had anything to do with them. After a while, they started making sure I was their server. They leered at me. One always found ways to touch me. I found out later that he was the leader. He'd touch my butt. Leg. Thigh. Arms. Hips." I feel him tense as his eyes darken, but I plow on. "I told my dad, but by that time, he'd pretty much shut himself off from me. He was never really that lovey-dovey, but after my mom died, he'd totally shut down. No hugs. Nothing. I would bring him home straight A report cards. I'd get nothing but a grunt for approval. But I knew he loved me. He always showed me in his own way. He'd make sure I got paid and wouldn't let me pay any of it towards bills. Not at first. Later I did. And he would tell everyone to listen to me. I was just as in charge as him. He started showing me the books. And teaching me about finances. He was kind. He'd make sure I was warm when it was cold out by getting me a space heater for my room."

"So, not affectionate, but still caring."

"In his own way, yes. It's why I'm so…" I trail off, frustrated, and shake my head. "I mean, I know my problems and my battles are so minute compared to everything else. It's why I feel the way I do. Dwelling on things I can't change. Feeling left out and wanting some kind of normalcy." I look down at my t-shirt and jeans before looking back up at him. Tears sting my eyes. "I feel like the world's worst person because I'm thinking about all of that on one side of my head and the other is thinking about how I wish I had more than five pairs of panties and two bras. And more than two t-shirts and a sweater. And more than a pair of jeans and shorts. It's not like I've ever had much more than this, but I did have a few things that I loved. I didn't have to wash my clothes every other day to make sure I had something to wear. I had enough to last a week -"

"Harleigh, baby, you've gone off on a tangent. We'll come back to that because it's an easily solvable problem. The real issue isn't your clothes and feeling selfish for wanting basic necessities. It's your father."

I slump a little. He leans forward and kisses my chest before pulling me back into his lap. I love how he spreads his legs wide so I fall between him and fit so snuggly that I never want to leave. Like I'm being surrounded by him. I turn a little and wrap my arms around his waist.

"Thank you," I say into his chest. He wraps tighter around me, like he's engulfing me. Suddenly, I feel calm and safe. Protected from anything. Including my emotions. "He ignored me when I told him. It should have been a sign. But I just swept it under the rug. I did my best to just be a tough girl and take it. After a while, it became second nature. And about a year or so after the surgery, they started the shakedowns again. So, I wasn't so worried about the touches as I was about the money we were forced to give them. It took a toll on my dad. And that took its toll on me. I felt the stress. For three years, they took the same amount every Friday. And it was the same act. Touching. Being obnoxious. Making snide comments to my dad about me and how pretty I was. He'd hang his head and walk back to his office. And then ignore that it happened at all. He became so indifferent to it. Maybe it was all a mask. That the only way he could cope was to brush it all aside. Bury it deep down because he couldn't think of a way out. It never made total sense to me."

"Until the night they came for you."

I nod and close my eyes. I grip his shirt just above his heart. "I was so, so scared, Gavin. And so pissed. I didn't know which one to feel most. I was thinking of trying to figure out how to get away. And then how angry I was. And then how to get to safety. All I could think of was getting to Lucinio Tech because someone would contact the mafia. Then I started thinking of how angry I was again. Then of you. I was such a mess. And then adrenaline kicked in."

"And now you're left both pissed off at your father for doing that to you in the first place and not being able to understand why. And questioning how he could if he ever loved you."

I nod. "So, so many questions. And I'll never get answers. So, it leaves me feeling kind of empty and confused. I feel like everything I knew is just gone. And I'm scrambling in the dark trying to keep up and figure it out."

"You're not alone, baby." He kisses my head. "And there's nothing wrong with the way you feel. Be pissed. Fuck, yell. Scream. I'll take you to my gym and let you beat it out on my punching bag, if that's what you want. I'll even stand there and spar with you until it's all out of your system. There's nothing wrong with being angry. And when it's all done, I'll hold you while you cry. The point is, you don't need to feel bad for being upset. But you do have to deal with the emotions and own them before you can move on." He locks his arms around me tighter. "As for the clothes and everything, we can order whatever you need online. And before you argue about money, I have an American Express black card. That should give you some insight into my financial worth."

I blink a few times. "Okay, that's impressive, but I don't care about what you can buy me."

"Good thing I know that, huh?"

I sink into his embrace. "I don't feel like I deserve you," I whisper. "I was really shitty to you."

"Forgive and forget, right? Isn't that the point of us starting over and moving on after our talk? Promising no more secrets and lies? Always being open and honest?"

I smile and look up at him. I kiss his jaw. "You're too good of a guy."

He chuckles. "I'm not a good guy, baby. I've done a lot of things I'll never tell you. But I promise I'll always be good to you."

"I don't care what you say about it. You're a good guy. One who does bad things in the name of justice."

"Being a vigilante doesn't make me good."

I purse my lips and tilt my head. "Speaking as someone who was on the other end of that spectrum, I'm sticking with what I said."

He throws his head back and laughs. "Whatever you say, beautiful." He takes out his phone and texts something quickly before putting it back. "It's almost lunchtime. What do you say to getting some of that anger out? Then we'll spend the rest of the day doing whatever you want. I'll even cook dinner. And if you're a good girl, I'll give you a massage." He grins devilishly and waggles his eyebrows.

I laugh but blush. "I take it back. You're bad. All bad."

"Now she gets it." He shifts and lifts me with ease as he gets up.

I squeak and throw my arms around his shoulders. I'll never get used to how easy it is for him to do that. I might be short, but I'm still pretty curvy. My stomach isn't flat. I don't have abs that can be seen. I'm soft where I should be hard.

But Gavin doesn't seem to care. He makes me feel pretty when I don't think I am. Desired and wanted when I'm not feeling my greatest. Just with the simple action of lifting me like I'm nothing goes a long way in my self-confidence battle.

While I'm not sure of a lot of things in my life, the one thing I am sure of is my feelings for him.

Chapter Twelve

☙ Gavin ☙

I swing open my front door the next morning when a very loud and insistent knocking wakes me up. A low growl escapes my throat, and I glare a little more viciously than I intend.

"Couldn't even bother to throw a shirt on?" Dane, our resident early bird, says with a smirk.

"What the hell could you possibly want at five in the fucking morning?"

His smirk only grows wider. "Come on. Don't tell me you weren't already up and in the gym."

I don't flinch or even give him a grin. "Nope. I was upstairs with a beautiful woman in my arms. I'd much prefer to be looking at her gorgeous body than your ugly mug. What the hell do you want?"

"I need your expertise. Grab a shirt."

I just blink at him, unmoving. "My expertise this early is never a good thing."

"Well, it's good for us. Let's go. Josh is already having his fun."

I sigh and scrub my hands down my face. "I hate you all." I turn and stride to the stairs, jogging up them. I quietly enter my room and slip into the unnecessarily large closet I probably wouldn't have wanted had

Jessa not talked me into keeping it after Marissa was killed. She had already designed the house, but it was just starting to be built.

Her argument, though, was quite convincing. She told me my true love would enjoy it, and that I'd find her someday. I resisted, but only a little. Deep down, I've always wanted a love like what she shares with her husband. Not that I'd ever admit to that shit. I settled for Marissa because it was the right thing to do. So, I allowed the closet. And asked for the jacuzzi tub just because I fucking could.

After changing into jeans and a t-shirt and grabbing my Glock out of its safe, I step silently out of my closet. Harleigh is just stirring, and I have to pause at how pretty she is as she stretches and makes little whimpering noises when she feels I'm not in bed. How she slept through that knocking, though, shocks the fuck out of me. I must have exhausted her.

I smile and make my way to the bed. I sit on the edge and lean over her, kissing her shoulder and her neck, my Glock still in my other hand. I make a trail of soft kisses up to her eyes as she giggles and grips my arm, curling into me and it. I tickle her neck with my stubble because I love the way she laughs and squirms.

I kiss where I tickled with an even bigger grin. "Good morning, beautiful."

"Morning," she hums as she looks up at me. "Why are you dressed?"

"Because I gotta go to work." I kiss her nose. "It's still early, though. Why don't you try to sleep for a couple more hours?"

"Because you're not in bed."

I smile and chuckle, then kiss her. I pull back slowly and grab my pillow. I snuggle it into her chest, and she hugs it with a sexy moan. "How's that?"

"Perfect," she murmurs as she closes her eyes and hugs my pillow tighter.

I groan. She has no idea how adorable she is. I shift and kiss her naked ass before pulling the covers up. "I'll try to hurry back so my pillow doesn't take my place."

"Hurry…," she murmurs. "Miss you…"

I kiss the corner of her mouth and quickly stand before I ravish her and make Dane wait longer. I wrestle a little with doing just that, but it would be making Josh wait. We do not make Josh wait. So, I quickly leave the gorgeous woman in my bed alone and slip out of the bedroom, closing the door behind me. I jog down the stairs, my gun still in my hand, and meet Dane at the front door. I grab my shoulder holster off the hook I hang it on right by the door and strap it on as we walk out, locking up behind us. I slide my gun in my holster.

"So? What's going on?"

"Last night there was a disturbance call."

I wait for him to continue, but he doesn't. I raise an eyebrow. "The fuck does that have to do with me?"

He gives me his best asshole grin. "I'm so glad you asked."

I shake my head as we make our way to Josh's house. "Dick."

"I have one. Pretty proud of it."

I throw my head back and laugh. "You fucking fit right in with us."

"Damn good thing I'm such an asset. Anyway. There was a disturbance. A neighbor called and said she thought she saw a prowler around the house next to her. Nice old lady. You'd like her."

"Fuck, get to the point. I could have my face between Harleigh's thighs right now. I might just go back there and do just that\," I growl as grumpily as possible.

He laughs. "Okay, okay. Don't shoot. As she was on the phone with dispatch, she thought she heard someone trying to get into her house. She has locks on all her windows and doors. Checks them religiously every night. Dispatch tells her to go somewhere she can lock herself in and stay quiet. Not to hang up. Call goes out over the radio. I'm close. I was just coming back from serving a warrant. So, I decided to swing over there. Guess where it was located?"

"I'm guessing you're about to tell me."

"I am. West Garfield."

It takes me a moment, but it hits me. "Son of a bitch. Harleigh's neighborhood."

"Not just Harleigh's neighborhood. Harleigh's next door neighbor. Turns out he was searching through the ashes of her burned down house, then spent a bit of time prowling around the neighbor's."

"Please tell me you fucking caught him."

"I did. Just as he was crawling through a window he broke open. He keeps saying he won't talk without his lawyer."

I grin. "Well, let's see if I can change his mind."

Dane laughs and opens the door to Josh's house. "Josh is with Cole in the basement."

"Is Dallas here?" I ask.

Dallas Cassidy has been spending a lot of time around here after school because it's quiet, and she can focus on large projects. Apparently, being the little sister of the president of Chicago's chapter of Viper's Venom makes her a bit of a target for leering men. Of course, they'd never do it in front of Alec. He'd kill them on the spot. So, when she needs a break, she comes here. It's a good thing for her that Josh is Alec's best friend. And that Alec is Jessa's long lost brother. Dallas has family here. And if she feels safe and can concentrate, that's all we really care about.

"No. Josh took her home last night."

"Good. I don't want her waking up in the middle of this."

"I wouldn't have taken him here if she were, dude."

"Didn't figure you would. But I had to ask."

Dane opens the basement door. "Want me to call the cleaners?"

"You know me well. Have them on standby. I'll send Cole up." I walk down the stairs, surprised that it's silent. I nod to Cole Westwood and send him upstairs. He works with the Chicago P.D. and is on Dane's major crimes taskforce, but he's been with us for years. Cole gives me a wink and heads up the stairs.

"Who's he? Another guy who's supposed to scare me into talking to the big bad mafia boss?" the guy cuffed to the chair and sitting across from Josh asks.

Josh chuckles darkly. He doesn't move an inch, keeping his arms crossed over his chest. "You don't want to fuck with him. He's almost as sadistic as I am. You're better off talking with me." Not taking his eyes off my new play toy, Josh grins. "According to his driver's license, this motherfucker's name is David White. And given all those nice patches on his pretty leather jacket, he's part of our new friends' little gang, the Ruthless Warriors. He was caught trying to break into a little old woman's place. Nice grandma type. She makes the best sugar cookies I've ever had."

I raise an eyebrow at that. "You don't eat sugar cookies."

"Nope. But who can say no to an old lady who adopted you as her grandson within five minutes of meeting you?" Josh's grin widens, but his eyes are still satanic. "I was happy to take him off her hands in exchange for some more of those cookies. They're upstairs in the kitchen if you want some."

I smile. "Must be delicious if she got the world's biggest health nut to eat them."

Josh throws his head back and laughs. "Not that bad. I know good junk food when I see it." He leans forward and rests his arms on the small, metal table we keep down here. It's temporary. We have a house we'll be taking people to as soon as it's built. Almost there. The smile drops from Josh's face. "Alright. I'm tired of fucking around with you and being a nice guy. You're going to tell me exactly what I want to know, or things are going to get messy for you real quick."

"I told you six hours ago, asshole. I'm not telling you shit. You can kill me."

"That's definitely on my agenda," Josh growls dangerously. "The only question you need to answer is how quickly you want it to end for you."

It looks like Josh has already started to have his fun. The fucker's nose is already broken. One eye is swollen shut. Pretty sure the slices across his chest came from the pocket knife Josh always carries.

David glares and spits at Josh, hitting his arm. Daring son of a bitch. "Fuck you."

"Well, that wasn't very nice," Josh says, looking at his arm. "Remind me to make you pay for that." He stands up and walks to the wall where we have a rack of towels hanging. He grabs one and wipes the spit off his arm. Keeping the towel in his hand, he walks back to the table and cocks his hip onto it. "What were you doing there? Why that house?"

"Fuck -"

Josh cuts him off with a hard backhanded slap that makes his head snap to his left side. "Wrong answer. Want to try again?"

"I'm not telling you anything," David growls.

"I think you will." I sit on the table next to Josh and backhand David again. His head snaps back towards Josh. "Just need the right motivation."

"You have nothing you can use against me. I have no family." He smirks. "Nothing you assholes can use against me as leverage."

"Oh, there's always something. Hidden deep down in the corner of some dark closet," Josh says with a half smile as he looks at me. "Like… a certain five-foot-eight, two hundred and eighteen pound, brunette with a taste for wearing red panties. Not my thing, but it does make that ass pop."

I watch with a smirk as he tosses a photo down in front of the fucker. I glance down at it and whistle. "Fuck me. He looks pretty good sitting there in your lap, don't he?"

"You son of a bitch!" David screams. He tries to launch at us, but we both move out of the way. He crashes into the table and falls, chair and all, face first into the cement floor.

Josh kneels in front of David and picks up the picture off the floor. "I wonder if all your little biker friends know about this secret fetish of yours." He pulls out another picture. "Or if they know you like to play dress up in little red thongs, too."

"Where did you get those?" David growls.

"We have our ways." Josh takes out his cellphone and shows it to me.

My eyes widen. "Oh fuck. That's not good." I grin. I'm the demonic to Josh's satanic. We make a good team. I take the phone and kneel next to Josh. "How long do you think it will take your boyfriend to drown?" I turn the phone towards him. On it, there's a live video feed of the guy in the photo tied to a dock. I recognize it as just outside our compound in our lake.

"I have one of my guys out there ready to cut the rope tying him to the dock," Josh calmly explains. "His arms and legs are both bound together with rope. He's also cuffed and shackled, just because I can. Now, he might get lucky and float for a little bit, but we both know that can't happen forever. Especially since it looks pretty choppy out there with that big storm coming in."

I look at the video again and make a tsking noise. "Sure looks like he's already getting tired."

"Come on. He has nothing to do with this!" David yells as he fights against the cuffs he has no hope of escaping. "Let him go, and we won't kill you for this!"

"Nah," I say with a wider grin. "This guy looks like someone I've been personally looking for. I think I'll play with him a little bit after we're done with you." I show the phone to Josh. "Doesn't this look like that guy who backed up into my Camaro a few months ago? Took off on me."

"Oh, yeah." Josh nods. "You were out for blood."

"Still am." I hand the phone to Josh. David has no idea that I'm lying out my asshole. I've never seen this dude in my life. "Maybe I'll be nice. Tell me, David. Should I suck it up? Maybe let him go with a stern warning?"

He looks up at me, panting, and trying to figure out if I'm telling the truth. Finally, he nods. "Let him go. I'll talk."

"You'll talk. And then we'll let him go." I haul him upright in his chair as Josh rights the table. We both stand on either side of David.

"What were you doing there?" Josh asks again.

David sighs. "I had my orders. She's the next door neighbor to someone we've been looking for. We had a lead that the bitch we've been after was there."

My heart beats a little faster, but I keep my expression dangerous and dark. "Huh. So, you break into the house of a little old lady." I look at Josh with a grin. "I thought we had no morals."

He shrugs. "We don't. Unless we're talking about that woman's sugar cookies."

"Didn't know you liked your women dried out and frail," David glowers with a glare.

I kick him in the shin at the same time as Josh. "Enough fucking around," I growl, getting impatient. "I want to know everything. Who gave you the order? Who is the girl? What the fuck do you want with her? And what the hell were you doing in our fucking territory?" I watch him as he glares at us both. He says nothing.

Josh kneels next to him and takes David's hand in his. "You remember that kid's lullaby?" Josh asks as he looks at me. "This little piggy went to the market." He bends David's thumb down. "This little piggy went home." He bends David's index finger down. "This little piggy had roast beef." He bends David's middle finger down. David swallows hard, but stays still. "This little piggy had none." He bends David's ring finger down, and I grin. "And this little piggy…" Josh grins when David tries to jerk his hand away. "Well, he went wee, wee, wee, all the way home…" Josh bends the finger backwards quickly and breaks it with a snap. Before the guy has a second to scream, Josh breaks his arm. "That was for the spitting."

"Ah! Fucking fuck!" David screams. Josh doesn't flinch.

Neither do I. I just grin wider. "I do remember. It was a nursery rhyme my mama always used to say just before she'd tickle my feet." I kneel next to his feet as David keeps screaming and rip off his shoe and sock. "Whew. Fuck. Someone needs some foot spray." I wrinkle my nose at his foot odor, but David continues to howl in pain over his dangling arm, his elbow bone protruding disgustingly through the skin.

Josh stands and has David in a sleeper hold in seconds. "Don't make me make a mess down here. I'm not in the mood. Talk, or things will get a lot rougher. Who gave the order?"

"My boss! Fuck. My boss," David cries.

"Good boy. What's his name?" I ask.

"Gregory Franklin."

"Who's the girl you're after?" Josh asks.

"I… can't… tell you that. I can't! He'll kill me."

"You're going to die either way," I growl. I grip his ankle and twist until his ankle breaks.

"Ah!" he screams again. "Ah! Fuck!" He tries to get away. "Her name is Harleigh! Okay! Fuck! Harleigh!"

"Good boy," Josh rumbles. "And as a show of good faith…" He holds his phone in front of David as he leans over his shoulders. He types something into his phone as I stand. "I'll tell my guard to let your boyfriend out of the water."

He switches back to the video feed. We all watch as our guard, dressed all in black and in a ski mask, roughly pulls the guy, dressed in a sparkly red bra and matching panties, out of the water. I hold back the gag because that isn't a sight I ever wanted to see. The guy is full of hair. He looks like a gorilla wearing women's lingerie. He gives a bad name to Drag Queens. He's more of a crossdresser wannabe because he hasn't quite met the level of good crossdresser yet either.

I wince at his makeup. "I'm choosing to assume that's caused by the water. Please don't try and change my mind. I'll happily live in the lie. What do you want with this Harleigh chick?"

David looks like he's weighing his options, but he's in a lot of pain and gasping for air. Finally, he chooses wisely. "Assure me of his safety."

Josh chuckles. It wouldn't matter if we assured him or not. We could let him go on the camera and do whatever we want to with his boyfriend after we kill him. He'd never be the wiser, but it's lucky for him we aren't like that. Maybe he knows a little more about us than he's leading us to believe.

"Consider it assured. He goes free. You talk. I'll even be nice and not break any more bones," Josh says. We both sit back on the table and watch him.

David takes a deep breath. "Harleigh Harlow. She was promised to my boss' son."

"Name of the son," I command.

"Charles Franklin. The Harlow chick was promised to him in some deal. Her dad agreed to marry her off in order to pay his medical bills off. He was promised that she'd have a good life. College. Best of everything. He resisted quite a bit, but we kept telling him that his bills were piling up. Getting more and more."

Things start clicking into place. The "why" that Harleigh needs to move on is becoming clearer. I'm just hoping to Hell there's nothing sinister behind her father's actions. That it was all him just wanting the best for her and being a complete fucking idiot on how he gets it for her.

"What changed?" Josh asks.

"Him. He changed his mind. At first he said he needed time to say goodbye. Then he begged us to wait until she was eighteen. Then he said he was sick again. He asked us to wait until he was healthier. He needed her to help take care of him. We had a guy that was good at forging the hospital invoices. We kept reminding him that even though we paid his hundreds of thousands of dollars for the surgery itself off, there were still tons of other bills. All the prescriptions he couldn't afford to keep his heart beating after the surgery. The aftercare. The tests he was required to do every six months to make sure things were still working as they should. We showed him that we paid them and his debt was adding up exponentially. He'd never be able to pay us off. When we got sick of the excuses, we went to collect. Ended up killing him because he wouldn't cooperate. Harleigh disappeared. She ran to Lucinio Tech. We assumed she was under your protection, but we haven't been able to find her. She hasn't been seen."

I resist the urge to glance at Josh. "I smell bullshit," I finally say. "One of our guys was made watching you. Next thing we know, you're going after some chick's next door neighbor."

He glances at me and closes his eyes. "Fine. The truth? We know she's here. With you." He opens his eyes and looks directly at me. "We've been watching her for a long time. We know you had a night together. We know she contacted you when we went back. We expected surveillance, but we saw nothing for weeks. That's why we chose to just deal with him and take her."

"Why the old lady?" Josh asks. But we both already know the answer.

"Because we knew we'd lure you out. It was your territory."

This time, Josh and I do look at each other. "Wire?" I ask as I cross my arms over my chest.

Josh shakes his head. "Checked. This is something else. He knew he'd get caught." Josh mimics my pose. "Do you have someone on Harleigh?"

David chuckles. "Tick-tock, motherfuckers."

All at once, I get it. This wasn't an interrogation. It was a fucking distraction. He knew his fate long before we ever caught him. He drew the short straw and is the Ruthless Warriors sacrifice to the big bad wolves while the sheep try and grab their prize out from under the wolf's nose.

Josh puts his phone to his ear without taking his eyes off the fucker. "Kill him." He hangs up.

I take out my Glock and shoot David between the eyes just as they widen at Josh's command. I turn and run up the stairs behind Josh, who had already started moving before the fucker had opened his mouth for the last time. Probably to plead for his boyfriend's life.

My house has bulletproof windows and steel reinforced doors. Everything is locked, but Harleigh doesn't know all of the guards. She could have let anyone in that house and trusted they work for me if that's what they said. We haven't had that conversation before. I should have known better because it's not the first time our perimeter has been breached.

Our feet pound the pavement as Cole and Dane follow us unquestioningly towards my house. My heart races. If anything happened to Harleigh because I stupidly trusted she'd be safe in my house without me or anyone else to protect her, I'll tear the world apart to avenge her.

Fuck. Fuck. Fuck.

I pray to a God I don't believe in that we're wrong. That she'll still be in bed sleeping, curled around my pillow when we get there. But if not... whoever touched her better pray I don't ever find them.

Hold on, baby. I'm coming.

Chapter Thirteen

 Harleigh

"Mmm…" I yawn and stretch, slowly opening my eyes. I smile shyly to myself as I think of yesterday with Gavin and bury my face in his pillow.

He wasn't kidding around when he said I need to work out my aggressions. Hitting the hundred pound punching bag over and over was good for the soul. But I'm pretty sure it was Gavin showing me how to throw the punches that really heated my blood.

I bite my lip. His body in nothing but a pair of gym shorts hard against mine as he guided me… I blush and can't stop the giggle. His coiled muscles weren't the only hard thing hard against me. And when all of my anger dissipated, he was happy to relieve his own edge with me on the gym floor.

After, he made lunch and then we went shopping online for everything I need and so much more. I was happy with one pair of jeans. He made me get five. I put a couple of t-shirts, tank tops, and a hoodie in the online cart. He added several more. When it came to underwear and bras, I had very little say. Gavin ordered a lot of things he liked, but he was so sweet in making sure it was okay with me and wouldn't be uncomfortable for me to wear them. He even had me get several things that are nicer, in case we go anywhere that requires formal wear. Like anywhere his parents might decide to go if they visit him.

And then we ordered dinner in and watched movies until we went to bed. Then spent hours in each other's arms, connected on the most intimate of levels. I can't believe how far we've come in such a short amount of time.

Just as I'm losing myself in the memory of his lips and hands all over me, I hear yelling. My head whips to the door leading to the balcony. My heart drops into my stomach, which then relocates to my throat.

"Gavin?" I squeak.

The thought that he could be hurt sends me running for that door, but before I reach it, something crashes into it. I scream and fall, scurrying away in a backwards crawl towards the bed. Something else crashes into it.

Foot?

Body?

Is someone trying to get in?

I hear a pop and more yelling.

Gunshots.

"Ah!" I scream again, scrambling up and looking for anywhere I can hide. My eyes dart around the room. I leap towards the closet and close the door, praying for a lock. Anything to keep whatever is going on outside as far away from me as possible.

The closet is pitch black, but I refuse to find a lightswitch. Instead, I crawl along the floor as my eyes try to adjust and find a corner large enough to tuck myself into. I'm disoriented, so I don't know if I'm close to the door or not. I hope I'm not, but if I am, I pray I'm hidden enough that no one will see me if they open it. I make myself as small as possible, pulling my knees as close to my chest as possible. I tremble and squeeze my eyes shut.

I jump and let out a terrified squeak when something crashes downstairs. I quickly slap a hand over my mouth. I have to be silent, but it's not easy when I hear people running around the house. My heart is racing so quickly that I wouldn't be able to hear anyone if they were actually talking or yelling.

But I can hear the pounding footsteps.

They sound like an 808 drum and rival the fighter jet in my chest. I feel dizzy and light, like I'm crashing and floating at the same time. It makes me curl into myself even more and tuck myself as much as I can into the corner.

I shift slightly. The cubby next to me has a couple of shelves built into the wall. The first one starts just below my shoulder. I use it for leverage to wedge myself back even more, being as quiet as I can. My hand falls on something hard and metal. I grip the unmistakable handle of a gun and pull it from underneath some kind of fabric I'm guessing is Gavin's t-shirts or something.

I've never shot one before, but I'll be damned if I let anyone take me without a fight. "Please, God. Please don't let there be a safety... I don't know how to use this. Please just let it be point and shoot."

"Harleigh!" someone yells.

Oh my God, he's in the room! I hear the closet door open.

"Harleigh!" the person yells again. I don't recognize his voice, but it's hard. Dangerous. He flips the light on, and I know immediately that I'm not hidden well enough. If I can see him, he can see me.

"No!" I scream.

The man's eyes widen when he sees the gun pointed directly at him. "Harleigh, don't!"

I squeeze the trigger. He dodges behind the wall. The bullet hits the doorframe. Not prepared for the recoil, my arm flies upward and slams against the wall behind me. "Ah!" I refuse to let go of the gun. I clutch it tighter and bring my arm down. It's shaking just as much as my hand is. "Go away!"

"Harleigh, for fuck's sake! I'm on your side!" the man yells.

"How do I know that?" I scream back. I hate the tremble in my voice. I hate that I'm scared. I need to be strong. I have to be.

"Because I ain't stupid enough to fuck with Gavin and Josh! You don't have to put the gun down. They should be here any minute since I raised the alarm. But stop pointing it at me!"

My heart sounds like thunder in my ears. I'm sure it's going to pound so fast, it will rip through my chest. "Stay away from me!"

"Honey -"

"Don't call me honey!" I keep the gun trained on the door, but it's getting heavy. My arm is sore from the recoil. I'm trembling.

"Okay! Okay. Harleigh. I'm Zekeih. I'm the head of security for the compound. I used to work directly under Taylor Reddick for the

Chicago PD, but I left his taskforce after some seriously fucked up shit went down because my wife hated it and feared for my life. I'm a lot safer here in this job. And so are you with me leading the security team."

I see one of his hands slowly slide into the doorway. It's raised, but I still don't know who he is. "Don't! Don't come any further."

"I'm just showing you my hands, Harleigh. See? No gun."

I suddenly remember all of the cop shows I've ever seen, and my eyes widen. "Then throw your gun in here."

"Harleigh, I can't do that. If someone does come in here, I need to be able to defend you."

I sniffle. I see the logic in that statement, but I'm still terrified. On the verge of a complete meltdown. "Then stay out there."

"I'm not going in there, Harleigh," he says. His voice is so calm. Like he's trying to coax a scared dog out from under the bed in a thunderstorm.

"Call Gavin, then. If you work for him, get him here."

"I can promise you, he's already on the way. I alerted Ryan as soon as we saw someone attempting to get over our security wall. He would have already called Josh."

"I'm not moving until I see Gavin or someone I recognize. And this gun is staying in my hand. I may not be a great shot, but I'm sure I can hit at point blank range."

"I understand. I'm going to leave the room, but I'm keeping the door open so I can see if you need help. And I'll speak loud enough for you to hear me. Okay?"

I nod and swipe my eyes. "Okay." I hate that my voice cracks.

"You're being really brave, Harleigh. I know Gavin would be proud of how strong you're being right now. You might not feel that way because you're scared and you don't know me, but you are," he says softly to me as I watch his shadow make slow movements as he stands.

I say nothing. When I don't see his shadow anymore, I slink further back into the closet. I keep the gun clutched in my hand and my eyes on the door. If anyone comes through it that I don't recognize, I don't know what I'll do. Shoot my way out?

I choke on a sob. The truth is, I don't think I'm capable of killing anyone. I hope I'm not forced to.

"Only Gavin or Josh come up here. When they arrive, tell them she is safe in the bedroom. I'm up here with her outside the door," Zekeih, if that's really his name, says. His voice is low but still powerful enough that I can hear him if I focus.

So, that's what I do. I focus. I concentrate on every sight, smell, and sound that I can. I don't hear anymore shooting outside. Or yelling. I don't know if that's because I'm deep in a closet, or if it's because it really stopped.

But the silence doesn't last long. I slink as far as I can into the shadows of the closet and train the gun on the door again when I hear people crash through the door downstairs again and start pounding up the stairs.

"Stay down here!" someone commands. Josh? Please let that be Josh. I blink away tears.

"Harleigh!" someone else yells, closer than the other voice.

"Gavin…," I whisper. "Please let that be Gavin." My heart, seemingly knowing what my head still isn't convinced of, starts to slow immediately at the sound of his voice.

"She's in the closet with a gun," Zekeih says. "She already shot at me."

"Jesus. Fuck, baby. Harleigh? Harleigh, it's me baby. See my wrist?" he asks cautiously.

Knowing what he's asking me, my eyes zero in on the silver bracelet he never takes off of his left wrist. He makes sure I can see it and the tattoo he has. The light is still dim, considering the curtains are still closed, but I can see enough to catch a glimpse of the bracelet and tattoo.

"Gavin," I choke out. I lower the gun to the floor, too weak with relief to hold my shaking arm up any longer.

"You're safe, Lei," he says, his voice calm and completely cool, like he has women holding guns on him every day. Maybe he does. I don't know. "Can I come in?"

I sniffle and wipe my eyes. "Y-yes."

The next thing I know, Gavin is sitting on the closet floor with me in his lap. His arms are wrapped around me, and I suddenly feel safe. Nothing can hurt me. Nothing can get through him. With that realization comes the tears that I've fought so hard against to fall freely.

After what feels like hours, I hear movement outside the closet in the bedroom. Gavin doesn't release his tight grip on me, though, so I don't bother opening my eyes or moving from where I've burrowed into him.

"As much as I hate to interrupt, would you mind getting the formal introductions out of the way, so that if something ever happens again, I'm not likely to get a bullet in my brain when I try to do my job? Or would you rather my wife be on the warpath again? I'm sure you remember the kick to the balls you got last time I got hurt." Zekeih says with a hint of snark.

A low chuckle coming from Gavin's chest vibrates against my ear. "She didn't get my balls. But I had a fuck of a bruise on my thigh." When he shifts, I cling to him, not ready for the safety of his arms to leave me. "I'm not going anywhere, baby," he whispers. "But I need you to look up for me."

I keep myself plastered to him as close as possible, but I do look up. Leaning against the closet door with his arms folded across his chest is a tall man. He has dark hair and is very much in shape, though I don't think his muscles are as defined as Gavin's.

"I'm Zekeih Collins," he says.

"I'm sorry I tried to shoot you," I say just above a whisper.

He holds up his hands with a huge grin. "No offense taken. It was impressive as fuck. But you might want to tell that asshole boyfriend of yours to run you through the security we have around here. And maybe point out the important guards. Give you a safeword that we use just for you. You know. So you don't try to shoot us."

"Alright. Get out," Gavin growls with a low chuckle.

"And for the love of fuck, don't forget the family! Wouldn't want the women after your ass, Vandenberg!" he calls over his shoulder as he walks away, laughing.

"I'm sorry about him," Gavin says.

I sniffle. "I'm sorry I shot at him."

"Don't. Don't be. You did the right thing. You didn't know him. I'm glad you missed, but you can't blame yourself. I've been holding off on things that I should have shown you. That's my fault. Not yours."

I clutch his shirt and say nothing. Instead, I bury my face in his neck and let myself cry again, this time because I nearly shot one of the good guys in my panic. I didn't stop to think. I just shot. If my aim had been better, I would have killed someone who is seemingly close to this family. So, I sob uncontrollably until there are no more tears to cry. And then I dry sob just because I can.

Gavin holds me tightly the entire time, not letting me go once. "Ssh… I got you, baby. It's okay. Let it go. You're safe." He runs his finger through my hair and keeps me tight to his body with his other arm. His lips are against my neck as he whispers soothing words.

When I finally stop sobbing, I have no idea how much time has passed, but I wipe my eyes and sit up slowly. "I'm sorry I broke down like that."

"Lei, you need to stop apologizing, baby. You went through a very scary thing. The adrenaline coursing through you that was keeping you alive just crashed." He tugs my hair a little. "You're obviously going to break after something like that. You didn't have any idea what was happening. Fuck, I don't even know what happened. But I assume you heard the gunshots and came to the safest place you could find."

"It sounded like they were hitting the door to the balcony. I heard yelling. I…" I take a breath. "I was so close to the door, Gavin. I don't know how I wasn't killed."

Gavin sighs. "I'm so fucking sorry, baby." He kisses my temple. "I should have taken you through the security features. You've been here long enough, and I'm not ever letting you go. I should have told you."

I sniffle. "Maybe you could now?" I whisper hopefully as I look up at him. "Maybe then I can do something to defend myself better."

He tugs my hair again, a little harder this time, and kisses me. "Don't do that. You're blaming yourself for my actions, Harleigh. I won't let you do that. I've tried to keep the dark part of all of this away from you, but I should have known better than to do that. Not only are you an obviously capable, strong, and intelligent woman who can handle it, but I also know from past experience that leaving anyone in the dark like I did to you isn't an option and always comes back to kick us in the balls."

He nudges me up but doesn't break contact with me in any way. I'm so thankful for that because I'm still having a hard time processing everything that just happened. When we're standing, he takes my hand and kisses it before leading me out of the closet and into the bedroom. I cling to his arm and grip his hand tightly.

My heart leaps into my throat, and I make a strangled whimpering sound. "I could have been killed."

"No, baby. No. I'll show you." He links our fingers and pulls a very hesitant me over to the window. He pulls the shade back, and I hide my face in his arm. A few moments later, he drops a sweet kiss to my head. "Look, Lei."

I shake my head, not caring in the slightest that it might seem childish. "I'm really scared."

"I promise nothing is going to hurt you. I won't let it, baby. Now, look for me. I want you to see."

I take a deep breath and look, but I stay behind him. The glass on the door is shattered in several different places. "Oh God," I choke out, tears I didn't know I still had inside me are stinging my eyes.

Gavin turns to me and cups my cheek with his hand, not letting go of mine with his other. "I know it looks scary. Do you trust me?"

I nod. "I do." I trust him without question. It's a strange feeling for me, yet it feels so normal. A conundrum.

"Good girl." I watch as he reaches out and touches the glass. "Feel it."

I shakily do as I'm told, and my eyes become as wide as saucers. "But..." I trail off as I take a closer look at the glass. The bullets never got all the way through. The glass inside is still smooth.

"Nick West, Ryan's and Josh's brother, has been in security for a long time. He's designed some incredibly high tech shit that keeps all of our asses safe, and has for years. He's really smart and only uses the best products. If he can't get what he wants, he has it specially designed. This glass can't be found on the market, but it's used in all of our houses and every single one of our businesses on both the Crane's and Lucinio's side. Nick found a flaw in bullet resistant glass. So, he figured out a way to fix it. This glass is actually acrylic. It's stronger. It's treated with a bullet resistant film on both sides, layered with another layer of acrylic that's treated on both sides with the film, then another, and finally another. It's almost four inches thick."

My eyes widen, and my mouth drops. "It doesn't look like it."

"That's the point. We want it to look just like real, everyday, normal glass." He reaches for the door handle and opens it slowly, being mindful of my complete terror. I take a breath and follow him. He sticks a finger carefully into one of the bullet holes and pulls a bullet out before gesturing for me to do the same. I do and bite my lip as I look up at him. "Feel that?"

I furrow my brows. "It feels sort of like plastic." I push on it. "It's flexible."

He nods. "That's the film. And if you look closely, you'll see the bullet penetrated that first layer of acrylic but didn't quite get all the way through. That leads me to believe that the bullet didn't come from a very high-powered rifle." He holds out his hand. "I'd say a handgun. Probably similar to the one you found in the closet. We would normally have Dane have his lab run this. When he sends things, it goes to specific people and is top priority. So it won't take us long to get results. But in this case, we don't need to."

"Why?" I tilt my head curiously as he leads me back inside and closes the door.

"Because our guards caught the motherfuckers. They're being dealt with now. As for what happened, though, we'll need to wait for Josh to brief us. Usually, I'd be right there at Josh's side for something like this, but not today. Not when you need me. You come first. Always."

I don't know why, but his words make the butterflies in my heart take flight. I let him fold me into his arms and hold me tight. It's not that he said I come first. It's that those words solidify everything I already knew.

He'll protect me with all he is. I'm Gavin's.

Heart and soul. All of me.

But what's more?

He's *mine*.

Chapter Fourteen

❦ Gavin ❦

I put my phone back in my pocket after checking the text. "Josh will be here in a few minutes to explain what happened." I kiss Harleigh's hand, which I haven't let go of since we left the floor of the bedroom closet. I've been leading her around the house showing her security features that she didn't know about previously. Features I should have told her about long ago. If I had, she never would have been as terrified as she was.

"Okay," she says quietly.

I hate that she's still scared. I can tell she is by how quiet she's being; the way she's clinging to my hand. So, I continue on, hoping to make her feel better. Safer. She can squeeze my hand as tightly as she wants to if it means she feels protected.

"One of my favorite features that we have is the code. There are only an elite selection of people who have a code to this house or any of our houses. Only close family. People like Ryan and his wife. Or Alex and his fiance. Josh. Jessa and her husband. Family. And the head of security for the compound."

"Zekeih."

I smile and kiss her forehead. "Very good. They also have keys, but they don't need it with the code. We have very smart technology. There isn't a keypad, thumb print pad, or anything like that. It's just a black screen that comes up with numbers when it's touched, but when you enter the code, the panel recognizes you and your fingerprints. We'll need to get you scanned and everything. Another thing I haven't done that makes me feel like a fucking jackass."

"No…" She rubs my arm and kisses it. "Don't feel like that. It wasn't until recently that you learned to trust that I'm not going to run away again. I had to earn that."

I really hate that she's right. It's like a kick to the chest. So, instead of saying anything, I kiss her forehead and lead her to the living room. "There are only two other people who don't live here who have all of our codes and access to our homes as well as any Crane or Lucinio building in the entire world."

She looks up at me. "Who?"

"One of them is Alec Cassidy. He's an ally, one of Josh's best friends, and Jessa's brother. The other is Lyric. She's like a little sister to all of us. She was with Josh for a while, but they decided they were far better friends. Best friends. Josh is like her big brother. Well, we all are. She's happily married now, but she knows if she ever needs anything, she has us. She lives in Florida, but she comes here often to visit. If she gets busy, though, she always makes time to come once a year." My smile slips a little. "She and Josh had a child together that was miscarried. We hold a memorial every year."

"That's both so sad and so heartwarming all at the same time. It's so sweet that you all are still so close."

"We very much are." I take a breath. "Alright. Last thing. I forgot about this when we were upstairs, so remind me to show you where the one upstairs is located." I move a trophy I won back in high school for a baseball championship aside. Behind it, on the mantle above the fireplace, is a black button. "Panic button. There are four throughout the house. I'll show you where all of them are. When you hit this, the house goes into lockdown. And I mean that in every sense of the word. Reinforced steel comes down over all of the windows and doors."

Her eyes grow wide. "That would have been nice to know."

I grin because I can hear the tease in her voice, but I'm pissed off at myself for not telling her before today. "The only people who can override the system to all houses when this system is activated are me, Josh, Ryan, and Luke Massena. He's Ryan's second in command. We're the only ones who have the codes, and the only ones who can enter any of the houses when this system is activated because it overrides the entire security system in the house. No one in. No one out. Now, we know that it's possible the four of us are out at the same time. Maybe on a mission. We try not to let that happen, but anything is possible. If it happens, we have a backup. Nick is Ryan's and Luke's backup. He designed the system, so he should know how to use it. But he has his own backup code. He doesn't have ours. He needs to specify on the pad outside that it's a backup code. If he enters it without doing that, the system locks down and the only people who can override that are those of us with main codes."

"You, Josh, Ryan, or Luke."

I nod. "Good girl."

"That's actually super comforting."

I lead her to my office, then to the kitchen to show her the other panic buttons while I talk. "Alex is backup for me and Josh. Again. He has his own code. And if Nick or Alex are doing something off the compound property, we have Zekeih. Who also has his own code."

"And regular codes?"

"Yep. In the event that something big happens and none of us are here, there are two others who have their own set of codes."

"Lyric and Alec?"

I nod. "Yes. And I know where your mind just went." I smile and lean down and kiss her, slowly and deeply. When I pull away, she sways slightly and blushes. I kiss her forehead. "We don't expect a doomsday scenario to ever happen, but we are a mafia. Two very powerful ones. It's unlikely, but we always have a backup to our backups. It's one way that we've survived this long and grown to be as large and as powerful as we are."

She nods. "I understand." She takes a deep breath. "You have some very serious security measures in place."

"We do. They're necessary, though. We're in the process of having one more system installed. It's an alarm that will circulate through everyone's homes and send alerts directly to everyone's cellphones if

127

something happens, like what happened today. Don't ask me how. I have no idea. That is Robby's and Nick's expertise. When that system is installed, we'll have a button in every single room. Today, when you heard those shots, your protocol, if we had that system already and if I'd told you about the panic button, would have been to hit the alarm to alert everyone something was happening. Then when those shots hit the glass, hit the panic button."

"So the steel panels would have come down."

"Very good." I squeeze her hand. "Last thing." I nod behind her to the laundry room door. "This might sound like overkill, but we're having a bunker built underneath the compound. It's large enough to accommodate everyone. When it's finished, there will be enough food down there to feed everyone in this compound for a year. That includes all of the guards. And there are a lot of them. We have several rooms with bunkbeds for all of them. We have a huge food room. There's an air filtration system. Running water and sewage. Electricity. Air conditioning. Heat. Refrigeration. Private rooms for the entire family and the kids."

"Jesus. It sounds like a hotel."

I chuckle. "You're not wrong. It's the brainchild of Ryan and Josh, designed by Jessa and her husband, Jason, secured by Nick, and linked to the outside world by Alex and Lance. You haven't met him yet. He's on assignment. It will take time to build, but we have a lot of people working on it. The door to it is through the laundry room and hidden. If anyone is looking for it, they won't find it because the other side of the wall isn't hollowed out like most secret passageways are. It's reinforced steel and can only be accessed by code. Which is different from the house code and inaccessible by anyone except me and you. Every house has their own entrance and their own code."

"There's so much to remember," she says quietly.

"There is, but it will become second nature to you. I promise. You only have two codes to memorize. When we get your security clearance dealt with, I'll show you how to access it."

She tilts her head. "What about Lyric? I mean, if she's here and something happens? You said she lives in Florida. And Alec."

I love how she already cares about people she's never met. "Lyric has Josh's code. It's unlikely for her to be staying with anyone else while she's here. If she's visiting someone else, she wouldn't need to worry because someone in that house will have the code. Alec also has Josh's, but he's based in Chicago. His compound is just on the outskirts of the city. Not far from ours, actually. We're on the outskirts as well. He's a little further. But if anything were to happen, they'd be safe."

"Good." She nods. "That's good."

I kiss her head. "I know I said last thing already, but I just remembered you need a secret word or phrase. Zekeih would be one of the few people who know it. We have a few people under him who are also high in ranks. He has his own team of commanders, if you will. They would have it. The rest of the family would have it. You'll have to think about what you want it to be because if we ever have another situation like today, it's an extra layer of security for you. Peace of mind. If we do go into lockdown, the safest place is the bedroom. Lock the door. Have the steel panels down. Don't unlock the door for anyone who doesn't give you your phrase. Make it as off the wall as you can. That way you know it can't be guessed or used by anyone who doesn't have it. It would be used in multiple situations. Including if a guard comes up to you that you don't recognize. We'll never send anyone to you for any reason who doesn't have your keyword or phrase."

"I hate grapefruit and seashells."

I blink before cracking a smile and then laughing. "That's perfect."

"It's also a lie. I love grapefruit and seashells."

"What's your favorite color?"

"Deep red."

"Your phrase is I hate grapefruit and deep red seashells."

She giggles as she nods. "I love it."

I turn towards the door when I hear a knock. "That would be Josh."

Keeping her hand in mine, I lead her to the front door, but I'm tempted to bring her upstairs and wrap completely around her while she sleeps. She looks exhausted. I can't blame her. After an adrenaline dump like what she experienced, I'm lucky my girl is still functioning.

"Hey," Josh says when I open the door. His eyes meet Harleigh's. "Doing okay?"

"I'm not sure, honestly." She leans her head against my arm. "I'm still kind of in a daze. No idea what happened. All I really remember with clarity is nearly shooting someone close to you all. Everything else is there, but it's strange. It's like I can see everything that happened. It plays in my mind. But I feel like I wasn't really a part of it. Like it all just happened as I was watching from somewhere else."

Josh chuckles. "You won't believe me, but that's actually normal."

"Not for me," she whispers with a sniffle. "Why didn't I remember what happened at the diner like that?"

Josh steps in as I move to allow him to. I close the door behind him. "Every situation is different, sweetheart." Josh shrugs. "I have things that happened in my life that I don't remember at all. Others I remember vividly, but it's like I was an outsider watching it all happen, just like you feel. And still others, I was very actively playing my role, and I remember every second of it just as I should. Just like you remember the diner. I can't tell you why it happens, but I can tell you that as time progresses, you'll start to be able to process it better. At the risk of sounding like a fucking shrink, lean on Gavin. Having his support and the support of those you're close to and have come to trust will be your saving grace."

I smile as I lead them both to the living room. Josh sits on the couch. I pull Harleigh into my lap as I settle into an oversized chair near him so we can talk. Harleigh's body melts into mine when I wrap her in my arms and hold her tightly. Tension I'm not completely sure she even realized she was carrying begins to dissipate as soon as I start lazily rubbing her thigh up to her hip.

"So?" I ask when we're settled.

Josh rubs his head as he leans back and closes his eyes. "It wasn't this Franklin fuck who ordered this fuck of a day." He opens his eyes. "It was his son. Charles. And the shit last night?" He turns his head towards me and Harleigh. "All Charles. The old lady? She was a pawn for them. Charles' fucking grandmother."

I blink and shake my head. "Sugar cookie girl?"

Josh nods with a chuckle. "Good fucking thing I never ate them. The results from the tests I had run on them? Laced with fucking arsenic and fentanyl."

"Holy shit. Grandma ain't fucking around."

"I'm so lost," Harleigh says with wide eyes. I'm sure all she understands out of any of that is that someone tried to kill Josh.

I kiss her neck with a sigh. "Dane came over this morning. He went to a call last night in the neighborhood your house used to be in. The

130

call was from the old woman next door. She said someone was prowling next door and trying to break into her house."

Harleigh blinks at me, confused. Like I'm missing something huge. She takes a breath. "There's no old woman that lived there. My house was on the corner. On the other side of us was a party house. College kids. Across the street was a well known drug house. Police were there a lot. There were never any older people around my house. Not as long as I can remember. We lived in that house my entire life."

Josh and I lock eyes as he slowly leans forward. He rests his elbows on his knees. "The call that came in was what Gavin said, but what you said makes sense with what we know now. Dane caught the prowler. He called me. I talked to the woman a little bit. She tried to shove the cookies down my throat. I finally agreed to take them with me, but I gave them to Dane to take to his lab. I brought the prowler back here. I interrogated him for a few hours before I sent Dane for Gavin."

"Everything he gave us was a made up story. Something he was fed," I growl low.

"Not everything. I don't think he was lying about the shit that had to do with Harleigh."

Harleigh sits up a little. "What about me?" she asks. She's trembling slightly, like she doesn't want to know even though she does.

I keep her held tightly to my body. "Well, he told us a lot of shit you already had. But we got the son's name. The one you were promised to. The rest? We found out that they manipulated your father. He didn't say it outright, but I'm sure there were a lot of threats. They made it look like all of the medication they were paying for and the bills they were paying off were just adding up. They made the bills larger than what they were to show him that he'd never be able to pay them off. That he didn't have a choice but to take the only option they were putting on the table."

"Which was me." She sinks against me and buries her face in my neck.

I tangle my fingers in her silky strands and rub the back of her neck soothingly. While my heart breaks for her, my veins start turning to shards of ice throughout my body. Who the fuck agrees to something like that? But more than that. What the hell kind of evil fucking person thinks it's okay to purchase a human being? Arrange a marriage? Whatever the fuck is happening here.

"That's not even the half of it," Josh continues. "Our guys caught the motherfucker shooting up at your bedroom. His entire purpose here was to grab Harleigh. When our guards showed up, fucker started shooting in a panic. Our guys wounded him. It didn't take much to get him to talk, but what he said is a cause to ring the alarms here." He looks pointedly at Harleigh and flicks his eyes towards my office.

I give him a slight shake of my head. I know he's asking if we should do this in private because Harleigh is still processing everything else up to this point. "Harleigh?"

She sniffles and nudges my chin. "Yeah?" she whispers.

"I'm going to sound like a complete asshole for asking you this, but are you going to be okay with what Josh is about to say? Because whatever it is I'm sure is about to change things. Not only for us, but everything that this entire thing with you involves. I need to know you're all in. Because I sure as hell am."

Her hand deliberately moves up my chest, making me shiver at her touch. Not the fucking time for my libido to shift into overdrive. She trails it up to my neck, across my jaw, and to my cheek, letting her thumb run over my bottom lip on the way. She gives me a soft smile, but it's what's hidden behind those gorgeous amber eyes that tells me all I need to know.

"I am."

Those two words are all it takes for me to squeeze her hip with one hand and tighten my fingers in her hair with the other. I pull her closer and crash my mouth to hers in a feverishly delicious kiss so hot that all of the blood rushes directly to my dick. I harden underneath her as her fingers tug at the short length of my hair.

Before I can give into my baser needs, though, and give her what she so clearly needs from me, Josh clears his throat. "I hate to break it up, and I'm not just saying that because of you, Harleigh. I know what you both need right now. I hate to be the asshole, but we did get time sensitive information."

I pull back slowly from Harleigh's lips after nipping her tongue and look at Josh. I let out a long sigh. I hate where I know he's going. For the first time since becoming a part of Lucinio Mafia when I was barely a teenager, I don't want to go on any missions. Anywhere that takes me away from my girl when she needs me, no matter the distance, is too far.

"Did they give up his whereabouts?"

"Daddy is in Paris," Josh responds. "Son is at a hideout in Canada. He has a second hideout in Greenland, and a third in North Pole, Alaska. Don't ask me how the fuck Lance got me that information."

"What else did this guy tell us?"

He flicks his eyes towards Harleigh again. "That today, if he fails, Harleigh may as well not bother ever leaving this compound. Because there are people watching her everywhere."

Harleigh hisses out a breath. "But we knew that, right?" she asks quietly. "That people are after me?"

I kiss her neck as I let out a breath and run my nose along her sweet skin. "It means that this is bigger than just some small-time gang, baby."

"They want you for a reason, Harleigh. Whatever that reason is, I don't know. But we eradicated them when we went after them weeks ago. There's no way they could have regenerated this quickly. They're bigger than we thought they were. What's disconcerting about that is we do our research. So, it means they're well connected and very hidden. I don't like it. I'm sending four teams. One to Paris, where I will be. One to Canada, where Ryan will be. One to Greenland, where Luke will be. And one to Alaska... "

I sigh. I knew this would be coming eventually. "Where I will be."

Josh nods and looks at Harleigh. "Which means you'll be here. I'll set you up with Alex and Raleigh."

Harleigh says nothing. She just bites her lip and turns away from our conversation. I can't really blame her, but I really hate that she seems defeated. Like she's given up completely. I need to figure out how to put her beautiful smile back on her face because I hate how down she is. There's no way anyone is getting near my girl. I'll happily do all I can to prove that to her.

Time to end this bullshit gang once and fucking for all.

Chapter Fifteen

 Harleigh

The conversation Josh, Gavin, and everyone else are having feels strange. Josh asked Ryan, Luke, Alex, and a few other people I've never met to come here and be a part of all this planning thing. Someone will be somewhere. Another somewhere else.

Massive numbers…

Overwhelm them…

Do this…

Grab this gun…

Don't let him get away if you see him…

It's like I'm not even here, and it's all culminated into a Russian sized headache complete with launching missiles and atomic bombs that have all hit their targets in my brain.

Which is why I find myself in the kitchen with my head down on the counter. I feel like my heart is being squeezed in my chest. My entire left arm feels like it's both on fire and numb. I'd think I'm having a heart attack, but I know the signs of those. Watching my father have one was one of the worst days of my life. I still haven't figured out what's worse. Watching him die and not being able to do anything about it, or watching him fight for his life and not knowing how to help while thinking he was going to die right in front of me as I clumsily tried to save him while calling for help.

I force air into my lungs and count backwards from ten to steady myself. Thankfully, it helps, so I do it again. I lock my fingers behind my neck and stay bent over the counter until my breathing returns to normal and my heart doesn't feel like it's going to escape from my chest.

"Are you okay?" a soft voice asks next to me.

I jump and snap my head towards her. "S-sorry. I didn't hear you come in."

"Well, you were pretty busy breathing," she says. Her pretty auburn with hints of red hair glistens in the sunlight streaming through the window. "We haven't really been properly introduced. I'm Dani West."

I nod slowly. "I remember," I say quietly as I look down at my hands folded on the counter.

Jessa told me who everyone was and pointed them out, but I don't remember all of their names, and I haven't really seen much of them. When I was staying with Ryan and Arianna while Gavin was away, I decided quickly to steer clear of them. The animosity radiated off of them. I didn't understand it right away, but the more I observed, the more I got it. It wasn't until after I talked with Arianna and then Gavin, though, that it really sunk in. I wasn't even really angry with them anymore.

"Look, um. I know when you first got here, it was pretty rocky and rough. I'm sorry for my part in that."

I shake my head. "No, I understand. I see how close everyone is here. I never expected that I'd be welcomed with open arms. It was a shock how cold everyone was, but I really do get it."

Dani is quiet for a few moments before she takes a deep breath. "He's such a good guy. I don't know him as well as everyone else, but I do know he went through a really hard period of time when Marissa was killed. I didn't help that. I had only just found out that she was my sister." She smiles softly and looks down. "I grilled him for as much information as I could get about the woman I never knew. I thought there had to be some redeeming qualities about her if he stayed with her for so long."

"Marissa wasn't all bad," Jessa says, appearing behind us. We both turn to her as she steps in from outside. I'm not sure when all of the other girls and even guys got here, but the backyard and pool area is full of people, and someone is manning the grill. Though, I can't see who because his back is turned.

"I must have been completely focused if you all are here. I didn't notice at all," I say quietly and shake my head. "Anyway. I know I hurt him. I guess I didn't then, but I do now. We talked and worked through it all. It was self-doubt on my part. Which isn't an excuse… Just… true. It does very bad things to people. At least, that's what I've learned from all of this. And also not to doubt Gavin. And ignore signs."

Jessa smiles softly. "We're all very protective of each other. But it's different with Gavin. I've personally known him for a long time. He's always been dark and a little mysterious, but out of all of the guys on the Lucinio team, Gavin is the one with the biggest heart. It's also why he's so distant. He doesn't like to open it for anyone." She leans against the counter and crosses her arms over her chest. "I always thought there was more to the reason why, but there really isn't. Gavin takes a long time to open up to anyone. It scares him to death because he doesn't want to lose anyone he's let into his circle. Everything that happened with Marissa, and then her death, affected him a lot more than he let anyone see."

"But we saw," Dani says.

"Gavin has always been like a brother to me," Jessa continues. "I've always wanted him to be happy. I knew he wasn't with Marissa. I think everyone did. But he's loyal. Once he committed to her, it didn't matter that he didn't fully love her with all he is. He felt like she needed him. That was the end of it for him. Eventually, it just became comfortable for him."

"His normal in a rocky world," I finish quietly. "He mentioned that. When we first met. He opened up so much, and I just…" I shrug sadly and bite my lip. "I don't think I'll ever forgive myself for ignoring so much of everything he was trying to show me. I hate that I made him feel like it was him in any way, but I really hate that I hurt him."

"Truthfully, now that I think about it, maybe it was all for the best." Dani shrugs with a smile. "You both are stronger for it."

"Maybe," I agree.

Jessa gives my arm a friendly squeeze. "We're setting up for a barbecue. Everyone came in from back by the pool." She smiles and lets me go. "If you want to let them know everyone is here, we'll be out back."

I glance towards Gavin's office where everyone moved to when they got here. I don't really want to go back in there, but I know I should. This entire thing involves me and the sick and disgusting plan the Ruthless Warriors concocted around me. I still don't understand what they want with me. It can't seriously be just some deal made with my father. It has to be more. It's something I've been thinking about more and more lately, but definitely since today.

I nod and smile softly. "I can do that."

They both smile as I steel myself and walk back to Gavin's office. I slip back in as quietly as I walked out of it. The conversation is still just as lively, only I think it may have gotten a little more heated.

"No!" Gavin says. "No. Absolutely not. We're not doing that. Why the fuck would you even suggest that? If it were Arianna, do you think Ryan would allow that?" Gavin pinches the bridge of his nose as he paces the room. "Would you?"

"I'm just throwing out ideas, asshole. Didn't say it was fucking happening," Josh growls. I'm suddenly sorry I left because I really want to know what was said to make Gavin so upset.

"Well, you can shove that one up your fucking ass." Gavin drops in his chair and puts his head down. "Next idea, please."

"I... was just... coming to say everyone is here. What did I miss?" I ask quietly.

Gavin looks up at me and slowly sits up. He holds out a hand for me. I furrow my brows as I walk to him and take it. He pulls me into his lap and buries his face in my hair. I glance at Josh, confused, but it's Luke who speaks.

"We're coming up with ideas on how to lure the Franklin's out without having to go in, guns blazing," he explains. "One of the ideas was using you for bait."

"Well, wouldn't that be the easiest way?" I ask curiously.

"It's not happening," Gavin growls dangerously. "I want you here, in this compound, surrounded by people who will protect you."

"I get why -" Josh begins.

Gavin cuts him off. "No. Fucking no."

Josh crosses his arms and leans back in his chair. "You're fucking testy."

"And you're a fucking asshole," Gavin says back to him.

"I think Josh has a point," I say to Gavin as I kiss his cheek.

He furrows his brows. "Josh? He didn't come up with that bullshit plan."

I tilt my head and look over at the man sitting across from us with an amused smile, then back at Gavin. "Is… that not Josh?"

The other twin I thought was Alex sitting on the couch on the other side of the room waves. "That would be me."

I blush a furious shade of red at not being able to tell them apart. "Oh God. I'm so sorry."

Everyone in the room laughs. Alex grins. "Come on. Confusing me with him? I'm a lot prettier than that fucker."

I can't help but giggle as I look between them. Josh actually looks a little bigger, muscle wise. He's got a far darker and more dominant look about him. His eyes are the same piercing blue as Alex's, but Josh's have hints of something a lot more sinister. Dangerous. Mysterious. He holds himself confidently with a generous amount of don't-fuck-with-me attitude.

Alex, though still very intimidating and commanding, is different. I'm sure he could still take anyone he wanted to down in any manner he desires. To me, it seems like his personality is more CEO instead of mafia boss. Dominating in the boardroom. Far kinder when he's not in front of executives around a conference table. He holds himself far differently, though still confidently.

Josh stands. "Alright. Enough of this talk. We're not using Harleigh as bait because there are way too many fucking unknowns. We have no idea how big these guys are. Lance is working on it, and he's enlisted Robby's help, but we can't assume anything."

"The truth is, a small gang isn't going to have four hideouts in different parts of the world." Ryan begins as he leans forward. "And these are the only ones we know about. We know very little about this gang. I think the shit we do know are only things they want us to." He nods to Josh. "You've already been set up by these fuckers twice. And I'm not being a dick in saying that. I'm saying it as your mentor and family. We need to research. We have time. Harleigh is safe here. We've proven that. Gavin showed her the security features in the house. We need to take the steps." His dark gaze falls on me and Gavin. "If you're really serious about each other, then we need to get Harleigh set up with her clearance. Most importantly, though, the family all needs to come together. Harleigh knows us all, but there's a huge disconnect that we all need to fix."

"She's here to stay," Gavin says for me. The sureness of his words goes straight to my heart, but it's the deep growl of his sexy voice as he kisses my neck that has me blushing.

"I am," I say softly. "I don't want to be anywhere else."

"I think the plan needs to stay conservative," Luke says. "We research. We do surveillance. There's a reason we've survived as long as we have. Tried and true methods. We took Matthew Lucinio with it. We've taken down every enemy we've come across the same way. We'll do the same with these assholes because it's what we fucking do. Patience. I said it before. I'll keep saying it. No reason to sit here and try to hash out a plan. We've already got one."

Gavin lets out a breath. "I have to agree, I guess. But I don't want to be away from Harleigh. Not that I don't trust our guys, but being away from her for that long of a period of time..." His head drops to my shoulder, and he nuzzles me. "Fuck, I don't know what the hell to do. I'm torn."

"I know, Gav," Alex says. "But they're right. Coming up with other plans is pointless. We know what we're going to do. It's why I've been coming up with the most off the wall ones. To get you to see that the original plan is the right one. We investigate. Research. Figure out their hideouts. Get surveillance on them. You figure out where the fuck they are. You take them down. Harleigh stays with me while you all are taking care of business."

"We strike both of them at the same time -" Ryan begins.

"Wait," I say quietly. "I'm sorry. I don't mean to interrupt, but why do I need to stay with Alex?"

"Because it's the safest place for you," Josh answers. "Gavin could stay, but he's my second. We need to split up and take both father and son down at the same time. Coordinated attacks. We decided that we're going to send some guys to do some surveillance and pinpoint where they are while Lance gathers as much information as he can about them. From there, we need two teams. I'm taking one. Gavin is taking the other. I can't always rely on Ryan to bail my ass out, and I need someone keeping an eye on our issue in Texas. Ryan offered to help me out with that. Regardless, you being with Gavin would distract him from what he needs to do. That could get him or others killed."

The thought of that scares me, but another thought occurs to me. I look at Gavin because I'm not sure I should say anything. I don't feel like it's my place. My heart beats a little faster, nearing that state of panic again.

Gavin kisses my neck and hugs me tighter. "I can tell something is on your mind," he says softly. "You don't need to hesitate. No one is going to make you feel stupid or stop you from talking."

I glance at everyone before looking back at him and taking a breath, inhaling his intoxicating and calming scent. "What… if… your attention is split anyway…? Wouldn't it be easier if we were together…? I mean, couldn't we take extra people with us?" I tilt my head. "People who could stay with me while you're doing what you need to? I'm… not going to lie. I'd feel better with you near. Not just because I want to be with you, but because I just… I guess I just feel like the better option is for us to be together." I glance at everyone else again and lower my eyes. "Maybe I'm off base."

"No, honey. You're not." He hugs me closer. "That's what I was saying. And I was shot down because of the possibility of you being a distraction to me out there. My argument is that Ryan had Arianna with him when he felt she was in danger. And the lesson we've learned on so many different occasions is that being together is never a poor option. Especially since I can't sit here and lie to any of them or you and pretend that my mind would be fully on the job knowing that you're however many miles away from me. Not that I don't trust anyone to keep you safe. Especially Alex. But my attention would be diverted. There's just no other way to say it."

I let out a breath and stand slowly. "Is there a reason I can't go?"

"Because it isn't safe," Josh says matter of factly. "Here is safe. Out there? Not so much."

I shake my head, deflating a little. "But if Gavin's attention is going to be split, wouldn't it be better if we were together."

"I'm not allowing -" Josh begins.

I hold up a hand. "Please let me finish. I don't mean to be disrespectful to you and interrupt, but I think I have a good idea." I bite my lip as I watch him.

He sighs and waves his hand. "Fine."

"Well, would there be a way that we could sort of make it seem like it's undercover? Like, what if some of the family went one place, and the other half went to the other? Wherever it happens to be that they are. That way, it's just a family on vacation. No one would think anything of that, would they? And it would be extra protection."

Ryan shakes his head as he stands. "No, that wouldn't work." He paces the office slowly as he thinks. "Unless…"

"We paid off the tabloids," Alex continues. "Not like we haven't done that before."

Ryan sighs. "I was thinking that, but no. We all bring a lot of attention wherever we go. If we all showed up in North Pole, Alaska, as an example, people will know we're there. Even without the tabloids." He shakes his head. "No. It's better if we let you go with Gavin."

My heart both sinks and feels like it's floating because while I won't be separated from Gavin so soon after what happened today while I'm still feeling scared and vulnerable, I also won't be able to have a chance at bonding with anyone else. I thought if we could make it like a family thing, it would also help me to get to know everyone while Gavin was focusing on what needed to be done. Thinking about it now, it seems like a stupidly selfish thing to even suggest. Here they are trying to figure out how to save my life, in a sense, and I'm thinking about how to get people to like me.

"If you were mine, I would spank your ass red for those thoughts," Josh growls, startling me into looking back up at them.

I blink. "What?"

"You just said that you were stupidly selfish for coming up with an idea that could have merit all because you wanted the chance to bond with the rest of the family," Josh rumbles. "If you were my girl, your ass would be red for those negative thoughts. Lucky for you, you're not mine." His eyes flick to Gavin. "But going by the look on his face, you're in for some kind of punishment." His gaze returns to me. "You didn't give us the chance to expand on your idea to figure out if it's something that could work or not."

I blush in embarrassment at speaking those thoughts out loud. "But Ryan just said no."

"And we would have discussed it more," Gavin says behind me as he stands. His gaze darkens as he speaks to the other people in the room, but he doesn't take his eyes off me. "Come up with a plan. Tell me what it is." He takes my hand. "You know what I want. Try to make it work."

He turns and pulls me behind him, not saying another word. I watch him with wide eyes, jogging to keep up with his long strides as he pulls me out of the office. I glance back at everyone else because I'm confused about what's going on, but I can't ignore the fire igniting in my belly.

No one pays any attention to what Gavin is doing, and as he closes the door behind us, their conversation regarding the plan continues without us. Very suddenly, I'm aware of the sexual tension crackling through the air. I look up at Gavin in surprise, but he still says nothing. Instead, he pulls me down the hallway, holding onto my hand tightly.

"Where are we going?" I ask, already knowing the answer.

Gavin's low chuckle seems to vibrate through his entire body and straight into my arm, continuing directly to my clit. When he turns for the stairs, I know I'm in for whatever punishment Josh alluded to. I must be crazy, though, because thinking about Gavin's hand on my ass makes my body hum; my pussy tighten.

I blush a deep shade of red because I can't wait.

Chapter Sixteen

❦ Gavin ❦

I close the door to my bedroom behind me and turn quickly. Harleigh's eyes widen in surprise at what I'm sure is a slightly demonic and absolutely dark glare that makes my eyes probably look like they're on fire.

"We need to discuss what this family is like," I begin. "But first, you're going to learn a valuable lesson in thinking or saying that kind of shit about yourself." I tug her to the bed.

"I didn't say anything bad!" she squeaks out.

"Selfish. Stupid. All for wanting to move past what happened with us and start a new life with the man you love and his family." I reach down and grip her hips. I lift her with ease and toss her on the bed.

"Gavin!" she squawks. She tries to sit up, but I have other plans.

I grab her ankle and tug her towards me, forcing her to land flat on her back once more. "I don't think so, my little lioness." I pause with my hand on her ankle and grin. "Nala. I'm calling you little Nala from now on."

She blushes a pretty shade of pink, and her eyes sparkle. "From the Lion King?"

I grin. "Yep."

"I love the Lion King."

"I know." I tug her down closer to me so her ass is almost off the bed. "I remember everything you've ever told me." I lean down and grip her hips. I effortlessly flip her and tug her back so her ass is against my dick. I grind into her as I lean over her. I kiss her neck with a grin when she lets out a moan. "I'll give you all of that." I grind into her harder as she wiggles her ass against me. "But first…" I swat her ass. Hard.

"Ah! Gavin!" She looks over her shoulder at me and jerks away from me, but her fingers fist the bedspread underneath her. Her gaze heats up. Her eyes are hooded with desire. She's enjoying this just as much as I am.

The simple realization makes my semi-hard cock grow to a full hard on in seconds, and it makes me groan. "Fucking hell, baby."

I reach around her and unbutton her shorts. I yank down her zipper and tug her shorts down to her knees, binding her. I don't need to see how wet she is for me. I can smell it as I drop to my knees. I push her legs apart and dive into her pussy with my tongue because I can't fucking resist.

She jerks and pushes back against me as I slide my tongue through her sweetness. "Oh, fuck yes…"

"Christ, I'll never get enough of you." I dip my tongue into her pussy and slap her ass again.

"Ah!" Her pussy clenches and gets wetter.

"I'm going to have to think of new punishments for you. You like being spanked too much."

"Oh, Gav…," she moans as her pussy pulses around my unrelenting tongue as I fuck her with it.

"Something you won't enjoy so much," I say, low and deep into her pussy right before I suck. I slap her ass again.

"Oh my Christ, yes…" She clenches around my tongue, and I know she's close.

"Something like…" I grin devilishly as I pull back slowly. My entire body protests. My tongue tries to dive back into her sweet and savory warmth. But I force myself to stand. I slap her ass once more. "Something like stopping just before you come."

Her whimpers and panting are the sexiest thing I've ever heard. Her head snaps towards me. Her eyes crash into mine. "Please, don't stop," she begs.

I can't help but laugh. "If you think for a second I'm going to let you come after that." I nod towards the door and shake my head. I take off my shirt and toss it. She watches my every movement with wide, hungry eyes. I unbuckle my belt, not taking my gaze off her, and slowly undo the button on my jeans. "You have another thing coming, little Nala."

She blushes. Her eyes travel down my body to my hips. I push down my jeans slowly, freeing my hard cock. I'd groan in pleasure at the strain that fucking hurt like hell finally being ended, but I have far more important things to do.

Like drive my dick into her pussy.

Hard.

I grip her hips as she cries out and arches into me, grasping for anything and everything she can to keep herself from falling off the edge of desire I've already brought her to. I dig my fingers into the soft flesh of her hips and thighs as I keep her close to me. I keep myself buried deeply inside her, not moving a single inch.

She squirms. "Gavin! Please!"

"Fuck, I love when you beg," I rumble with a grin. "But that's not how this is going down. What kind of punishment would this be if I gave you what you wanted?"

She whimpers and pants, clenching around me as she tries to get me to move. It's really too bad for her that I have a lot more resolve than that. I grit my teeth when she clenches again and again, squeezing my cock. But I still don't move.

"Gavin, I'm so close. Please!"

I slap her ass again and pull all the way out. "Probably shouldn't have told me that."

"Ah! No!" She collapses against the bed.

I wrap her silky hair around my fist and tug her up, gently but forcefully enough that she knows I'm not fucking around. Keeping her hair wrapped around my hand, I tug it until she bares her neck to me. I lean down and bite it, then lick to soothe the sting. She moans. I grin into her neck and kiss where I bit as her head falls back against my shoulder. I let my free hand wander under her shirt and grip her tits over her bra. Since all of her new stuff should be here tomorrow, I put a rush on the delivery. This ratty one that doesn't fit her at all is about to meet its new home in the fireplace.

But not before we have a little fun.

I hold her tightly against me and grip my dick. I slide it through her wetness slowly. She moans and moves against it. I know damn well she's trying to make herself come, but I've gotten good at knowing when she's close. If she wants to keep edging herself, I'll gladly let her, but I'm not letting her come. Not yet.

I let go of her hair and hold my dick as she rubs her hot pussy over me. I grab the hem of her shirt and pull it up. Like a good girl, she pulls it off and throws it on top of mine. When her thighs start trembling, I pull back again with a wicked smirk.

"Gavin!" she yells, obviously frustrated, as she spins around.

"What?" I grip her ass and tug her close. My lips crash to hers as I smack her luscious behind once more.

She jerks towards me, falling into me with a moan as her eyes roll back into her head. "Okay. Okay. Lesson learned. I promise."

I chuckle darkly. "And what lesson would that be?" I let go of myself and her and push my jeans to the floor, stepping out of them. I keep my eyes on hers as I kneel in front of her. I grip the waistband of her shorts and panties as I look up at her, but I don't make a move to pull them down. A very deliberate message on my part.

Her shaky fingers tangle in my hair. "Not to call myself selfish or stupid or think that way about myself."

I grin and look at her pussy. My prize and her reward. "And…?" I lean forward slowly until my nose is against her skin just above the part I crave the most. I pause, waiting.

"A-and not t-to feel bad about w-wanting my b-boyfriend's family to like me."

I grin and lick her from her sweet pussy up to that little bundle of nerves that makes her go off like a rocket. "I love hearing that word on your lips," I growl low against her clit. I take it into my mouth and suck. Hard.

"Oh…" She grips my shoulders and falls against me. "Oh God, yes." She's already trembling for me.

I slide my tongue deep inside her. She's quivering; pulsing for me. She's not going to last much longer. "Should I let you come? Do you think you've been good enough for it?"

"Gavin, please… I can't take much more…," she breathes.

I swirl my tongue around and flick it inside her. "Then you better answer me, Lei." I moan deeply into her pussy. I know it sends vibrations through her that bring her closer to her peak because she collapses against me. Her pussy clamps down on my tongue.

Her fingertips dig into my shoulders. Any normal person would probably wince at the sting, but I fucking love it. I push her shorts down to her feet, helping her step out of them, and slide my hands up her satiny legs. When I reach her thighs, I squeeze. I lavish her pussy and suck while I moan. She's so close, I know she'll fall as soon as she crests.

"Come, baby. Come for me. I got you." I keep licking her pussy and sucking on her clit, alternating between the two like I'm a starved man who doesn't know what to eat first. I feast on her like she's my last meal. Holy fuck, if she was, I'd die a happy man.

"Gavin!" she screams, arching into me. My stomach clenches and my dick hardens at the sweetness of my name on her lips.

As I thought, Harleigh collapses against me, holding on for dear life, as her orgasm washes over her. I wrap my arms around, keeping her steady as I continue licking her, slowing my rhythm to help her come down. Her body rocks against me as her pussy clenches uncontrollably while she comes.

"Fucking sweetest thing I've ever tasted." I slow my licks even more until her trembles slow and the aftershocks subside. I kiss her pussy after licking her clean and slowly stand, keeping her wrapped in my arms. I crawl into bed, guiding her into it with me.

"Oh… God, Gavin." She cuddles as close to me as possible, and fuck if it doesn't make me harder. Her in my arms is everything I've ever wanted and didn't know I needed.

I kiss the top of her head. "I had other plans when we came up here. I was going to slap your ass until it was red for the bullshit that came out of your mouth down there. And then when I realized that spanking you makes you wetter…" I trail off as I grin down at her.

She giggles. "I think that might only be when you do it. If Josh did it, I'd probably cry and beg him to stop."

I laugh, even though the thought of another man touching her, family or not, makes the jealous and possessive motherfucker who lives inside me rear his head. "Josh or anyone else touches you, I might end up killing them. You're all fucking mine, little rebel."

She smiles and props her chin on her hands on my chest and looks up at me. "I thought you were calling me little Nala."

I grin again and kiss her nose. "I was. And still might. But right now, it's little rebel."

"Why little rebel?" She tilts her head adorably.

"Because it's exactly what you are. A rebel. One who likes getting in trouble and driving me up the fucking wall, but I can't complain because you appeal to a side of me that no one ever has before."

She smiles and leans her ear over my heart. "I've always been the good girl. Do whatever I'm told. Don't make anyone mad. Take care of dad. Put college aside. Stay quiet. Be seen. Not heard." She's quiet for a few moments. I run my fingers soothingly through her hair. "I really do love my father, but he was a flawed man. He had ideologies that are outdated. Women shouldn't go to college. They should cook and clean. I didn't need a business degree to help with the books. My job, in his eyes, was to take care of him and help him with the diner But he really did have good qualities." She falls silent once more. Finally, she sighs. "Is it wrong of me to feel so conflicted? I keep going back and forth. I'm so angry with him for what he did, even though I understand that he really didn't have a choice."

I shake my head. "Baby, there's always a choice. Always. He chose himself and that diner over you. He knew that if he didn't agree to what they wanted, they'd kill him and take the diner. He'd have nothing but you. That was scary to him. So, he agreed to the deal. Maybe he thought he could get out of it, but his fear still overruled. He made a poor decision that cost him his life and damn near cost you yours. They would have taken you. Who knows what they would have done with you. You can love him and still be pissed off at what he did. Maybe one day, you'll forgive him, but right now? It's okay to love him and be angry." I hug her tighter. "If you weren't such a fucking fighter, a rebel, they would have succeeded in taking you away from me that night. I know we weren't exactly together then, but you've been mine ever since that first day I saw you. I would've destroyed the damn universe searching for them if they'd hurt you or taken you from me."

I feel her smile before she kisses my chest. My heart beats faster at the sweet gesture. "You're still going to."

I grin because she's starting to know me quite well. "Fucking right I am."

She traces the lines of my abs. After a few moments, she shifts and looks up at me once more, a soft smile on her face. "What were the rest of your plans when you got me up here?"

I chuckle and kiss her forehead. "Curious little Nala."

She smiles and giggles. "You said you had plans. I feel like since I ended up with an earth shattering orgasm out of it, your plans were very ruined."

I laugh. "Oh, they were. There was the spanking. Then when I realized you'd get off on that, I figured I'd edge you again and again, not letting you come. But my fucking tongue got the best of me on that one. I needed to taste you." I grin when she squeaks. Her eyes widen. "And then I planned on fucking you with you bent over my bed, but that went out the window as soon as you screamed my name."

She bites her lip and blushes as she wraps her arm around my waist. "That was the most intense orgasm ever," she whispers.

"Many more of those to come in your life because watching you was fucking hot. But first…" I shift and push her slowly down to my cock. She moans, and I can hear her lick her lips. My dick twitches for her, and I groan when she wraps her hand around my length. I swallow hard. "Suck." The word comes out more raspy than I intended, but I don't care. I need her mouth over me. Now.

Her tongue flicks over my tip. She licks up a bead of precum with a moan that makes my balls hard. "Yummy," she whispers against my cock just before she takes it into her mouth and sucks.

I arch into her. "Oh, fuck!" My fingers automatically find the back of her neck, and I push down until my cock reaches the back of her throat. "Oh, fuck, baby."

"Mmm…" She keeps sucking as she slowly moves her head back up, scraping her teeth along my length as she goes.

"Christ, Harleigh," I hiss between my teeth.

Her tongue dips into the dimple below my tip, and she nips it. I jerk into her and push her head down again. I let my head fall back as I pull her back up, controlling the pace. Her tongue and teeth are everywhere at once. She's driving me insane, making me a quivering fucking mess underneath her.

I get harder and harder until I'm thickening for her. I bob her head up and down over me faster as I thrust my dick into her mouth at the same pace. Harleigh sucks, moans, and swallows around me each time I hit the back of her throat. I feel like my entire world is spinning as she catapults me to a height only she has ever been able to bring me.

I feel a powerful orgasm start to rip through me, beginning at the base of my spine. I want to lift my head and watch her swallow everything I give her, but I can't. I'm too far gone. My eyes fall closed as I moan and grunt. I start spilling into her mouth. My stomach tightens and clenches with each and every jet of come that erupts from me. She swallows every drop and licks me clean afterwards.

When I come back down to Earth, Harleigh is sitting on her knees in front of me. Somehow the bra is still on her. I crack a smile because it's one more plan I had that she ruined just by her being her. I sit up and hook a finger under the worn out lace and tug. She watches me with curious eyes.

"When are you going to get rid of this? I know you have a spare."

She blushes and looks down. "I do, but…" She looks back up at me with a deeper blush. "Okay, I have no idea why I still have it. It's comfortable…"

I raise an eyebrow. "It's stretched out." I run a finger along the under part of her breasts. "You're falling out of it down here. There's no support at all for you." I tug at the lace. "There's tears all over the place." I hook a finger in one of the holes and pull.

"Gavin!" She grips my wrist as her mouth falls open.

I can't help the smile that plasters across my face as I pull harder. The cup barely holding her in gives. Her tit spills out. I lean down and lick her exposed nipple. I do exactly the same thing with the other side, licking that nipple as well when it spills out for me. She moans quietly as she watches.

I reach around and flick the clasps. She spills out the rest of the way, and I remove the bra. I lean in and kiss her softly, though I want to ravish her. I love seeing her completely naked in front of me. Just for me.

"Go put a different one on," I command softly. "The others fit a lot better. And I know they're more comfortable because you're not constantly adjusting yourself like you were today."

That pretty blush creeps into her cheeks again, and she rewards me with that sexy, sultry smile. "Yes, sir."

That elicits a groan from me. I fall back on the bed. "I don't know what I like better. My name spilling from your mouth or the word sir."

She looks back at me when she reaches the dresser on the other side of the room. "You should probably get dressed, sir. There's people downstairs waiting for you."

I sit up slowly and narrow my eyes as I get out of bed. Fuck if my dick doesn't stand at attention at those words. "Run," I warn.

Her eyes widen. Her mouth drops as her gaze falls to my dick. Her clothes are clutched to her chest, but she doesn't move. I take a threatening step towards her. She squeals and runs to the bathroom, giggling. She closes the door behind her.

I grin and head directly for the door. Even if she locked it, I have a master key. But, like a good girl, *my* good girl, she didn't. So, I slip in and grip her hips. I lift her onto the bathroom counter and crash my lips to hers.

Then, as I've wanted to all fucking day, I ravish her until she's too exhausted to do anything but hang on for the ride. A ride she'll only ever get to take with me.

My little rebel.

Chapter Seventeen

 Harleigh

(Two Days Later)

Gavin's arms wrap around me. He bends to kiss my neck as he hugs me close to him while I look out the window of the Divine Spruce Bed and Breakfast. There's a gorgeous lake that I really wish was frozen over so I could ice skate. Its crystal blue water looks that inviting, but it's far too cold to swim in. I'm sure winter comes a lot earlier in Alaska than it does in Chicago.

The B&B is properly named. It's truly divine here. And it's surrounded by such beautiful spruce trees that smell so fresh and amazing that all I want to do is sink into their calming aroma and never wake up.

"You look lost in thought, beautiful," Gavin whispers in my ear. "Care to clue me in?" He tightens his grip and sways gently with me.

"It's beautiful here. Peaceful. The past couple of days since… well, since I almost shot Zekeih, have been so…" I take a deep breath, unsure of the right words.

"Chaotic and confusing? A lot of shit going on?"

I nod slowly with a soft smile as I lean back into him and hug his arms tighter to me. "I keep going back and forth about this. I don't want anyone to be upset with me and think I forced you to take me with you somehow. But I'm honestly happy I'm here with you. I'm just kind of scared to be without you right now." I shake my head. "I don't know why. I'm sure I'll be safe there with everyone."

Gavin chuckles and kisses the back of my head. He tightens his grip around me and rests his chin on the top of my head. "No one is upset with you, baby. Nor would they be. They don't have a reason to be. We both worked everything out with everyone the night of our family barbecue. We've put the past behind us. All of us. We're moving forward."

"Yeah. I know. It's just…" I turn in his arms. I put my arms around him and look up at him. "I just don't think they would have asked to go with their significant others if it was them in my situation. I don't want to be resented for it."

He chuckles and runs his fingers through my hair. "Everyone's situation is different, baby. Raleigh didn't want to be away from Alex. Jessa didn't want to be away from Jason. The issue is that they were both attacked or threatened at work. Arianna was with Ryan the entire time. They had two reporters chronicling their entire wedding and honeymoon to throw people off. In the end, though, it didn't matter. And it was the same with Breetana and Nicole. Neither of them wanted to be away from Chase or Taylor. And they weren't, but the threats still got to them. They didn't have to ask to be near their significant others because they already were. You wouldn't have been. Not unless you'd asked. The truth is, if they want you, they're not going to stop until they get to you. Or die trying. Which is what will happen because they're not getting through me or any of us."

I let out a long, slow breath and rest my cheek on his chest. His steady breathing and the soothing way he runs one hand through my hair and the other up and down my back goes a long way in calming my frayed nerves. The girls did share with me their stories the night of the barbecue, which went long after midnight. Gavin is right. Everyone's story is different, but there's one thing in common. Being together and united is the way to beat the enemy, whoever they happen to be. And every single one of them feels safer and more secure with their loved ones near.

It's the one thing I keep coming back to. My decision to stay with Gavin may have started out simply as an I-don't-want-to-be-away-from-him decision, but it's turned into something much more than that. Gavin has been adamant that he doesn't feel comfortable without me near him. I heard him talking to Alex before we left, and Alex validated his feelings on every level. It's not just about him being possessive. It's about him truly feeling that he needs to be near me right now.

He called it instincts. I'm not sure if that's what it is or isn't what it is, but I'm grateful that he feels the same way as I do. I can sense that he's more on his game knowing I'm close. I'm lucky that he feels the same as I do about it.

"I guess I just feel like I need to be close to you."

"And that's all there is to it, Lei. If that's how you feel, I'm never going to ignore it. You come first. I might be second in command to a powerful man, but we stand on the same principles. Love and family first. Always. You're mine. That makes you family to them. We'll always do anything we need to for each other. That includes you."

He doesn't know how much his words soothe me. How they ease my racing heart and tumultuous soul. I breathe another sigh of relief and stay wrapped tightly in his arms where I truly feel like I belong. But it's the declaration from him that I'm his. It's not that he hasn't said it before, but something about tonight makes it all sink in.

I don't want anyone else. I don't want to be anywhere else that he isn't. Gavin has brought me everything I've ever wanted. A fairytale love story. A family who truly respects and cherishes one another unconditionally.

And the hugs.

A person doesn't know how much they missed something until someone shows them. Hugging myself for comfort had become normal to me. When Gavin started holding me and hugging me, though, I realized just how much I missed hugs; how much I need them. Gavin isn't the only one in the family who gives them freely. They all do. And every time someone does it, I want to weep in happiness and fall at their feet in thanks. Dramatic, but so very true.

I pull away slowly and look up at him once more. "I know you have work to do, but thank you for taking me here."

He leans down and kisses me, softly at first, but he deepens, swiping his tongue across mine before pulling back. "You're welcome."

"I'm probably not going to be able to explore the town much, but this view is incredible." I turn in his arms again and smile. The sun is just beginning to set, and the colors dancing across the sky and the water are things I'm positive I'll only ever see once in this lifetime. I see it in Chicago, but this is different.

He hugs me tightly again and rests his chin on the top of my head once more. "I wouldn't say that. I'm not going to be gone all day and night the whole time we're here. I have a surveillance team. I have guards around for you, for when I'm with you and when I'm not."

I smile softly because the extra precautions he is taking are heart-melting. I hate that it's necessary, though, and I still hold a lot of guilt about feeling the need to be near him during this. He's working. Technically. I should be okay being without him. Especially since I want a future with him. I'd never expect him to stay home just for me. Not when there are so many places and people in need of his kind of expertise. Not that he'd stay home anyway. Gavin needs to be out there. It's simply who he is. And I love that about him.

"You need to get out of your head, baby," Gavin rumbles against my neck. "I don't know what you're thinking, exactly, but I have a few guesses. And I can assure you, they're all misplaced." He kisses my neck and hugs me tighter. "What do you think about dinner? Whatever they were cooking down there smelled delicious."

"It really did. I think it was a roast. I'm pretty sure that's what the woman who checked us in said." I start to turn but pause suddenly. "We brought a lot of people here..."

Gavin raises an eyebrow. "Yeah...?"

"What if they can't feed them all?"

Gavin bites his lip, but I know it's to keep from laughing. I swat his arm with a pout, and he laughs. "Baby, the only people here are the people for you. The rest of the guards I have with me are at different hotels. And they all took significant others or family with them so it looks like they are just enjoying time with their loved ones. People don't know who works for us and who doesn't. Especially the ones with us here. We work in the shadows. You might see Josh on the news, but you'll never know who his guards are. Same with Alex. They blend in. We all do."

"But you don't." I look up at him. "I've seen you in the news. Sometimes. I mean, not until after I started looking into the Lucinio Mafia and doing my research, but I did see you coming up in that research."

"My dad is a bank investor, baby. A lot of the stuff you'll see my face in are things to do with them. My name isn't tied to the mafia. At least not out there." He points behind me and outside. "The vast majority of people know Alex Lucinio as the businessman and Josh Lucinio as the leader of the Lucinio Mafia, a legit and powerful mafia who works with kids and throws their name behind good causes. But behind closed doors and in the deepest shadows that people keep a blind eye to, the Lucinio Mafia is feared. Josh's name is synonymous with his own brand of justice. And so is mine. But that world is hidden. Kept behind a carefully constructed wall. If people try to blow our cover, we have contacts everywhere who will help us keep it hidden. A lot of people refuse to believe that the man who organizes sports games, from girl's netball down the list to boy's volleyball, could ever be capable of such dark acts, like torture and murder."

I stand on my tiptoes and kiss the stubble on his jaw. "Including the United States Government."

He grins. "You think they're the only ones?"

My eyes widen. "What?" I squeak out. "Like MI5, or World Government?"

"M15, MI6, NATO, United Nations, international Governments all over the world, and top secret organizations, as well. The Queen and King call M16. M16 calls us. The President requests the FBI or Secret Service. They contact us. Everything all the way down to military intelligence. They know we have ways of getting information that their best hackers couldn't dream of."

I just stare at him in open-mouthed shock. Ryan eluded to all of this. Even Josh and Gavin did when we all sat down and talked about it. But I never thought they were that big. Sure, I knew they had factions everywhere, but I didn't know they worked with so many, including Governments.

I shake my head like I'm coming out of a daze. "I guess I'm still getting used to just how… powerful and into everything you are," I say quietly as I look down. "It's a little intimidating."

He hugs me close again. "It doesn't change who you know me as, Lei." He kisses the top of my head. "It doesn't matter how powerful I am, what I do, or who I work with." He cups my face gently in his large hands. "I love you." He kisses my forehead so tenderly, I close my eyes and melt into him.

"I love you, too," I whisper. I smile as I open my eyes and giggle when his stomach growls. "I should probably feed that monster inside you."

He grins and laughs. He teasingly swats my ass, and I giggle. "There's only one cure for that, little rebel. And you're gonna need the energy for later, so we'd better eat up."

I laugh as he takes my hands and tugs me out of our suite. The B&B is only two stories, but it's large. Gavin rented out all twelve rooms on the upper floor, leaving only eight rooms for regular guests. We're lucky we managed to pick a week where they weren't fully booked. Apparently that's a rarity. Truthfully, I'm not sure it would have mattered. I'm pretty sure that Gavin or the mafia, I don't know how that works, would have just paid everyone off somehow.

Gavin leads me down the stairs to the ground floor and towards the dining room where so many delectable scents are radiating from. When we reach the dining room there are a few large and very nice tables set up that seat six people. Gavin leads me to one of them with two seats open and settles next to me. Across from us is an older couple who looks so happy and in love with each other, it makes me see my future. I blush furiously when the man I envision is Gavin.

Are we there yet? Is that an appropriate thought to have about a man I just truly started seeing? Even if he's been my every thought ever since I first saw him? What if he doesn't feel that way? The thought makes me panic a little. I take a deep, shaky breath. Gavin takes my hand and lifts it to his mouth. He kisses it, righting my world once more. Looking in his eyes eases my anxiety because I see in them all that I feel.

I smile softly as he leans in and kisses me for everyone watching to see. I blush again, but for a completely different reason. I've come to know him well enough to understand that this is Gavin's way of claiming what's his in front of everyone.

He pulls away from the soft kiss slowly, and I feel like I'm on my honeymoon or something. I giggle giddily and let him hold my hand under the table like we're secret lovers, even though there's nothing secret about us.

"So, where are you all from?" Gavin asks the couple sitting with us.

The older man grins. "We're from Flagstaff."

"Arizona." Gavin smiles. "I bet it's nice to get out of there for a little while. Lots of heat."

"Oh dear," the woman says. "You have no idea. We enjoy it, but whenever we need a break, we come here. To North Pole. We're regulars here. I'm pretty sure they just save us our room throughout the year." She laughs.

We all fall silent as someone starts wheeling things out of what must be the kitchen and someone else stands in the middle of the room. She's an adorable woman who must be in her seventies. She reminds me a little of Mrs. Claus. For a brief moment, I wonder if she just might be. They say North Pole, Alaska, is a magical place.

"Everyone," she begins. "We have lots of familiar faces here tonight, and several new ones. I'm delighted to see everyone down here tonight because our chef has prepared something very special for you all." She gives a brilliant smile as the man who wheeled out a tray with several dishes on it disappears once more. "We have a delightful roast tonight made from moose rump. That might sound odd to some, but I promise it's nothing like you've ever tasted!"

"Don't forget to remind them about the tiramisu for dessert! I worked hard on that!" a deep, rumbling male voice says from behind the wall.

The woman mumbles something under her breath and shakes her head. "Don't mind him," she says as everyone starts to giggle.

"Woman! Did you hear me?" he calls again. This gains more laughter from everyone around the room, including the Mrs. Claus lookalike.

Gavin squeezes my hand. "Sounds like it's going to be a good dinner."

"Don't ignore me, woman! I hear you all laughing!" the man says. Everyone laughs harder as the man pops out from the kitchen area.

My eyes widen, and I look up at Gavin. "I swear to God that's Santa and Mrs. Claus."

Gavin grins and shrugs. "Perhaps."

I watch them both curiously. Santa, that's what I'm calling him until he proves me wrong, and Mrs. Claus, it's only fair, she's obviously his wife, kiss each other lovingly. Santa, beard and all, disappears once more.

"Please start dishing up," Mrs. Claus says. "And I do hope you enjoy! After dinner, we'll be making Christmas cookies. We do hope you'll join us!"

"Christmas cookies. Yum," Gavin says with a smirk as he pulls me up with him.

He makes sure all guests, including the guards, are in line before us. He doesn't know it, but the simple gesture of him making sure everyone is fed before him makes me melt. Though he tries to get me to go ahead of the guards, I refuse and stay next to him.

I kiss his arm and look up at him. His eyes seem to be everywhere at once. Like he's calculating the food to the people ratio or something. As we get closer to the tray set up, Santa brings out more, seamlessly keeping the line moving. Gavin smiles as each and every person in front of us dish up healthy portions for themselves.

"Watching you make sure everyone, including the guests here and not just those with us, are fed is the sexiest thing I think I've ever seen."

Gavin grins as he looks down at me. "I'd blush, but that's unbecoming of someone of my stature."

I laugh as we both start loading our plates. "God, this smells so good. I didn't realize how much I missed home cooked food until being with you. I mean, I can cook, but it's just different."

"Couldn't afford to get much stuff for home?"

I love that he understands me and doesn't judge. I shake my head. "No. We really couldn't. After we paid everyone and he made sure I was paid, there wasn't much left over. It mostly all went to the Warriors," I say quietly. I don't really want anyone else hearing me.

Gavin guides me back to our table after we finish grabbing our food. "Not something you ever need to worry about again," he rumbles in my ear as we sit down. His voice sends tingles to my core, and I cross my legs. Gavin makes me gasp when he slides a hand up my thigh and pushes a finger against my clit from the outside of my jeans. I gasp and grip his wrist, but he doesn't stop. He grins and turns to the couple across from us without missing a beat. "So, what are your names? Or shall we just call you Flagstaff and Arizona?"

I smile when they laugh and realize something else about the man I'm so in love with. He fits in everywhere. Conversation comes easy to him. While I'm sure it's to gather information, he also has a way of doing it while putting people at ease. As I watch the older couple interact with him, though, I can't help but smile, giggling quietly as Gavin brings me the pleasure only he can.

As I watch our table mates, I don't think I'm the only one in love with Gavin Vandenberg.

Chapter Eighteen

❦ Gavin ❦

(Three Days Later)

"Vixen," I whisper in Harleigh's ear as I hug her close. She giggles and pushes back against me again, wiggling against my dick as we watch a baking competition. Holiday cupcakes are all over the presentation tables. It smells like fresh baked goods. But all I can think about is Harleigh.

I still her hips so she can't move anymore, but I pull her close to hide the growing lump in my jeans she's created. Harleigh, thankfully, gives me a break and leans back against me like a good girl as she watches the events going on around us. Something is wrong, though, because there are three people standing in the corner in a hushed conversation with clipboards looking all around the room. What they're looking for is something that has me slightly on edge.

After a few moments of tension between the three, one of them walks away shaking his head. He slams his clipboard on a table on his way out. I make eye contact with a guard near the door. He shrugs, signaling it's nothing to worry about. Huh. Interesting because my instincts say otherwise.

The other two frown and continue their hushed conversation as their eyes roam the room. One of them, a middle-aged woman with designer glasses and gray, business appropriate pantsuit, locks eyes on us. Seconds later, the man she's with does the same thing. Before either of them move, though, I can sense the guards in the room shifting positions and moving closer.

Good. I like not having to give the command.

I subtly shift Harleigh slightly so she's a little behind me and close to a guard who is pretending to be interested in one of the cupcakes in a display near us, but he's ready to intervene if he needs to. Just like the other eleven guards in this room. I'm not taking chances. Our surveillance confirmed that Charles is here. He's staying in a cabin not too far away from Fairbanks, but he was spotted here last night with a woman they discovered works at the general store here in town. They confirmed to me that she's here, but he's not.

If she knows him, it's likely others do. This is a small town. I've already learned quite a lot about the people, and we've only been here three days. Everyone knows everyone else. They all have favorite restaurants, diners, bakeries, and hotels. The B&B we're staying at is on everyone's list.

And Harleigh's theory about the owners being Mr. and Mrs. Claus themselves wasn't far off. The two of them play the two characters at every single Christmas event where Santa and Mrs. Claus are expected. They own a sleigh and fucking reindeer. Every year, they end the Christmas parade and hand out Christmas to everyone, not just the kids.

"Hi, I'm Mayor Triss Lutz." The woman holds out her hand for me to shake. "I haven't seen you around here."

I raise an eyebrow. "Uh. Yeah." I reach out and shake her hand. "We just decided to visit. Never been here before. My girl wanted to see what it was all about. She loves Christmas. I'm Drew." I let go of her hand and squeeze Harleigh's hand but keep her right where she is. "This is my girlfriend. Lei." I intentionally don't give her my real name or Harleigh's. It's what I've been doing the entire time we've been here. I've been using my alias. I don't need people dropping word to the wrong people that I'm in town.

"Drew and Lei. We need a couple of judges. We lost two tonight due to conflict of interest. You two aren't from here. You'd be perfect."

I look down at Harleigh. Her eyes widen. "What do you think?" I ask with a half-smile because I already know the answer.

She bounces on her toes. "Can we? Please? I've always wanted to do something like this!"

I smile wider and lean down to whisper in her ear. "You're fucking adorable." I kiss her neck and look back at Triss. "She says yes, so I guess we're yours for the judging."

"Great!" Triss says as she thrusts clipboards in both of our hands. "You'll be tasting each offering from each table. There are fourteen tables, so fourteen cupcakes. All different flavors. Some might be kind of out there. You up for the challenge?"

I glance at the clipboard and grin when my eyes fall on one of the flavors. "Who can say no to a cupcake with bacon in it?"

Triss laughs. "I think you'll do well. We're already late, so let's get started." Triss turns and addresses the crowd.

I look down at Harleigh. "You're going to love this."

Her eyes are so bright, my heart actually beats faster. She's so beautiful. "I'm so excited for this," she whispers. "Thank you. For everything. I know you're working, but this has been the best three days of my life."

I raise my eyebrow teasingly. "Seriously? I'm gonna have to step up my game."

She giggles and looks up at me shyly. "You know what I mean. I've never gone on vacation before."

I grin. "Then start thinking of everywhere you want to visit. I'll take you around the world." I kiss her softly, then guide her to the first table behind the other two judges.

The first cupcake is a peppermint candy one. I don't make any kind of facial expression at all, but it's obvious Harleigh doesn't like it. She tries to school her expression and give a kind smile, but it doesn't work too well.

"That was awful. So spicy," she whispers to me.

I smile. "That wince was pretty telling."

She pouts. "I thought I was good at hiding that."

"You need some practice," I tease.

The next one is chocolate with mint. The one after that tastes like a vanilla latte. I'm holding out for the bacon one, but this vanilla latte is good enough that I take the rest of it with me with a wink to the baker.

By the time we reach the tenth cupcake, red velvet with some kind of frosting inside that I'd rather forget exists, I'm about done. I've had so much that my teeth hurt. I'm crabby as fuck, but taking one look at my girl makes it all worth while. She's loving every single second of this, and I'm finding out quicker and quicker that I'm not capable of denying her anything.

I chuckle a little bit as I try the next cupcake. Alex told me this day would come. He's told me for years that when I found the woman I'm meant to be with, I would feel a lot of shit I've never felt in my life. Do things for her I've never dreamt I'd do for anyone. He knew as well as I did that Marissa wasn't that person. I was mad at myself for a long time for not giving her up a long fucking time ago, but then I look at Harleigh and realize that everything I went through during my life led me to her. Including the time I spent with Marissa.

"It's the bacon one," Harleigh whispers with a beautiful smile.

I lean down and kiss her forehead because I can't stop myself. "I love you, but this needs to end. I've never eaten so many cupcakes in my damn life."

She giggles. "Almost, my love."

I grin and lean down once more to whisper in her ear. "I love those words falling from your lips."

She blushes and hands me one of the cupcakes she picked up. She takes a cautious sniff, but I'm all in. Bacon. It makes everything better. Even if it's already good, bacon will always elevate it. I take a big bite and realize immediately that I was wrong.

So wrong.

I won't give off any clues as to if I do or don't like it, so I force myself to swallow the worst cupcake I've ever tasted in my entire thirty-six year existence. Maple syrup. Good. Candied bacon. Fuck yes. But the nutmeg. Far too fucking much. And why the hell does it taste like carrot cake? Did these fuckers put bacon and maple syrup with carrot cake? Why the hell would anyone do such a ridiculous thing? I can honest to God feel Nicole's disappointment.

Maybe I've been spoiled. Maybe Nicole Reddick is just the best baker I've ever come across. Maybe people like this shit. Maybe I'm one of the few who hates everything about it. I never thought I'd say I hate bacon, but the chunks of it mixed with everything else make me want to throw up.

I follow my way too polite girlfriend and the other two judges to a room off the large hall the contest is being held in. Harleigh immediately spits out the cupcake in her mouth while I look at the clipboard.

"Fuck...," I whisper to myself.

"So? What did you think?" Triss asks.

"I was looking forward to that last one," I say with a chuckle. "I don't know what the hell they did to it, but it was fucking terrible."

Triss laughs. "I agree. It wasn't good."

"I really loved that Vanilla Latte one, but my favorite was the Egg Nog. Oh my God, so good," Harleigh says.

"I liked that one a lot, too," the other judge I don't know the name of says. I don't really care to either, but if he keeps eyeing Harleigh, I'm going to kick his ass.

"It had the highest marks for me," Harleigh says quietly as she steps closer to me. Huh. So, she sees it, too. And it's definitely making her uncomfortable, which pisses me off even more.

"Heads up, Gav," one of my guards says in the earpiece I'm wearing. "Babyface is heading towards North Pole. Looks like we're about ten minutes out, unless he turns off and goes somewhere else."

My hand finds Harleigh's waist. I pull her closer and hand Triss my clipboard. "Sorry, ma'am. Can't stay for the results. Something's come up." I give her one of my most charming smiles with a wink.

She takes my clipboard and Harleigh's. "Aww. That's too bad. Thank you so much for the help!"

"Anytime," I say as I steer Harleigh out into the crowd.

"What happened?" she asks, looking up at me fearfully.

I keep her close. "Charles. He's on his way here."

"Oh my God." She turns pale and starts frantically looking all over the room.

"Hey, baby. I got you. You have more people here protecting you than you know." I squeeze her hip as I usher her through the multiplying number of people in this room. Where the fuck did they all come from? "No one is getting to you, Lei." I say it for her benefit as much as my own.

My eyes scan the room. Each of my guards are stationed right where they're supposed to be, and all of their eyes are on me. They're waiting for my command to move, but I don't want them to. Not yet. I want her to be surrounded, so if anything does go down, and my instincts say it's about to, Harleigh will be safe.

Completely protected.

Suddenly, Harleigh gasps. I look down at her just as she starts sinking to the ground. She's spun from my grip before I can adjust and take her weight. I turn quickly, and see the judge who was eyeing her dragging her through throngs of people. Why the hell does she look limp? Is he stumbling? I take off after them.

"On the exits!" I command. Why is she not screaming? What the fuck did he do to her?

I watch him tighten his grip around her and pick her up, throwing her over his shoulder. The movement causes the people around him to let out shocked squeaks or quiet screams. They all stare after him, paying no mind to me.

"Move!" I push a couple of people out of the way. "Move! Out of the way!" I push a couple more people as I give chase.

The fucker heads straight for the main exit, even though there's no way he can't clearly see that it's blocked. As I gain on him, I realize with a start exactly why he thinks he can get through. He shifts Harleigh and throws her into the two guards who got there before anyone else. They both catch her, but fall backwards onto their asses. Knowing I have others around me to chase him, I slow.

"Go!" one of my guys cradling Harleigh says. "Go! We have her!"

My heart doesn't want to listen, but my brain propels me forward. I crash through the door after him and launch myself off the top of the three steps leading up to the entrance. I grab him around the waist and take him to the ground with me. We both land hard. I know I'll feel it tomorrow, but for now, I ignore the pain shooting through my knee and hip because he's immediately fighting me.

"Get the fuck off me! You have no idea who I am!" the douchenozzle screams at me.

"I don't give a fucking shit. But going by your looks, I think I'll stick with Scowlyfuckface," I growl as I slam his face into the ground. He moans, but doesn't quit fighting. "You shouldn't have fucking touched what's mine."

"She's not yours! She's never belonged to you!"

"Well, that was the wrong thing to say," I grunt. I've had the upper hand this entire fight, but having enough of his whiny voice, I shift my hands to his jaw and the side of his neck. I lean my weight down, pinning him more firmly to the ground. "Your choice, Scowlmeister. One more fucking move, and I twist. Wouldn't that be something? One quick flick and poof, Scowlyfuckface is no more." I growl into his ear with some snark and no little amount of sarcasm. Even if the idea is really fucking appealing, I know Josh would rather he be alive, at least long enough for me to get some answers. Like who the hell gave him the orders to attempt to grab Harleigh when I'm right fucking there.

"Fuck," he moans as he falls limp.

"Good boy." Keeping my grip on him, I look up and see five of my guys with me. "You four with me. The rest of you, get Harleigh back to the B&B. No one leaves her fucking side," I order the rest of the guards through the earpiece. "Brayden." I meet the eyes of one of the guards nearest to me as I stand. Someone else takes my place and cuffs the dipshit sprawled on the ground.

"What do you need, Vandenberg?" Brayden asks with his low, growly voice. I like him. He's quiet. Ex Army. Joined us when his sister was murdered by a rival mafia, and has been with us ever since. He's one of the men I always make sure to take with me on missions because he's just as dangerous as I am, and even better with a gun.

I pull him aside as the other four deal with our prisoner. I look around. "It's eerily quiet out here."

"I think it's because everyone is in there." Brayden points to the building. "And our guys are keeping them in so we can deal with this piece of shit."

I nod. "Still don't like it."

Brayden shoves his hands in his pocket. "I don't either. Probably has something to do with Babyface. Fucker probably has this town sucking candied assapple out of his dick."

I scan the empty streets one more time. "Get Harleigh out of -" I look at him incredulously. "Candied assapple out of his dick?"

Brayden shrugs with a grin. "Must be something. You've seen pictures of the douche. Ain't no way he's getting any otherwise. Ugliest motherfucker I've ever seen."

He's not wrong. Charles Franklin looks like he was dipped in a van of teen spirit or some shit. Complete with pockmarks and the greasiest skin I've ever seen on a man his age, which we've recently discovered is just under thirty. He's got a scar that goes from his ear to his neck and a fucked up lip. Not cleft. More like half of it is paralyzed. He even has a beer belly that I'm pretty sure he's deluded himself into thinking is a six pack. I can't figure out how the fuck he was seen with a girl who can obviously do much better than him. But maybe that helps to prove the theory of him owning this town.

"I'll get our shit from the B&B. I want Harleigh on a plane back to Chicago. And figure out what the fuck he did to her that knocked her out like that. Get a doctor if you need to."

"He gave her a dose of something in her neck. Pretty sure the needle is still on him. Adam saw him put something in his left pocket right before he grabbed her. There's a medic with her right now."

I scrub my hands down my face and nod. "Good."

"We're pulling into North Pole. You need to fucking move. Get Harleigh out of there," my guard says in my earpiece.

I look up at Brayden as another guard hands me the syringe. "Take good care of her. Get her the fuck out of here. Anything happens to her, Brayden, I won't be responsible for my actions." I hand him the syringe and lower my voice. "She'll be scared when she wakes up. Her safe phrase. Use it."

"Got it, boss." Brayden hurries away as I turn back to the fucking mess in front of me.

Another guard flies up in one of our rented SUVs. "Get him in there," I growl. "We need to get the fuck out of here." I take a last look at the building as I climb in the passenger seat.

The idiot is spouting off threats of how we're all going to pay for doing this to him, but my mind is completely on the earpiece in my ear as I listen to the guards moving Harleigh. Brayden pays the doctor to go with them, and although I hate the fact that I'm leaving Harleigh in the hands of anyone but me, I know she's safe.

So, while they take her away, I force myself to focus on the asshole who won't shut the fuck up in the backseat and trust everyone else to get Charles fucking Franklin. He doesn't know it yet, but his days are numbered. No one touches my girl or hires someone to do it for them.

Not unless they want their arms ripped from their fucking body…

Chapter Nineteen

☙ Harleigh ❧

Why do I feel like I'm flying? I reach up to rub my eyes, but my arms feel heavy. My entire body feels like lead. Like I was thrown into a lake while I was passed out and suddenly woke up. The thought makes me tremble. *Is that what happened? Am I dead? Dying?*

"What happened?" I croak out.

"You were hit with a drug that immobilized you and made you instantly pass out," a deep voice says to me. I feel whatever is under me shift. The subtle movement makes the panic rise to a full blown attack.

I thrash my body because it's the only way my limbs seem to work. My eyes fly open when a strong grip grabs my upper arms. "Get off me!"

"Harleigh! I hate grapefruit and deep red seashells!" His grip tightens, though not tight enough to leave marks, and I immediately stop struggling because that is my safety phrase.

I take deep breaths as he loosens his grip on my arms. "Fuck... Oh God." I slowly move my arms to my face to rub my eyes. It's not easy. They feel really weak. "What the hell happened? Who are you? Where is Gavin?"

"I'm Brayden, Harleigh. We met a few days ago. Gavin assigned me as your personal bodyguard. Remember? You have twelve of us assigned to you, but I'm the head one. I'm the one who will be with you all of the time."

I let my hands fall. I try to hug myself, but I can't, so I let myself fall back down. I feel him shift and raise my body, so I'm leaning against his chest. It's like he can sense my panic attack and is doing all he can to help. I feel myself calming now that I can see my surroundings, even though my mind is still murky.

"Why am I so weak and exhausted?" I feel tears sting my eyes, but at least the fog is clearing, and I remember who he is.

His grip tightens. "Do you remember anything?"

I give in and close my eyes. I feel far too tired to keep them open, and now that I know I'm safe, I relax even more. "All I really remember is Gavin saying something came up. He guided me out of the room we were in with the other judges. There seemed to be a lot more people in the competition room. Gavin had me close to him and was maneuvering us through. The next thing I know, I'm waking up here feeling like I'm flying, even though my body wouldn't move."

I can feel him nod. "You were poked in the neck with a needle and injected with a sedative. Liquid X, or propofol. Depending on the dose, it can knock you out for ten minutes to a couple of hours. In your case, you were out for a little over an hour. People recover quickly from it. They're groggy for a few minutes. They feel like they are coming out of anesthesia, which would make sense, considering it's used for that."

"I feel more tingly than heavy right now. But I'm tired."

"You will be. That's normal. You're okay. We had a doctor check you out. He's on the plane if anything happens, but Gavin told me specifically that the only one in this room when you wake up is me. We knew you'd be in a state of panic."

"Where is Gavin?" I ask as I open my eyes.

"Gavin is in North Pole still. He's dealing with the asshole who came after you. And hopefully, they found Charles and were able to catch him. I contacted Ryan and had his jet sent up there for them when they're ready to leave."

"So, Charles… He's not… the one who injected me and tried to kidnap me?"

"Nope. But it was someone working with him. We know that for sure. We're a little unsure just how deeply Charles is in that town. How many people are in his pocket? Rather, his fathers. What we do know about him is that he doesn't do shit. All of his money comes from his daddy. We still don't know who the fuck he's working with, though, and how he has so much money and so many resources. Everything we know about the Ruthless Warriors points to them being very small. No factions elsewhere. So, how they have all of these hideouts and money to flaunt is beyond us. But we also have the best hackers in the world at our disposal. So, all of those secrets won't be hidden for long."

I sigh. "I just want this all to end."

"I know, sweetheart. It will. I promise. You're safe."

"I know I am, but what about Gavin?" I can't help but worry about the man I love. His safety has been the only thing on my mind since my mind started clearing more and more. It's why I kept asking him where Gavin is.

"Gavin is safe, Harleigh. He kept four of your guards and has at least twenty more. They tailed Charles into North Pole. He was alone. All of the surveillance we've done over the past three days showed him alone. No guards. No nothing. He was out once with a woman, but that's all."

"But you don't know how many people he has working for him in the town."

"No. You're right. We don't. But that doesn't mean Gavin doesn't know what he's doing. I can tell you that the guards tailing him grabbed him as soon as he parked his car in Town Square. We took off from Fairbanks just after they got him and the fucker who tried to grab you to our secret location. We rented a cabin way out in the sticks. No one around for miles. Nowhere to run. Gavin has a lot of people with him. But you want to know a little something about your boyfriend that he probably wants to keep away from you?"

I nod. "I want to know everything," I whisper. "Good and the bad."

"Gavin Vandenberg is a completely different person when it comes to protecting those he loves. He has a lot of blood on his hands, all bad guys, because he's not afraid to do what's necessary to keep those he cares about safe. To the outside world, he's the son of a really rich dude in Los Angeles, California. He plays the role well. But when the moon rises, he's cold and cruel. Feared. His name holds just as much threat to the bad guys as Ryan Crane and Josh Lucinio. People do not fuck with him. To you, those walls come down. He's the man you see. The real him. He trusts you because you accept him for who he is. Just like he does you. But to them? They know he won't hesitate to rip out the spine of the fuckers stupid enough to mess with him or threaten those he loves or who he has claimed as his."

I blush. "Me."

"You. His family. Those who are blood and those who aren't. You want my opinion? If there is anyone up there who might be on the wrong side of the law, it doesn't matter if they're getting paid off by the Franklin's or not. If they've heard of the Lucinio Mafia, then they've heard of Gavin and why he makes such a good second in command to Josh. And if they know that, then they also know putting themselves on the opposite side of the line he's drawn is a death wish."

I take a deep breath. "You're saying I shouldn't worry myself into a panic because he's okay."

"I'm saying to have faith in him. I'll never tell you not to worry. He has a far more dangerous job than a cop. Even a soldier. And I can say that because I was one."

I look up at him. "You were in the Army?"

He nods. "I was. I wouldn't trade my time in for anything. It taught me a lot. Helped shape me."

I let my eyes fall closed again and crawl back into the bed so I'm laying down. I yawn. "How did you get involved with the Lucinio Mafia?"

I feel him shift and pull the blanket over me. "I owe Josh my life."

"Really?"

"Mmhmm." He tucks the blanket around me then lays on his back over the blankets and next to me. I smile because it makes me feel much safer.

"I'm not getting more than that, am I?" I say softly.

He chuckles. "About ten years ago, my sister was killed. I left the military and dedicated my life to hunting down the assholes who took her. A few years ago, when I found out who they were, I planned out a mission. Go in. Take them all down. Probably go out in a blaze of glory, but at least the fucker who killed her would be dead. He was the first one I planned to take out. I went in just like I planned. Only there were a lot more of them than I planned. I did take down my primary target and several others, but I took a bullet. One that would have cost me my life if Josh hadn't been there that night. He had gotten information, apparently, about them and was doing his own takedown for completely separate reasons. He finished what I couldn't and got me to a hospital. I've been on his team ever since, and he'll always have my loyalty."

"I'm glad you're here…," I murmur. I know he says something, but I drift off before my brain can process it.

🐞🐞🐞

"We're home, Harleigh," a soothing voice says as he gently wakes me up.

"Mmm…" I slowly open my eyes and rub them. "I'm awake." I smile softly at Brayden. I didn't really notice before, but Brayden is a big man. I think he's taller than Gavin. Definitely more muscular. I have to wonder if he is a closet bodybuilder or something.

Brayden chuckles. "Looks like you're awake."

I yawn and stretch as I get up. "Have we landed? I feel different."

He nods. "About five minutes ago. I wanted to let you sleep. The doctor checked you out already. Gave you a clean bill of health, but I'm still under orders to make sure our doctor sees you. I just sent the doctor I paid back to North Pole on a private jet."

I blink a few times. "Geez. You all get things done so quickly. It's like a whirlwind of crazy that just never stops."

"Welcome to mafia life, honey." He laughs. "It takes some getting used to. I'll give you that. But when we want something, it gets done. And we have the money to make sure of it if a simple request doesn't work." He stands and offers a hand to help me up.

I take it. "And if money doesn't work?" I ask as he pulls me up gently, making sure I'm steady on my feet.

"Then we resort to other measures. The kind that gives us our ruthless reputation."

I can't help but giggle as he leads me out of the bedroom in the back of the plane. He guides me to the exit door and stops on the landing. "I bet you don't get to say those words everyday."

He grins. "Nope. I also don't get to use these words everyday." He sobers up, but his eyes still dance with humor. "Come with me if you want to live." He puts on his best Arnold Schwarzenegger accent, and we both crack up laughing.

I follow him to a waiting, black, SUV. He has his gun ready as he scans the tarmac for any threats. He uses his body to shield me. When we get to the SUV, he opens the door and ushers me inside. I follow his subtle commands not only because he demands it, but also because I have come to realize in the past few days just how dire and volatile this situation with me is. I have had two attempts on me now. Whether it's to take me or kill me, I suppose I really don't know for certain. I can't imagine they'd let me live. And if they inject me with something to make me play nice, I may as well be dead anyway.

As Brayden pulls out of the airport, I let out a small sigh. "Have you heard from him?" I ask quietly.

He glances at me before his eyes fall back to the road. He nods. "Yes."

I watch him for a few minutes before I focus on the traffic in front of us. Not a lot. Most people are probably sleeping right now. It makes it easier for Brayden to fly through the streets at speeds that would make me uncomfortable if I didn't trust him and just want to be home.

Home.

I think it's the first time I've ever really admitted to myself that I feel like I've finally found home. A place I belong. At first I thought it was just with Gavin. Wherever he happened to be was home to me, as long as he was by my side. But it's more than that now. The Crane and Lucinio compound is home. The two families who have merged into one while still managing to keep their mafias separate is home.

"You're not going to tell me anymore than that," I say quietly.

"I have my orders, Harleigh. I'm sorry. Something you're going to have to get used to is not being told everything you want to be. There are some things that are going to be kept from you. It's the same with the other wives and girlfriends. I get my orders, and I follow them. It's what has kept us all alive. "

I sigh because I realize the conclusion he just jumped to, and it's one that isn't true. "It's not that, Brayden." I shake my head. "And I'm honestly a little upset that you felt like that needed to be said. I realize that

I'm not going to be told everything. It's a conversation I've had with Gavin. My problem is that all you gave me was a yes. Not if he's okay. Not if he's coming home. Just a one-worded answer that fills me with so many other questions and fears."

Brayden says nothing more, so I leave it at that and watch the buildings blur as we pass by them. I try to ignore all of the things running through my mind, but it's not easy. Brayden still hasn't said that Gavin is okay. He could have been shot. He could be bleeding out as we speak. He could be hurt, and I wouldn't know. It's truly a chilling thought. Maybe Brayden doesn't feel like I deserve to know. Maybe I haven't earned his respect yet.

I wipe my eyes as he turns into the compound. The guard at the gate waves us by, and Brayden navigates through the streets until he reaches Gavin's house. I'm shaken right now. I'm not sure I can consider it mine. If Brayden doesn't accept me, how can anyone else? I take a breath because I know my mind is wandering away with me and nothing I'm thinking is probably true. But I can't help thinking it anyway.

I open my door when Brayden stops but he grabs my arm. "Hey," he says quietly. "I didn't mean to upset you. I'm not good at this emotion, relationship, talking thing. I'm good at being on my own and following orders."

I sniffle and nod slowly. "It's no big deal." I start to get out of the SUV.

"Harleigh, you and I are going to be spending a lot of time together with me being assigned to your protection detail. You'll never hear me say this again, but I don't want you to be upset with me and start this off on the wrong foot."

"I get it. Something happened, and he doesn't want me to know because he doesn't want me to worry about him. Even though he knows I'm going to anyway."

"That's not it. At least not all of it. Gavin is fine. He's not injured. He's okay. But he found out a lot of shit. And it's all things he wants to be the one to tell you. Not me. And because I respect him as not only a friend, but one of my bosses, I'm respecting his wishes not to tell you everything he told me."

My heart hammers in my chest at the same time it stutters to a stop. "I wish you'd just said he was okay."

"I honestly didn't think that's what you were asking me. And I'm sorry I got it wrong. I'll do better. I'm still getting to know you and your needs. But I will. You just gotta bump along this road with me. I've never been put on someone's personal protection detail like this before. I'm usually the one out there at Gavin's and Josh's side taking out the bad guys. I'm doing this for Gavin because I've gotten close to him during the time I've been with them. But that doesn't mean I intend to be an asshole to you or treat you like a favor I'm doing for a friend. I'll work on it. Just call me out a little, okay?"

I smile softly and nod. "Okay." I get out of the SUV when he lets go and does the same. It's then that I notice lights are on. My heart slams into my ribcage and I stop cold. "W-why are there lights on?"

Brayden chuckles. "The girls are here. Something else you'll need to get used to. They all take care of each other and all of us. Doesn't matter how low on the totem pole we happen to be. These girls care about all of us."

I let him lead me to the house and stay behind him as he opens the door. "Considering how I started out with these girls? I kind of wonder if they might try and murder me in my sleep. Even though we've seemingly worked things out, I sort of feel like I'm still on very thin ice with them."

"I realize that's probably how it works out there in the wild." He grins down at me as he steps inside. "Crazy bitches stabbing each other in the back and shit. It's not how these girls work."

"Oh my God! Harleigh! Are you okay?" Arianna is a small woman, but her grip is hard and tight.

"Harleigh!" Raleigh wraps me in an even tighter hug than Arianna, but between the two of them, I feel like I'm being squeezed to death. "Are you okay? What happened? We were told you were drugged and nearly kidnapped!" She pulls back and runs her fingers through my very snarled hair, something I didn't realize until right now.

I'm suddenly very self-conscious. They all look incredible. I have to look a mess right now. "I… I'm okay." I swallow hard when I see all of the other wives in the living room. "Were you… all waiting?"

"Oh God, honey," Jessa says. "Of course we were!"

I bite my lip and blink away the tears as Raleigh and Arianna take my hands and pull me into the living room. "I should clean up," I whisper.

Secretly, I don't want to, but I feel so inferior to all of them. I feel like I have to at least brush my hair.

"Nonsense," Breetana shakes her head. "What you need is a hot cup of tea and your family surrounding you."

The words make the damn burst. I feel myself being tugged to the couch and surrounded by everyone hugging me hard and tightly. I'm sure they all think I'm crying because of the ordeal I've been through, and maybe I am. But while it was scary, the overwhelming emotion I'm feeling right now is happiness that I can't even describe.

For so long I've felt like it was just me, alone, fighting the world so my dad and I could survive. It was hard. Cruel. Sometimes, I just wanted to give up and run away. I didn't because I could never do that to the only family I had. I've wanted this for so long.

Comfort from a family I've longed for my entire life makes me cry harder because I feel like all of my dreams are coming true. That if I move too quickly, I'll wake up. I don't want to wake up. Ever.

I want the found family.

I want Gavin.

I want them all for the rest of my life.

I want… home.

Chapter Twenty

☙ Gavin ☙

"If you don't shut the ever living fuck up right now, I will knock your fucking ass out. Again." I wave my gun menacingly. "Dare to test me?" I growl and level the sick fucker handcuffed and strapped to the chair in front of me with the most dangerous glare I can muster.

To his credit, Charles Franklin glares right back. "He's going to kill you. Right after he kills your fucking boss."

The snickers around us turn to full laughs. The corner of my mouth turns up into a small but threatening half smile. "Well, that's not a nice thing to say." I gesture around the cab of Ryan's plane. "Here I am being such a nice guy. Flying you in luxury on an incredible private jet that probably has more fucking security than Airforce One." I lean forward and rest my elbows on my knees, keeping my gun trained on my prisoner. "And there you are spouting off threats and accusations and whatever the fuck else is coming out of your mouth. No 'thank you, Mr. Vandenberg.' No appreciation to me for keeping your ass alive and conscious. Tsk… Tsk… Such an ungrateful son of a bitch, aren't you?"

"He's probably putting a bullet in his head right now," Charles snarls. This earns him more laughs from the other guards on the plane.

I smile a little wider. "Well, you're right about that. He is probably putting a bullet in his head right now. Only it's Josh pulling the trigger. Not the worthless fucking asshole you call a father. Tell me, what do you think is going to happen to you when daddy can't give you money to pay for all your expensive cars anymore?"

"You're not going to touch him. Just like you're not going to touch me. Because he's coming for me. And when he does, you'll all be sorry."

More laughs. I lean back in my seat. "Man." I shake my head. "For someone with an MBA who is supposed to be so fucking smart, you sure are dumber than a box of pencils, aren't you? I'd feel bad for you, but I truly don't give a fuck. It was quite entertaining listening to them tell me how they followed you all that way and caught you in the middle of the Town Square and you didn't notice them. But I think my favorite part hasn't happened yet. I'm going to have a lot of fun watching you sing like a fucking canary."

"Yet you haven't been able to do it. Losing your touch, Vandenberg?" he sneers.

I growl and stand slowly. He cautiously watches me as I loom over him. I lean down so I'm inches from his face. "I haven't lost anything. But you're about to." I slam the butt of my gun against the side of his temple and watch him jerk against his restraints and pass out slowly. I sit back down and grab a towel to wipe his blood off my gun. "Fucking hate when they make me get messy." I look up at the guard nearest to me. "You heard from Josh?"

"Yeah, he's on his way home," he responds. "Sans Gregory. Fucker disappeared out some secret passage way. I think he figured out he was outgunned and outnumbered. By the time Josh and the team moved in, he was gone. He left a nice little trap, though. Too bad Josh is fucking smart."

I raise an eyebrow. "Bomb?"

He nods. "On a timer. Sixty seconds. Josh saw it and moved everyone out. Thing is, it wasn't hidden that well."

I put the towel down and holster my gun back in the shoulder holster. "Sounds to me like it wasn't so much a trap as it was a warning."

"I'm not so sure, sir. I just don't think he expected Josh to see it as quickly as he did. I also don't think he expected the house to be cleared as quickly as it was. I got the feeling he underestimated the forces Josh would have with him."

I nod. "Or maybe it was the plan all along. Maybe he knew exactly what Josh would do. I bet you this fucker can answer that."

"He can also answer the questions we have about a leak," he says quietly. "You know the boss has considered that he has one lately."

I sigh. "Yeah. I know. I'm not sure I can even really argue it. I think Ryan even thinks it, so it's not just Josh being a still rather new boss being paranoid." I lean my head against the back of my seat. "Not that I think he's paranoid any other time."

"Nah. I get it. I've never worked for anyone who has the instincts he does. Even when his fucking father was running us. I learned early on to trust Josh. Fucked up on that serum or not, his instincts are unparalleled. It's why so many of us followed him."

I chuckle as I close my eyes. "Wise choice. Because everyone else is dead." I yawn and open my eyes to look at my watch. "Fuck, this flight is taking forever. I miss my girl."

"Well, give her a call. Not like we can't handle him."

"Not a bad idea." I take a last glance at Charles. "He should be knocked out for a bit." I stand and make my way to the back room. I sit on the edge of the bed and pick up the in flight phone and dial Harleigh's number. I look at my watch again. "Shit." It's almost four in the morning. She's probably fast asleep.

"Gavin?" she answers on the first ring before I can hang up, but she sounds like she just woke up.

"How did you know it was me?"

"It came up with Ryan's name, and Brayden said you were taking his plane home."

I smile as I lean back in the bed. "I'm sorry to wake you, baby. I just needed to hear your voice so I know you're really okay."

She sniffles. "Gavin... I needed to hear from you, too," she whispers. "I wasn't sleeping. Are you okay? Are you hurt?"

"No. No, baby. I'm not hurt. I'll be home soon. We have a lot to talk about."

"I tried to sleep. The girls made me drink soothing sleepy time tea, but I'm wide awake. I think I just need you to be here. Is that needy of me?"

I chuckle. "No. It's fucking adorable. I was with Marissa for a long time and not once was she worried about me not coming home. The fact that you are makes me love you more. I never thought I'd ever be the one to say it, but I like having someone at home who worries about me as much as I do her."

"And someone who misses you so much it hurts?" she asks with such obvious hope I can't help the smile that spreads over my face.

"I love that, too."

She's quiet for a few moments. "I love you, Gavin," she finally whispers.

"I love you, too, my pretty little rebel."

She giggles. "Hurry home, okay? The girls are all here still. They don't want to leave me alone. Even though Brayden is here."

My heart actually feels warm. "Good. That means they've given you what your heart desires."

"Family. A home. I may have cried a lot when I first got here and saw them all."

I look up at a knock on the bedroom door. "Hang on, baby," I say to her. "Yeah?"

"Just letting you know we're landing, sir."

"Thanks." I breathe a sigh of relief at being almost home. Back to my girl. "We're just landing, beautiful. Be home in about an hour. I need to make one stop."

"Okay." She kisses the phone. "See you soon."

I smile. "See you soon." I hang up and stand, making my way back to my seat. I buckle myself in and see Charles is still unconscious. "Well, fuck me. Hope I didn't cause him any brain damage." I grin.

"No, sir." The guards laugh along with me as we land.

"Someone wake this fucker up. Ryan said the interrogation house is ready, so we'll take him there. He's considered high priority."

I don't need to say anything more than that. They all know that means no one is allowed in the house except me, Josh, Ryan, Luke, or Zekeih. It means that the cameras in and around the house will be manned by no one other than Zekeih's Code Red team. And it means that no one goes near the house without one of us as an escort or they will be shot dead on the spot.

It may sound harsh, but it's how we keep any and all leaks from releasing prisoners that are of top importance. We're a big mafia. We know that not everyone who works for us is or will remain loyal. We also know that other mafias will always try to plant leaks into our ranks. Some might succeed, but we'll always find those stupid enough to betray us.

After we land and move to the SUVs, I let myself relax a little. Not enough to let my guard down. Enough to finally let myself think about going home and, if I'm lucky, snuggling my girl into me while we sleep for the rest of the day.

"Motherfucker just needs to be put down quickly," I say. "I need a damn break."

"You?" the guard driving asks as he laughs. "I never thought I'd hear those words out of Gavin fucking Vandenberg's mouth."

I can't help but laugh with him. "It doesn't happen often, but sometimes, disappearing to Tahiti doesn't sound like a bad fucking idea." I yawn as my phone starts ringing. "Josh can't get back here fast enough." I raise an eyebrow when I see my father's number flash across my screen. I answer it with a raised eyebrow. "This can't be good. It's just past five in the morning. Which means it's three for you."

He sighs. "It's not, Gav. I need your help. And before you protest, this isn't the kind of help you're thinking. I don't need you at an event playing the proud son and making me look good while I scour for clients. I need... the other... kind of help."

My heart catches in my throat. My pulse immediately starts racing. "What? What happened? Are you okay? Is mom?"

"We're okay for now, but I don't think that's going to last. Not after the letter I received. I emailed you a copy."

I put my phone on speaker as I check my email. I pull up the one my dad sent and scan it. "When the hell did you get this?" My temper spikes to damn near the level my pulse is. "Fucking hell, dad. When the fuck did this start?"

"I just got the letter, Gavin. I opened my email this morning over coffee. I couldn't sleep. It's fucking hot here. I haven't even taken a shower yet. I called you right away because I know this is above my paygrade."

I pinch the bridge of my nose. "I'll book you a flight and send you a driver. You can't be in L.A. right now. Wake mom. The driver will be there in thirty minutes. Pack for a few days."

"Okay."

I didn't have to read the letter to know things are bad. My dad agreeing to leave L.A. in the middle of a work week without argument or question is enough. But I did read the letter. And now my hackles are raised. First Harleigh, and now my father? What the fuck is happening right now?

"Get ready quickly. Do not open your door for anyone unless they say…" I furrow my brows. "Fuck. Forget that. Don't open the door for anyone unless I say. When they get there to pick you up, call me."

"Okay." He hangs up. I know he's jumping into action. If he's afraid enough to call me, I know I don't need to tell him to move quickly.

And he should be afraid. The letter threatened his life, my mother's life, and mine if he didn't comply with their demands, which were outrageous. They wanted ten times the amount of their investment of a hundred thousand dollars in a cash payout to be given to them in cash today. There's no way my dad would be able to pull that off. It's not like he has a million dollars sitting around his office. He has to go through channels, proper channels, to get that kind of money.

The Ruthless Warriors are the fuckers who signed the damn letter. Which means they're either brazen as hell or stupid as fuck. I'm going with the latter. I rub my temple as I call our contacts in L.A.

"Hey, Gavin. What can I do for you?" Noah, our lead guy for our L.A. faction, asks when he answers, sounding tired as hell.

"I need guys on my parents. Right away. Three SUVs. I want them in the middle. Full security escort to the private airstrip at LAX. I'll have a jet waiting."

"You want us all to travel with them?"

"No. I want you and your second with them. When you get here, I'll have people you can hand them over to. I don't want them opening the door for anyone but you and not without my code word. I didn't give it to them over the phone because I don't know if their phones are bugged."

"Ditch the phones?"

"They leave the phones at the house. Code word is dew. When you walk up to that door, say Code Dew. They won't open it until I give them the okay."

"Okay. You got it. We're on the way."

I hang up and call Josh. When I hear him pick up, I start talking, slightly in a panic. "When does your flight land?"

"Uh… A couple hours. Why? What happened?" he asks, suddenly on high alert.

"The Ruthless Warriors have been investing at my father's firm. They sent him a letter this morning saying they want a return of ten times the amount of their investment, a total of a million dollars, by the end of the day or they will kill him, my mom, and me."

Josh cracks up. "Are they that fucking desperate? Need money that badly? Maybe they just realized beating us is fucking impossible. Do you have them coming here?"

"I'm booking their flight as we speak. Will you hang out and grab them? I think they'll be landing around when you will."

"I'll take care of it, Gav. What about Charles?"

"He'll be going to the interrogation house. High priority level. We're pulling into the compound now." I finish booking the flight. "And my parents will be landing in just under three hours."

"Perfect. I should be in about then."

"I want Charles to fucking sit for a day or two. Fuck with the climate control in the house. Let him sit in heat and freeze in the cold. He can have water. Just enough to keep him alive."

"I agree. Give the orders. See you soon, and don't worry about your parents. I got them."

We both hang up, and I growl low as I put my phone away. When we're parked at the interrogation house, I step out of the SUV and storm back to the SUV we have Charles in. I pull the door open with far more force than necessary and glare at him. He looks up at me with complete fear in his eyes.

I give him a demonic smirk. "I do hope your daddy tries to come to your rescue. I'm gonna enjoy taking a peeler to every inch of his skin and relish in his screams as he begs for a mercy that will never come."

As if he's accepted his fate, he hangs his head. I grab his arm and yank him out of the SUV. He stumbles when his feet hit the ground. I don't stop him from faceplanting on the hard pavement, but I do grab his arm again and hoist him up.

He struggles to keep up with my pace, but I don't care. How the fuck dare these people come after me like this on a personal level? Honestly. This can't have everything to do with Harleigh. Ryan has helped us many times in taking over territories and cleaning shit up. As far as I know, these assholes aren't going over the Crane Mafia.

Less than thirty minutes later, after handing down orders regarding our new guest and sending the women back to their homes with a promise of an update later, I'm crawling into bed behind my girl. She turns towards me with a sleepy smile, and I wrap her up in my arms, relaxing for the first time in hours. I bury my face in her hair as I feel her melt into me. She falls asleep quickly now that I'm home, and I love that I have that effect.

My mind refuses to settle, though. It's racing faster than a fighter jet. I know there's more at play here. I feel it in every fucking bone that makes up my being.

Before I can figure all of this out, though, I need to figure out if they're going after the Lucinio Mafia as a whole…

… or just me.

Chapter Twenty One

☙ Harleigh ☙

"I'm sorry we had to meet on these terms, Harleigh," Emily Vandenberg, Gavin's mother, says to me as I hand her a cup of tea.

"Oh. Think nothing of it, Mrs. Vandenberg," I say with a soft smile. "I've learned rather quickly Gavin's life is quite fast-paced. Anything can happen at any given moment. I'm learning to just go with it."

She smiles softly and nods as she takes a dainty sip of her tea. "So, Harleigh. How did you meet my Gavin?"

I nearly drop my cup. I'm able to catch it before I make a big mess and set it on the counter. "Um… Well, we… um… Oh… Well…" I take a deep breath just as Gavin comes into the kitchen.

"Mom," he chuckles. He bends and drops a soft kiss to her perfectly made up cheek. "Are you giving my girlfriend the fifth degree already?"

I blush furiously and turn towards the sink. I pretend like I'm arranging the few dishes to wash just so I can get myself under control. I decide it's just best to do them, so I start filling the sink with water.

"I was just trying to figure out how the two of you met, darling."

"We met at a diner after a mission I was on," Gavin answers smoothly. He drops a kiss to my head and taps my ass, making me squeak softly. "She knocked me off my feet."

"A diner. How… quaint."

I don't need to see her to know she's staring down her nose at me with one perfectly tweezed eyebrow arched. This is the reason people like me don't get involved with people who come from money like Gavin. I'll never fit into that world. The better-than-everyone-else attitude just isn't me.

I let out a breath before turning after putting the dishes in the sink and give her my best smile. "I loved it there. The customers were amazing. Most of them, anyway. We had really good, hearty, and delicious food."

Gavin puts three bottles of water on the counter. "It burned down a little while ago. Long story, but it was hard for Harleigh to lose it. It was all she had."

"So, you… worked there?"

I open my mouth to answer, but Gavin beats me to it. "Her father owned it. He lost his life just before the diner was torched."

I look down and focus on the tea in my cup. I say nothing because I can feel the judgment and resentment coming off her in waves and slamming into me like torpedoes. I was excited to meet Gavin's parents when he told me they were here. A little scared maybe. As soon as I saw them, though, I knew right away that I don't fit into their world. They're very posh. Gavin's father, Simon, is dressed in a suit. I'm pretty sure it's his casual wear. And Emily is dressed in a sleek, navy blue business type of dress that I'm pretty sure is everyday wear for her.

Gavin's look at his mother is a little dark. Almost like he's daring her to say anything else. It's nice to know he'll defend me against her comments, but it's also very sad because he shouldn't have to defend me at all.

"I'm sure there are much better options out there for you," Emily says after a few moments. "It may have been for the best. New doors open everyday!"

"Mom," Gavin rumbles warningly. "Don't. Don't start. You know I love you, but don't pull the status attitude. Harleigh and I are very happy together. She's just getting her feet under her again. Don't do the holier than thou shit."

"Gavin, honestly. I was just trying to get to know her."

"No, you were interrogating her." Gavin picks up the waters. He kisses me on the forehead, then walks back out of the kitchen towards his office. "She'll report back!" he calls over his shoulder.

Emily shakes her head. "That child enjoys thinking he's always right."

I smile softly and take a small sip of tea. "Gavin has been my saving grace," I say quietly. "I don't know where I'd be without him." I set my tea down and slowly turn back to the dishes.

"Darling, let the housekeeper do that. We can drink our tea outside and watch the sunset."

"We don't have a housekeeper," I say quietly as I start washing. "Or a chef. I'm happy to keep things tidy. It's the least I can do for him. He works hard."

More silence. I hate silence. It's so loud.

"I… hope… I don't say this the wrong way," Emily begins. I brace myself for the worst. "It's just that this is a large house. You could spend all day long cleaning it."

I chuckle. "It keeps me busy."

"I don't like to get into the darker side of my son's life, but I'm not naive to it. I'm pretty sure the long story he alluded to is something to do with that. Which would mean that he's probably protecting you from danger of some kind. But that won't last forever. Not with Gavin on the job. And Josh. They've all been working together since Gavin was very young. I know what they're all capable of. Even if I pretend I don't. When it's over, you'll want to do something with your life. I don't need to know you well to see the fire and passion inside you. You'll never be happy just waiting for him to come home. Cleaning the house and cooking as a distraction for him being gone. I tried that when I first got together with his father. Simon has always been very driven. I was happy to let him shine. But I quickly realized that letting him shine didn't mean my own star had to dim."

I'm quiet as I finish the dishes. When I'm done, I dry my hands, and turn back to her, nibbling my lip. "I have a lot of dreams. I just don't feel like they're attainable." I put the towel down and take my tea. I sip slowly.

"Nothing is unattainable if your heart is set on it."

"Dreams cost money. I don't have that. They don't pay insurance to people when arson is involved. I'm sure Josh and Ryan can pull strings and get me something, but it won't matter. I don't want any of it. I don't want anything from my father. I want to make my own way in life without money from the man who sold me to a horrible man in order to save his own life."

"Oh, honey…"

I shrug. "I've cried many tears. I'm to the point right now where I loved him for who he was. Not for who he became. He didn't deserve to die. Not like he did. But I didn't deserve to be sold to someone either. Right now, I'm just angry."

Emily stands and walks to the other side of the counter. She shocks me when she hugs me close and hard. I let out a surprised and quiet squawk. I stay very still for several moments before I finally hug her back.

Before I know what's happening to me, I'm hugging her harder and spilling my entire story. When I finish, we're sitting outside by the pool, and she's rubbing my back. I wipe my eyes having no idea how we ended up here, but forever grateful that she didn't push me away. Maybe I was wrong about her.

"That's a very heartbreaking story," she says with a soft smile. "But what I took from it is that you met and fell in love with an amazing man. One who will treat you like you deserve to be and love you unconditionally with all he is. And one who will support you in your dreams and aspirations. You mentioned being a veterinarian when you mentioned school, but how you put it off."

I sniffle and wipe my eyes. "Yes, ma'am," I say softly.

"I can tell you aren't one to take handouts. So, think of what I am about to say as a parent speaking to a child. Because if I received my message correctly, Gavin isn't going to let you go. Which means I might get to see my boy happy after all. He deserves to be after that wretched woman, Marissa." She shakes her head with a scowl. "I never liked her. But I digress. If college is really something you want to do…" She trails off.

"More than anything," I whisper. "I just can't aff-"

"You can," she says resolutely. "Because there are so many ways to do it without going into debt. You could take grants, and I'm sure there are scholarships. All of those are just fine, but you don't need them. Because you have Gavin. And you have us."

My eyes widen when I catch her drift. I shake my head vigorously. "Oh my God, no! No way could I accept something like that. I don't know about grants and scholarships and how they work, but I have time now. I'm sure I can figure it out."

"I can tell you with all certainty that Gavin would never allow it. He'd pay for it anyway. Even if we didn't. So, it's settled. When you're ready to enroll, your tuition and fees and books will all be paid for."

My mouth falls open. I try to find the words to argue, but they don't reach my lips. So instead, I blush and lower my eyes. "Thank you... I don't know what to say."

Emily stands. "You've never had a real family. It's time. And I apologize if I came off judgmental of you. It's been ingrained into me from my own family. Sometimes, I revert back to it, even if I try not to. Simon and Gavin have to bring me back."

"I understand," I say quietly. "I suppose it's not everyday you have a son who marries a woman who ends up portraying something she isn't and then betrays him on such a disgusting level."

"No, it's definitely not an everyday occurrence. I suppose the attitude I have stemmed a little bit from that. But truthfully, I think it was a subconscious test to see how you and he reacted to it. I didn't do it intentionally. It was a defense of sorts. I never liked Marissa. You, however, I do."

I blush again as I stand slowly. "I was thinking of making some lemonade and sandwiches for the guys. Would you like to join me?"

"I'd love to. I'll tell you all of Gavin's secret food likes."

I smile brightly. "Oh, yes. Please. I want to know everything!"

We both laugh as we walk back into the kitchen. Emily starts taking everything she needs out of the fridge to make sandwiches. I begin to make lemonade with freshly squeezed lemons, much to Emily's delight.

Several minutes later, we're both carrying trays filled with drinks and food to Gavin's office. Without knocking, Emily pushes the door open and walks right into the meeting Gavin has called with his father and Chase. It's like she owns the place. I both admire her and fear her as I follow tentatively behind her.

"Mom," Gavin says with an amused half-smile. "We're right in the middle of a meeting."

"A meeting you've been in all morning." She sets the tray down on Gavin's desk. "It's time for a lunch break. Or at least lunch while this secret meeting is going on."

Gavin chuckles and moves his chair back a little. He gestures with his head for me to set the drinks down on the desk. I do so as quietly as possible. He wraps an arm around my waist and tugs me into his lap. He kisses my arm as Emily busies herself handing out drinks and sandwiches.

"It's not exactly a secret," Simon says. "You know I've been talking about retirement. I want to be able to enjoy the money I've worked so hard for. Splurge on vacations a little. Maybe get a house in a retirement community down in Florida." He takes a drink of his lemonade. His eyes widen and a huge grin plasters his face. "My Lord, that is incredible. The perfect balance of sour and sweet."

I blush. "Thank you. We also made cucumber sandwiches. And tuna sandwiches with mayo and cut up pickles. Which, for the record, I think it's weird."

Gavin laughs. "It's fucking amazing. You'll love it. I promise." He offers me a bite of his.

I sniff it cautiously before taking a tiny bite. I chew thoughtfully. "It tastes like a regular tuna fish sandwich."

"That's because you took the tiniest bite known to man. Come on. Try it. I wouldn't steer you wrong. You didn't think you'd like alligator skewers with watermelon barbecue sauce or chips with curry sauce. You ended up loving them and ask for them all the time."

I can't help the giggle that bubbles up my throat. "Okay, okay. I'll admit those were amazing. And I need to meet Lyric because her curry sauce and chips is literally one of my new favorite things. I don't know if she invented it, but she gets all the credit. However, if I die because this is fish, and I hate fish with a blinding rage, I am coming back to haunt you."

"I wouldn't have it any other way."

I wrinkle my nose and take a deep breath before I give in and take a regular sized bite. I expect my gag reflex to force me to embarrass myself and spit the sandwich out into my hand, but it never happens. Instead, the explosion of flavor on my tongue makes my eyes widen in both wonder and delight.

"Oh my God," I say over my mouthful as I look at Gavin.

"See? I told you! I've been eating this since I was a kid. I never knew what she did to make it taste so good until I realized she added a little bit of pepper to it and rosemary. It's why you'll never see this house without pepper, rosemary, tuna, mayo, and bread." Gavin smiles as he munches on another of the tuna sandwiches while he lazily rubs my hip.

"So… can I ask what all of this is? The meeting?" I ask Gavin quietly.

He chuckles. "I don't want to take over my dad's firm. He's an investment banker. For years, it was a pretty big source of tension for us until my dad finally realized that our relationship was more important than his company. I knew how hard he worked, so for a while, I had agreed that my son or daughter could take over. Then, I realized two things. The first was that I didn't want kids. I didn't trust Marissa, and I don't feel like I have the time to dedicate to children. So, I got a vasectomy. The second was that forcing my kid, if I did have one, into a life I didn't want for myself without giving him or her a choice was a pretty shitty thing to do as a father. I sat down and talked to my dad, and we both came to the same conclusion. He was wrong to try and make me do something I didn't want to, and I was wrong for even thinking of making that same mistake with my child."

"I've never wanted kids. I always thought that was so selfish until I met you and we talked it through."

Gavin kisses my shoulder. "This meeting is for my dad. He hates the idea of selling his company to a large firm with a bunch of employees who treat their clients so impersonally. He always said he'd close the doors before he allowed that to happen. But I've been talking to Chase about it for a while. Dad wasn't really open to Chase buying him out until recently."

"We've had a few meetings," Chase adds. "I've flown out to L.A. to talk to him. Gavin knew he wanted to retire soon but hated letting his company go."

I tilt my head slightly confused. "I thought he was an investment banker?"

"Well, I am," Simon says. "But that's what Chase's company does."

I furrow my brows. "You're a financial firm."

Chase nods. "I am. I control accounts and invest them to gain more profit for my clients. Well, I oversee that. My company employs people like Simon. And we're the best in the business. We've helped companies like his grow. In his case, I'll be buying him out."

My eyes widen. "But… what about the people he employs?" My heart hurts at the potential loss of jobs.

Chase smiles wider. "That's what we were discussing when you brought lunch in. We're deciding if we want to close down and transfer people to wherever they want to go, give them a payout, or if we want to bring them all into my L.A. branch. That and other numbers. Like how much he's going to make me pay."

I giggle at that because I know Chase is a billionaire. "I think a billion dollars sounds fair."

Gavin, Chase, and Emily both laugh. Simon laughs and points at me. "I like this one, son! We're keeping her!"

I blush furiously as I get up. I lean down and kiss Gavin on the cheek. I follow Emily out of the office and help her take our lunch out to the patio where we both talk and discuss our lives. While they're very different, we also have a lot in common. We love animals and, though I didn't know until today, both wanted to be veterinarians. While I want to work with all animals, Emily specialized in horses. She closed her company a couple of years ago because her hands became arthritic, but she spent years in the field she loved.

I make plans to talk to Gavin about school and what I want to do, but one thought keeps rolling around in my head that makes me giddy.

I really hope they all keep me.

Chapter Twenty Two

❧ Gavin ❧

(Three Days Later)

Gripping Harleigh's thighs tightly, I pound my dick into her tight, wet little pussy as the water from the shower rains over us. I lean down and lick the water droplets from her neck as she pants against my shoulder and hangs on for the ride with everything she is.

"Oh, baby," I growl against her cheek just before thrusting my tongue between her lips and tangling it with hers. I grip her ass tighter.

"Gavin... yes. Yes!" Her legs tighten around my waist. She hugs me tighter. Her nails dig into my back as she slams herself over my hard cock and clenches hard around me.

I groan. "Fuck, Lei." I kiss down to her neck and push her against the wall of my shower with every thrust into her.

I kiss back up to her lips and slam my tongue into her as I plunge my dick into her over and over again. Her mouth hungrily moves against mine. I swallow her moans and fuck her mouth just as thoroughly as I'm fucking her sweet pussy.

"Gav, oh... Oh! Right there!" she moans against my neck. Her pussy pulses erratically around me.

I grin and suck on her tongue before pulling away and making my way down to her throat. I kiss and lick and nip as I pull my cock all the way out of her and slam into her again and again. I drag myself over her clit and make sure I'm hitting the spot deep inside her that makes her pussy quiver and clench around me uncontrollably.

I let my head fall back when her pussy grips my dick harder as she gets tighter and tighter. "Fucking hell, baby. You feel so fucking good."

"Ah!" she screams when I start pounding into her pussy once more. "Gavin!"

Her thighs start to tremble. Her pussy feels like a vice around my cock. She's so wet for me that I know she's about to shatter. I slap her ass, forcing her to jerk into me and scream again. She bites down on my shoulder.

"Come for me," I growl with just as much possession as passion. "Right now, baby. I'm not holding out much longer." My dick is thick. She's clenching around me painfully tight, but I don't fucking care. I'll never get enough of her.

"Ah! Gavin! Fuck, yes!" She jerks her hips against mine and comes so hard, she slams herself against the wall.

"My fucking Christ, Lei!" I push as deeply into her as I can and start shooting my load, filling her pussy with all of me.

She clenches and pulses around me as we both pant against each other while the peak we've been chasing is reached. Except we don't stop to admire the view. We crash right over and tumble our way back down the other side.

When we reach the bottom, I pull out slowly and gently set her down. I keep my hands on her hips to steady her. Her eyes are closed as she hugs me, snuggling herself against my chest. I drop my hands to her hips and hold her while she regains her bearings and a little strength.

After a few moments, she looks back up at me with a soft smile and just fucked eyes. "How does sex feel so much better every single time I'm with you?"

My grin is cocky as hell, but the words about to come out of my mouth are completely genuine. "Because you're falling more and more in love with me. And sex is always better when you're truly in love."

She giggles and lets her arms fall from my shoulders, down my chest, and to my stomach. She traces my abs and leans forward to kiss my chest. "I'm so in love with you."

"Well, that's a damn good thing. Because I love you, too. And I'm a possessive motherfucker, so I'd probably pull the mafia card and keep you safely hidden away for only me to enjoy if you weren't here willingly." I'm kidding. Or maybe not. I'm not sure I could live without her at this point.

Harleigh laughs. "You want to know the slightly scary thing about that comment?"

I grin. "What?"

"I think you might actually be serious."

I laugh. "Maybe a little." I lean down and kiss her gently before grinning again. "Or maybe a lot. I guess you'll never know. You said you love me. Can't take it back."

She giggles. "You'll have to buy me a diamond ring." Her eyes sparkle, and her voice is laced with humor.

I grin because I wonder what she'd do if she knew that my mom gave me my grandmother's engagement ring the very night she and Harleigh met and talked. It's just been a couple of months since she landed back in my arms, but we haven't been together that long. I wonder if it's too soon to ask her to marry me. What has it been? Maybe a couple of weeks? I almost wince at the phantom slap to the back of my head for overthinking this. When it's time, I'll know. Something my mother told me when she handed me that ring.

"I guess that means you'll have to marry me, then."

"I'd marry you right now. Get a priest."

I laugh. "You honestly think I'd let a priest marry us? Fuck no. I'd walk into a church, and it would crumble around me."

She giggles as she starts washing her hair. "I think it's burst into flames."

I shake my head and start cleaning up. "Nope. I'm not fucking Satan. That title belongs to Josh. I'd walk in, and it would be painful. The walls would crack and start crumbling. But I'd survive it. Josh, on the other hand, would take one step inside those doors and the entire building would combust. He'd get sent back to Hell to recover, and come back with a vendetta against the fucking church."

By the time I finish my spiel, Harleigh is laughing so hard, she's red in the face. "So, what you're saying is no church wedding."

I grin. "And no priest. Because he'd douse me with holy water, and that shit fucking hurts."

She laughs harder as she rinses her hair. "No church. No priest. I think I can work with that."

We finish in the shower and step out to dry off. "On a serious note, you'd really marry me?"

"Yep." She tilts her head. "Want to take me to the courthouse right now?"

I shrug as I towel dry my hair. "What for? Ryan has a license to marry us. He can do it as soon as we get the shit we need."

She smiles at me so brightly, I could probably shut the light out, and she'd light the room. "Are we really talking marriage right now?"

I lean down and kiss her softly. I deepen it, swiping my tongue over hers, then suck on her lower lip as I pull away. "I knew the second I saw you that I was going to marry you," I whisper against her lips. "Today. Tomorrow. Next week. Next year. Though Raleigh may castrate me if we have ours before hers and Alex's. They've had to wait long enough."

She giggles and reaches down. She grips my dick. "She can't castrate you. This…" She gives me a couple of strokes that feel so fucking good, I almost melt into her hand. "It's all for me."

"She'd get it made into a dildo just for you."

"Gavin!" Harleigh's face flames red, and she laughs. I'm starting to realize that her laugh is musical, and I need it in my life.

I sigh mock sadly. "That Brit has been such a bad influence on the girls. Sometimes, I'm pretty sure my entire family likes Lyric more than me."

She giggles. "Well, I don't know her, but she sounds like a lot of fun."

"You'll meet her. She's always here around Christmas. Josh's mom won't have it any other way." I catch a glimpse of my clock. "Fuck." I drop a kiss to her forehead. "I really need to get going. We've left Charles in the interrogation house for three days. We've only given him water. I'm not sure he'll survive much longer without food, and I want some damn answers."

She nods. "Honestly, so do I. Now that I've had time to decompress and really think about it, I have questions that I just can't figure out the answers to. I still don't really understand how they got my father to agree to selling me off. It's so out of character. I mean, he was never really all that affectionate, but I do know that he loved me." She shakes her head. "There has to be more to the story. I just don't know what."

"Truthfully, baby, you're not the only one with questions." I kiss her again and take her hand. I lead her to our closet, where I've made room for her things as well as mine, and start getting dressed. "I think I'm going to have Josh come and get you when he gets in. He can bring you to the guards quarters. You can watch the interrogation in the camera room with Zekeih. I don't want to bring you in right away, because things get a little messy in the beginning, but you can feed me questions that you want answers to through an earpiece."

"Is it wrong of me to say I hope you skin him alive?"

I pause as I'm putting on my shirt and look down at her. She doesn't meet my eyes as she sits on the chaise lounge chair and pulls a pair of jeans on. After a few moments, I clear my throat. "I'm not going to lie to you right now and tell you that I've never done dark shit like that."

She shrugs as she frowns. "He's the one from the picture you showed me the other day, right? He was one of the men there that night. He's the one who held my father down over the grill and burned him." She sniffles and shivers, immediately hugging herself.

I instantaneously drop to my knees and pull her in my arms. Her trembling body and the wetness on the shoulder of my black t-shirt are the only signs she gives me that she's in tears. I can't blame her. Seeing what she saw that night would be traumatizing to anyone.

I run my fingers through her still wet hair and kiss her neck as she clutches my still half off t-shirt. "It's okay, baby," I whisper. I keep my lips against her neck and sway gently with her. "I had a feeling you weren't ready to say it, but I knew from your reaction when I showed you the picture of him that he was probably there that night. I knew you'd tell me when you found the words."

"I hate him!" she screams out suddenly, pushing me back as she stands. "I hate him! I hate them all!" She throws her shirt against the wall.

199

"How could they do what they did? My father didn't deserve that! None of us did! How could they do that? Why?"

Before she can swipe her arm across a shelf filled with shoes and a couple of guns, I wrap my arms around her and haul her out of the closet. I pull her against me and hug her close and as tightly as possible. She flails against me and pushes at my arms as she screams and cries. I let her, dodging her fists, because I know she needs to get it out.

When she's exhausted, she slumps against me and cries. I swoop her up and carry her to the bed. I sit and settle her into my lap, hugging her tightly.

"Good girl," I whisper. "Let it all out."

I know enough to understand that this isn't over. Harleigh went through something unimaginable to most people in this world. She was trapped in a dark world I'd much rather keep her away from completely. She saw things I wish she'd never seen.

As I hug her, I allow the anger I feel at her innocence of the world being taken from her in such a vicious and malicious manner. Let that mother fucker sit for a few more hours. Harleigh is the most important thing to me in this entire situation. I don't care if I have to spend hours with her holding her while she breaks. I don't give a single fuck if I have to spend days putting her back together again. Nothing is more important to me than her.

🍏🍏🍏

I take the cup of coffee Zekeih hands me as I watch the cameras in front of me and take a sip. "Fuck me, that's good." I look at the to go cup in awe. "Where did you get this?"

"I can't take credit. Nicole made it. I stopped by on my way here. Figured you'd need some coffee, but I'm fucking addicted to those vanilla rose muffins. She puts a vanilla cream cheese in the middle of it."

I take another sip and stare at the cup in awe. "I can't even figure out what this is. It tastes like a vanilla latte but there's something else."

Zekeih laughs. "It is a vanilla latte. But I told her it's for you, and that you're interrogating Charles today. She added a shot of espresso and put mocha into it. Then she did some fancy shit, put whipped cream on it, and handed it to me with my muffin. She told me to tell you that you can thank her later, then sent me on my way."

I laugh. "Something about being a cop's wife has done something to that girl. She's got some incredible confidence going on that she hadn't had when I first met her."

"You're telling me. She's also become best friends with my wife. That doesn't bode well for me in the slightest." He grins.

I laugh as I sip the coffee. I'm silent for a few moments as I watch our prisoner. "Charles looks pretty weak."

"He hasn't done a lot since you threw him in there. We've been keeping the temperature around ninety during the day and plying him with water. At night we put it up to a hundred. Yesterday, I thought he was dead when I went in to give him the water. But the fucker tried to strangle me. Lunged at me. He didn't get far because of the shackles, but I decided to be a dick and put the water just out of his reach. He finally managed to get it, but he used a lot of energy. Energy that he didn't have to spare in the first place. Today, he looks worse for the wear, that's for sure."

I nod. "Good. That's where I want him." I take the earpiece he hands me. "When Josh gets here, send him in. He's in a meeting. He'll have Harleigh with him. Keep Harleigh here, but give her an earpiece. I want her to be able to ask questions and see what's going on."

He raises an eyebrow. "I know how you get. Sure she can handle that?"

I chuckle. "She told me she wants him skinned alive."

Zekeih laughs. "Huge difference between saying and seeing. I'm removing the earpiece and taking her out of here if things escalate."

I grin. "Probably wise." I toss my empty cup after finishing.

He smiles as he follows me out of the room. "High priority client means you need an escort."

"I don't need one."

"Oh, I know. But that's not my rule. That's directly from Josh and Ryan. You get an escort. Two guards. Take your pick, Vandenberg. I'll be in the security cam room."

I roll my eyes and point to two random guards. "You and you. With me."

Two very eager looking guards scurry after me. I don't break stride, but I grin when I see Zekeih smile and shake his head, heading back to the security cam room. Most think that our guards are constantly busy, but the truth is, they aren't. We aren't always in a conflict. We don't always have high priority clients. Most of the time, these guys are sitting on their asses or training. Getting to escort any of us to an interrogation is something they all enjoy because it gives them some action in an otherwise mundane day.

I lead them across the backyard that they use for training sessions and stop outside the interrogation house. I put my thumb against the screen and wait for it to scan me. A few moments later, the screen turns red.

"Access denied," an autobot tells me.

I raise an eyebrow. "Excuse fucking you? Do I need to fucking shoot you again?"

Suddenly, Nick's ugly face fills the screen. And the asshole is laughing. "I'm fucking with you. Don't shoot my tech, asshole. They're my babies. And it costs thousands to replace. Just stand there a minute. I need to scan you."

"You're a fucking douche. You're lucky I like you."

"Shut up and stay still."

I watch as blue lasers seemingly jump out of the screen and scan me. "The fuck is this shit?"

"Like a fingerprint, a person's body is unique. Turn in a circle, then put up your left wrist. I need the tattoo."

I do as I'm told then hold up my wrist so he can scan the sword on my wrist that says 'Live and Die' underneath. It's a reminder to me that we all live and we all die. It's what we do between that matters. "So, what do you do if someone has a tattoo on their ass?" I grin.

"Fuck you. Christ." Nick laughs. "It gets scanned in. Then the next time, the high tech shit sees it through the clothing when they get scanned. I'm not even going to attempt to explain it to you."

I laugh. "Good. I won't understand it."

Nick laughs. "Alright. Give me your thumb again."

"Am I going to have to go through this shit every time I come here? Because I swear to hell, I won't be the only one who gets irritated with this shit." I put my thumb on the screen.

"No. You'll get in same as always. Thumb to the screen. The body scan will happen quickly and without the blue lasers. I already put everyone else through this. You were the only one left because you were holed up with your girl the past three fucking days."

"Access granted. Welcome, Mr. Vandenberg," the autobot says.

I blink and let his comment go. "That's it?"

"That's it. Thanks for flying Air West. Enjoy your stay in Casa de Infierno."

"Fuck me," I mutter under my breath with a laugh as the screen turns back to black. Nick's humor is as dark as mine and always manages to cheer me up.

I enter the house, and the second in command persona slips easily into place. The two guards who are escorting me each choose a corner and stand with their hands clasped in front of them. I chuckle a little bit because their stance has always reminded me a little of the Secret Service guarding the President. Stoic demeanor. Unmoving. Unflinching.

I stride across the room to my very weak plaything. He keeps his head down, but his eyes are open. His legs are shackled together and chained to a metal bar that's attached and reinforced to the wall.

I kick him in the ribcage hard, smiling sadistically at the sound of cracking bones under my steel-toed, black boot. He slumps to his side and falls to the ground with a groan. I kick him in the stomach just because I can.

I kneel in front of him with a grin. "I've been told you haven't wanted to talk to anyone. Now you get to deal with me, motherfucker."

Chapter Twenty Three

❦ Harleigh ❦

I let out a breath as I walk with Josh towards a giant house near the edge of the property. I was really excited to get to face one of the men who caused me so much hurt and heartache over the past few years, especially the past couple of months, but the closer I get to the looming house in the distance, the less excited I become. More anxious. A little terrified and angry. But mostly, an overwhelming sense of sadness feels like it has washed over me.

I let out another breath. "Maybe this wasn't a good idea."

Josh chuckles. "I can honestly tell you that it is."

I look up at him curiously. "How is me throwing up when I see him a good thing?"

He smiles as he guides me into the house we just reached. It's amazing seeing how everyone reacts to him. They're all suddenly very alert. "After I confronted my father the first time, I spent days decompressing. I couldn't believe it was finally over. I didn't know then that it really wasn't, but I thought it was. I still had a little of the serum in my system. I was fucked up. I spent most of the day sleeping and most of the night lying awake and puking my guts out and crying."

My eyes widen. "You? You don't seem like a crier."

"I'm not. It was part of the reason I felt the way I did. Far more fucked up. I didn't feel regrets or sympathy for him, so why the fuck was I crying over it? It took me a long time to realize that I was coming down from all of the shit I went through. It took me quite a while to realize that confronting him was a very important aspect of my life. It was closure. I went through a lot of the same shit over a quicker period of time when we put him down for good. This might not get you all of the closure you need, Harleigh, but it will go a long way." He opens a door and guides me inside.

"This... is... a lot of cameras."

"This is our central security footage area. We can see every inch of the property from this room. The only people who have any kind of offsite access are leaders and people we consider command. And we don't let anyone but each other know that information. It's another layer of protection in a very vast web." Josh hands me an earpiece and puts one in his own ear.

I mimic him and put the earpiece in my ear. I watch him to see what he does next. He leans down and taps a key. Suddenly, I can hear everything Gavin is saying, even though I could already hear him from the audio in the room.

"Can I talk to him?" I mouth the words to Josh.

He nods before looking back at the screen. "Gav? I have Harleigh with me. We're in the control room."

Gavin grins just before he slams a fist into the already bloody man laying at his feet. "How many hits is it going to take?" Gavin asks. His voice is deadly calm.

I tilt my head. "Did he hear you?" I ask Josh. "He didn't respond."

"He did. He gave us a smile." He points to the two other people in the room standing in corners like they're on guard. "See those two?"

"Mmhmm."

"They're there to protect Gavin. If anything goes down with our prisoner, Gavin has backup. But they aren't part of our high priority team. So, they don't have earpieces and have no idea that Gavin does. The smile is his signal that he heard us without giving anything away to them that he has voices in his ear."

"Oh." I nod. "Okay."

"When he's ready for us, he'll give us his code word. It looks like he's been here for a while, judging from Charles' condition."

"Here's the deal, Charles. I'm sick of fucking around," Gavin says as he stands. "So, you're going to start talking. Where's your father?"

"I don't know! I told you I have no idea. He has many hideouts, but his favorite is the one in Aspen."

Something about Aspen triggers me. "I remember something about Aspen. One time when they were in the restaurant the older guy mentioned it. Something about it being peaceful and hidden. He specifically said Aspen was his happy place. No one knew where his cabin was located. He bought it under a false name. Um…" I nibble my cheek as I think.

"Where is this place in Aspen?" Gavin asks. He leans against the wall on the other side of the room and crosses his arms.

"He never took me there. I don't know, and I'm telling the truth on that."

Gavin takes a knife out of his pocket. "You know I'm going to check it out. If Gregory Franklin doesn't come up as an owner, I'm going to slit the vein underneath your balls and let you bleed out." He flicks something on the knife, and a blade pops up, but he doesn't move from the wall. Instead he focuses on the tip of the knife like it's the most interesting thing in the world. That should send chills down my spine. Why doesn't it?

"It's not under his name. Do you think he's fucking stupid?"

Gavin pushes off the wall and slowly struts across the room like he has all the time in the world. "Then what name is it under? Or do I need to start cutting? I've always loved watching a man's life drain from his eyes right in front of me. Some kind of sick satisfaction to it. I'm probably a sociopath."

"I don't know. He said something about Jake Cooke once. Maybe that's the name."

I furrow my brows. "No… That doesn't sound familiar. He said the name. I wish I could remember."

Gavin kneels down again and yanks Charles up by his shirt. He slams him against the wall behind him. Charles groans and slumps a little. "I don't do well with maybe, Charles," Gavin growls menacingly.

With cool, collected movements, he runs the tip of the knife up the already cut pant leg of Charles. This time, though, he draws blood. There must be something wrong with me because that doesn't bother me either.

Charles jerks away from him. "Okay, okay! He always uses the same code name. Benjamin Sans. That's what it would be under."

I shake my head. "No. That's not it. I'm positive. I know when I hear it, I'll remember it."

Gavin chuckles. "Do you know how fucking much I hate being lied to?" He flips the knife in the air and catches it by the handle in his other hand. Without warning, he slices through the air and straight down between Charles' legs.

"Aaaaaahhhhh!" Charles screams.

It takes me a second to realize what he did. When I do, I cover my mouth and sway, catching myself from falling on the table next to me. "He just…"

Charles' screams echo in my head as I turn away from the screen to regain my composure. Holy fuck. Fuck, fuck, fuck. He stabbed him clean through his jeans and down through his dick and balls. I take several deep breaths.

Charles continues screaming in pain. Animalistic. Completely not human. My heart is racing. My stomach is trying to escape through my mouth. I squeeze my eyes shut and breathe until I calm enough to think.

"You okay?" Josh asks while keeping his eyes locked on the screen. "Do you want me to have Zekeih remove you and escort you home?"

I shake my head as I turn around and slowly open my eyes. "Is there something wrong with me that Gavin actually doing that isn't what bothered me? It was just the surprise of it happening. Does that make me a psychopath?"

Josh shakes his head. "It means you're a strong fucking woman who knows what her boyfriend is doing is for the greater good."

I give a soft smile as Charles' screams and sobs eventually diminish to whimpers. "I'm staying."

Gavin turns his back just slightly from the camera so that the guards can't see him. "Good girl," he whispers.

His words send my heart flying. I can do this. I can know what he does and how he does it. I can still love and support him. And I'm not crazy for doing it. Those eight letters give me the strength I need to keep going. I am a good girl. I'm strong. I'm capable. I belong here with him. With the entire family.

My family.

Gavin kneels down in front of Charles once more. "Tell… me… the… alias… now."

"George. The name he uses. It's George Bond."

"Like James Bond? Come on. That can't be fucking true." Gavin laughs.

"It's fucking true!" Charles yells. He shrinks as far away from Gavin as he can.

"Actually, I think that's true," I say quietly. "It sounds… familiar. I can't be positive… I'm sorry. I thought I'd know for sure when I heard it."

Out of the corner of my eye, I see Zekeih stand a little straighter as he focuses harder on the screens. I step to the side a little when he and Josh both furrow their brows and cross their arms over their chest.

"Did you see that?" Zekeih asks.

"Yeah," Josh says. He leans forward slightly and squints. "Zoom in. Right there." He points to one of the guard's left side. I'm suddenly on high alert because I feel like they are. The other guard in the room does as Josh says. "Keep an eye on it. Gav, guard in the far corner of the room reacted to that name. We're keeping an eye on him. He just got pretty fucking twitchy. He looks like he's holding something with his right hand. He just crossed it over to his left side. He's acting like he's holding his side or some shit."

Gavin stands again. This time, he angles himself slightly. Instead of being intimidating and crossing his arms over his chest, he keeps his hands at his sides. He looks ready for an attack but still completely in control. He flicks his eyes at the other guard and tilts his head just a little bit towards the guard in the corner. If I wasn't so focused on him, I would have missed it. The movements are so subtle that I wouldn't have noticed anything.

Obeying Gavin's commands, the guard nearest the door turns just enough that he still looks like he's completely focused on Gavin. His elbows move back just a little, so his hand is closer to his gun.

I take a deep breath and trust that whatever is happening is being dealt with, even if I don't understand it. "Can you ask him about my father? Why they killed him? I really just feel like there's more."

"Let's talk about what happened at the diner. Jake Harlow."

Charles looks up at Gavin. "What about him?" he asks weakly.

"I don't buy for a single fucking second that you killed him to get your hands on Harleigh. You could have easily just taken her. Why the theatrics? Why burn her house to the ground? Why kill him?"

Charles lets out a long and painful sigh. He coughs up blood. "Because he knew too much about the Lucinio Mafia. He was smart enough to know that we tapped his phone, but he didn't know we could also intercept text messages and email." He coughs again and pauses to look at the blood splattering his shirt. "We did the same with his bitch daughter's phone and email."

Gavin's eyes narrow. "Watch your fucking mouth. Remember. I can leave thousands of cuts all over you and watch you bleed out in the most painful of ways. By the time I'm done, you'll be begging me to kill you and end the fucking misery."

Charles looks up at Gavin once more. I can't help the smile that tugs at the corner of my mouth, and the swell of pride that lifts my heart at Gavin's protective demeanor towards me. But I can't stop staring at the guard in the corner. Is he a threat to the man I gave my heart to?

Charles heaves out another cough, spitting up more blood. I don't know a lot, but I'm pretty sure he doesn't have much longer. "We saw all of the texts you sent her. When she didn't respond, we thought he'd prepared her. Told her the truth of what was going to happen. He never sent texts. We were caught off guard and almost missed it. He sent a text to you."

I let out a quiet whimper. "You never told me you got a text," I whisper.

"I never got a fucking text from him," Gavin growls.

"That's because we intercepted it."

"How the fuck do you intercept a text message?" Josh mumbles, then winces. "I can just feel Lance getting ready to lecture us. It does make me wonder…," He trails off on a mumble as he pulls out his phone and sends off a message to someone without taking his eyes off the screen. He tucks it back into his pocket when he's done.

"How?" Gavin asks.

"When you understand apps and technology, nothing is that hard. We have a hacker on our team who can do it and did."

"What did the message say?" Gavin asks. "And don't even think about lying to me because I never ever ask a fucking question I don't have the ability to verify."

Charles sighs and coughs up more blood. He slumps against the wall even more, and I almost start crying. I really want to know what it said. Did my father really want to sell me? Or was he trying to protect me somehow?

"I don't know the exact wording. But he said that he needed help. He said the Ruthless Warriors were after his daughter. He also sent an email. That was what spurred us into action."

"What did it say? What the fuck did you want with Harleigh? And don't give me the bought and paid for bullshit. I'm smarter than that."

"He's fading," I whisper.

Charles tries to raise his arm, but it drops. "He…," he whispers. I have to push my earpiece in a little more just to hear him. The blood pooling between his legs is an indication to me that he really is bleeding out. He clears his throat and gurgles. "He really did agree… to… her… being sold to us."

"Wake the fuck up!" Gavin commands. It makes me jump.

Charles snaps his head towards Gavin. "He… knew… about you." His words are getting more and more painful. My heart starts to clench. My throat swells with emotion. But not for him. For my father. I knew there was more. "He knew… she… was in love with you. He… told… you everything. He… tried… saving… her…" His words get softer and softer as his eyes fall closed.

I sink to my knees and cover my mouth with my hand. Tears sting my eyes as the lump in my throat swells enough to start hurting. My stomach clenches as tightly as my chest. I let out a sob, but I don't know if I'm going to cry or throw up.

"Gun!" Josh suddenly yells.

I look up just in time to see Gavin diving to the ground as a barrage of bullets fly around him. I can see them hit the wall just behind him as he covers his head. Josh and Zekeih fly into a blur of motion and run out the door.

"Gavin!" I shriek. I scramble towards the door. "Gavin!" A strong set of arms wrap around my waist. Fight or flight instincts kick in, and I fight as I scream. "Gavin!" I hear more shooting and yelling. Screaming.

It takes me a long while to realize that the screaming is coming from me.

Chapter Twenty Four

❦ Gavin ❦

As soon as the word 'gun' hits my ear, I'm in motion and diving towards the furthest corner of the room. I grab for my gun as I cover my head from the barrage of bullets, but I have no idea where to shoot because I don't know where the shots are coming from.

With my arm over my head, I glance around the room. It's open space. There's nowhere for me to take cover. That needs to fucking change. One of my guards is dead. The other is crouched in the corner furthest from the door. Why the fuck is he pointing a gun at me?

Another barrage of bullets hit just above my head. I duck but quickly start moving. A running target is far harder to hit. I shoot as I run for the door, still crouched low, but suddenly, I can't breathe. I can't feel the gun in my hand anymore and involuntarily drop it as I stumble and hit the ground.

"Ah! Fuck!" I clutch my side and try to make myself as small as possible. Not an easy feat for someone my size.

I reach for my gun, but can't feel it. I force myself to stay awake, even though my vision is starting to get cloudy. I know help is coming. I just hope they get here quickly.

I finally find my gun, just as the asshole traitor of a guard takes aim at me once more. I can't get up, so I raise the gun just off the ground and shoot towards him. All I can do is pray I hit him.

I don't.

The guard laughs. "The great and mighty Gavin Vanderberg has lost his impeccable aim." He levels his gun at my head, so I shoot again. I miss. He laughs once more. "Too bad, you know? You could've made a great asset to us."

As if I suddenly have hyper vision or something, I watch as he squeezes the trigger in slow motion. His smile is demented. He's still across the room, but I feel like he's a lot closer than that. The walls are closing in on me. I shoot again, but I'm getting weaker. My breathing is slower.

I can hear Harleigh screaming. It's how I know I'm still alive. I take another shot. This one sends so much pain radiating up my arm that I cry out from the excruciating feeling of it. Harleigh's screams seem to be getting more and more distant, but I can still hear them.

"Gavin!" she cries.

The walls seem to be getting closer and closer; the room darker and darker. I force myself to take one more shot, but I can't squeeze the trigger anymore. I don't have the strength. I can't hear Harleigh anymore.

"I'm sorry, baby," I whisper. I lose grip on the gun just as the room goes black. All I can hear now is the roaring of my own heart as it slows more and more. "I... love... you..."

This isn't how I thought I'd go down. Maybe it was cocky and arrogant of me, but I know how fucking good I am at my job. I always thought that if anyone was able to take me out, I'd take everyone else down with me. I never dreamed one person would be able to end me.

I take shallow breaths.

"Gavin!" someone screams. A male. Josh?

More shooting.

"Gavin! Wake the fuck up!" someone else orders. I can't see them. Zekeih?

More shallow breaths.

"Get me a fucking SUV! Call Freeman!" Josh commands. At least I hope that's who it is. "Have him meet us at the hospital!"

"He's not going to make it by vehicle, Josh," Zekeih growls. "We need a chopper. Ryan or Chase can fly. Jason can."

I feel myself being moved. I grit my teeth and groan in pain, but everything is still dark. Maybe I'm imagining it all. Maybe I'm in some middle fucking ground between Hell and the afterlife.

"Ah!" My eyes fly open when I feel pressure on my side. I didn't know they were closed. I grip whatever is closest to me. Someone's thigh. I squeeze my eyes shut and inhale sharply as I growl.

"I know it hurts, bro, but I gotta do what I gotta do," Zekeih says.

The brief period of time my eyes were open, I could see the room was filled with a lot of recognizable faces. Josh and Zekeih are two of them, but there's one face missing. The only one I want to see right now.

"Harleigh," I ground out.

"Safe," Josh says. I feel a hand on my shoulder.

"What do you need, boss?" someone asks.

"Ryan," Josh says, tersely. "I need his chopper. Now!"

I try to open my eyes because his tone scares me more than fucking death itself. I'm used to Josh being commanding, dominating, and fucking intimidating as hell sometimes. But I've never heard that tone. Like he's freaked the fuck out that he's going to lose someone close to him.

If I'm going to die, I want my girl. "Harleigh."

"Coming," Josh says. "Stay with me, brother. Fuck, stay with me."

"Gavin!" Harleigh screams.

And just like that, the pain is gone. It's like her strength and love is all I need. I feel her head on my shoulder as she cries and clutches my arm. My head is against her thigh. Zekeih presses down harder, making me cry out in pain again.

"Fuck!" I grimace.

"Gavin…" Harleigh presses her head closer to my cheek. She kisses my shoulder. "Gavin, please, please don't leave me." She sobs intp my shoulder.

"Harleigh." I want to tell her I'm not going anywhere, but that numbness is coming back. I'm fucking freezing cold. I can feel myself shaking. Even though I try to stop it, the shivering is violent. "Harleigh?" I can't feel her anymore.

"I'm here. I'm here, baby," she whispers.

Or maybe it seems like a whisper because it's all getting dark again. I can't hear anything other than a powerful engine. Like a chopper.

"Ryan?" I whisper.

Zekeih presses down again. I groan, but the pain is lessening. I don't know if that's a good thing or a bad thing. "He's landing, man. Stay with us," Zekeih says, though he seems to be yelling.

"Harleigh…"

"I'm not going anywhere," she sobs. "I'm coming with you. I'm not going anywhere."

For a brief moment, I feel her hair against my face; her tear soaked cheek against my neck. I feel Zekeih's hand against my side. I feel myself being moved again, but then I feel nothing but the cold. Like I'm sitting in the middle of the coldest part of Antarctica. I don't hear the chopper. I hear nothing more than the slowing of my heart once more. My breathing becomes shallow once again.

I can't open my eyes, but clear as day in my mind's eye is Harleigh reaching for me. I reach for her like she's my lifeline and hold on tight when she takes me in her arms. I let myself fall into her as my entire world fades.

ꙮꙮꙮ

-ep… Beep…

I groan.

-ep… Beep… Beep…

I have a splitting headache.

Beep… Beep… Beep…

That beeping is going to drive me fucking crazy.

Beep… Beep… Beep…

Harleigh's alarm?

Beep… Beep… Beep…

"Harleigh, fuck. Shut it off…," I growl sleepily. My own voice makes the headache seemingly stab throughout my entire body.

"Gavin?" She sounds so fucking tired.

"Baby, please. I have the worst fucking headache," I say quietly. Weakly.

Beep… Beep… Beep…

"Oh, Gavin…" She sniffles and wraps her arms carefully around me. She buries her face in my neck. "Thank God. Thank all the Gods. Or demons. Or Satan himself. I don't even know."

"What…?" I feel her shift against my side and kiss my neck. I force my eyes open, but I do it slowly because fuck. That headache.

I don't recognize the room. I blink a few times. Thankfully, there isn't a lot of light coming in. I still don't have a fucking clue where I am. Why is everything so hazy? It's like my brain stopped working and can't focus on anything but the pounding in my head.

"I'm so happy you're awake," Harleigh whispers as she reaches over me and pushes a button or something. A control?

"What happened? Where am I?" I try to put my arm around her, but realize she's not in the bed with me. She's sitting next to me in an ugly brown chair I'd never buy in my life. "Why aren't you in this bed with me where you belong?"

She sniffles and breaks down into sobs. "You almost…"

Alarmed, I turn towards her to put my arms around her and pull her into the bed with me, but grit my teeth at the shooting pain in my side. "Oh, fuck," I groan.

Her eyes widen as she looks at me. "Don't move, Gav. Please!" she whispers as she puts her hand gently over mine on my side.

"What the hell is happening right now, Lei?"

Beep! Beep! Beep! Beep! Beep!

That beeping gets a little more intense, and I start looking around for the source. The door to the room flies open, and I jump. My heart thuds in my throat as instincts kick in. I grab for my gun and try to shield Harleigh, but my gun isn't where it's supposed to be. Panic rises.

"Gavin, it's okay. Please calm down. Please," Harleigh whispers as she gently pushes on my chest.

My eyes slam to the door where someone I recognize strides in. "Doc?" I croak out over the rapid breathing.

"Mr. Vandenberg," Doctor Freeman says. He's been our family doctor ever since Alex and I were teenagers. He's always been loyal to us. When we chose to move to Chicago from L.A., he came with us. I've never been so grateful to see him in my life.

"What the fuck is going on?" I ask, taking deep breaths as Harleigh soothingly runs her fingers through my hair. The nurse who followed

Doctor Freeman into the room starts taking vitals and checking the machines.

"You were shot, son. The bullet went through. You were lucky. It missed vital organs and your ribs. It made a very bizarre path. There's no other explanation other than someone was looking out for you. The way it went in, well, it should have hit something. Liver. Kidney. Spleen. It didn't hit anything. You lost a lot of blood, though. We had to do a transfusion."

"We were lucky Ryan is such an expert pilot," Harleigh whispers. "You would have d-died." She squeezes my hand as she lays her head down on my arm.

I close my eyes as everything comes back to me so quickly and with such force, it makes me sick to my stomach. Harleigh's screams. The guard shooting at me. The very second one of his bullets hit.

"What about Charles and the other guard in the room?"

Harleigh sniffles. "The other guard died. He w-was sh-shot in the neck." She takes a breath. And then another. "Charles bled out." Even through her tears, I can hear the venom in her voice.

"His vitals look good, doctor. Shall I grab his family?"

"Yes, but just his parents and Mr. Lucinio, please."

"Yes, sir." The nurse leaves the room.

Doctor Freeman pulls a chair out and sits down. "You gave us a scare there, Gavin," he says. "I've been with you boys for so long, I'm not so sure what the hell I'd do if one of you didn't make it." His eyes fill up with tears, but he blinks them away.

"I'm too much of an asshole to die," I say with a chuckle, but I hiss. "Fuck." I set my hand on my side.

"I'll get you something for the pain. The anesthesia has worn off. And don't give me the tough guy bullshit I know you're about to. You need something for it. You took a hell of a hit. Even though nothing major was hit, it's going to take time to heal. And you're going to be in pain. I'll order something and have it added to the IV drip."

I know better than to argue with the guy. I rarely get sick, but I had the flu once. Doctor Freeman had me laying down and resting. He showed up everyday and sent my mother to stay with me. By the time a week was up, I was feeling better and wanted to shoot both of them for how much they were fussing. I found out later, though, that Doctor Freeman never had kids. He thought of me, Alex, Josh, Damon, Lance, and Jessa as his kids. When we got hurt or sick, it pulled at his heartstrings. We're as much his family as ours. It's why he relocated with us.

Though, I'm pretty sure Jessa is his favorite, even if she is a Crane and treated by a different doctor now. Given how he reacted when he found out she was planning to cancel that original appointment for her anxiety, it showed us just how big his heart is. If the three hour long lecture he gave her was anything to go by. He still, to this day, checks in on her.

I look up as my parents come rushing into the room. Doctor Freeman moves back and stands. He starts talking to Josh as my mother hugs me carefully. Harleigh doesn't move from her place at my side.

"Gavin, my God. We thought we lost you!" my mom says.

"I'm fine, mom. Just a little sore."

"Gav, for fuck's sake," Josh growls as he sits on the edge of the bed as the doctor leaves. "You almost fucking died, man. If Ryan hadn't flown us to the hospital, I don't think you would have made it."

Harleigh whimpers. "They had to do CPR on you in the helicopter," she whispers. "I… had… to…" She cries into my arm. "I had to put pressure on your wound s-so they c-could…" Her body trembles against me. "R-revive you!"

I don't care that it hurts. I pull her onto the bed with me and hug her as closely as I can. "I'm sorry, baby," I whisper in her ear. "I'm sorry."

I whisper the words over and over again as I kiss her softly and rub my hand up and down her arm. My mom rests her head on my chest and hugs me, being careful of my injury. My dad pulls up a chair and rubs up and down my mom's back.

After a long while, I can tell my mom and Harleigh have fallen asleep. I doubt either of them have if I was that close to death. I'm sure no one has closed their eyes until I opened mine. My dad excuses himself to grab a cup of coffee. Josh stands slowly from the chair he sat in after I pulled Harleigh into the bed with me.

"Alex says the others are getting pretty restless. Jessa really wants to see you. He also said he's going to kick my ass for not letting him in here first. Something about having you first and me stealing you." Josh grins.

I chuckle. "You can send the others in. Just tell them to keep it down."

Josh nods and hesitates a moment before sticking his hands in his pockets. "I know we haven't always been on the same page. I did a lot of fucked up things -"

"Josh." I shake my head. "It's in the past. It's over. We've moved past it. I don't blame you at all for the shit your father did to you. I blame him."

"Let me get this out. I need to." He takes a breath, and I fall silent. "When I finally took my rightful place as head of the Lucinio Mafia, I honestly expected to do it alone. I thought you'd take over as COO or CFO and work with Alex. I thought he'd completely walk away. I didn't think Lance or Damon would stay. Cole. All of them were loyal to you and Alex. Not me. I didn't expect the help I got from Ryan. Especially after the shit that went down with Jessa. I guess what I'm trying to say here is that I don't just appreciate you sticking around and being both a friend and one hell of a second in command. I also appreciate that we've become close. Like family." He looks down a little sheepishly. "Brothers."

I grin. "We've been that since we were kids. We strayed a bit, but we found our way back. Stronger than ever, right?"

He chuckles as he looks back up at me. "I don't have a lot of people close to me. You know that. I almost lost a brother today, and it almost fucking killed me. Don't do that to me again."

"You got it, boss." I smile and wink at him.

He shakes his head with a grin. "Asshole."

"You wouldn't want me any other way."

He nods and smiles wider. "True."

I hug Harleigh tighter and kiss my mom on the head. My dad comes back in with coffee as Josh is walking out. Everyone in my growing and very fucked up family makes their way in and out of the room, telling me how grateful they are that I made it. There are a lot of hugs that wake up both Harleigh and my mom, but neither move from where they are. If I'm being honest, I can't blame them. I'm not sure I'd be any different if the roles were reversed.

By the time everyone leaves, and after my father convinces my mother that I need rest and so does she, I'm left in the room with only Harleigh and Alex.

Alex sits down on the chair my mom was in. "The last time I was that scared I was about to lose a family member was when Arianna was rushed to the hospital in Hawaii after Renza started that fire to kill her. Or maybe it was when Nick got poisoned. Or when Robby got kidnapped." He pauses with an incredulous look on his face. "You all need to stop fucking scaring me. I'm getting too old for this shit."

"I'm good, bro. Really. God doesn't want me. And Satan is afraid I'll take over the underworld. And I'm not ready to die yet. Too much life to live."

Alex falls silent as he watches Harleigh draw patterns on my chest. "I don't know what I would have done if…"

"Alex…" I reach for his hand and give it a squeeze. "I made it. I'm okay. You know better than to dwell."

He squeezes my hand back as I start to feel the effects of the painkillers. I yawn as my eyes start to fall closed and a small smile plays on my face.

I'm alive…

Chapter Twenty Five

🐚 Harleigh 🐚

(One Month Later)

"For several years, I've been in talks with Vandenberg Investments, a small investment company in Los Angeles, about buying them out," Chase says in a press conference he's holding that's being aired on CNN. "Simon Vandenberg, the owner and operator of Vandenberg Investments, is ready to retire, and we've struck a deal."

I look up at Gavin as I snuggle into his side on the couch. "You're an amazing son."

He chuckles and kisses me softly. "I'm not the one who bought him out." He takes my hand and kisses the engagement ring on my finger.

His grandmother's.

It's a gorgeous ring. The diamond is an oval cut. There are three small rubies, also oval cut, on the band on each side of the diamond. The band is white gold. I've always loved yellow gold, but this ring is so beautiful that I don't care at all. I've become a huge fan of white gold.

I smile when he kisses me again and snuggle closer to him. He placed it on my finger the day he got home from the hospital. No words were said, but there were a lot of tears and nodding on my part and lots of hugs from him.

"I want to make it clear here that no one is losing their job," Chase continues. "We're moving everyone who worked at Vandenberg Investments under the Shaw Incorporated umbrella. The move for all employees and clients will be seamless. There will be no disruptions to anyone's accounts or fees. While we expect some will leave, we do hope that all Vandenberg clients will trust us to continue building their investments and portfolios. We've spent years building our brand, but we understand we're always building trust."

"Chase is really good in front of people," I comment.

Gavin chuckles. "He's spent years in front of them. It's second nature to him at this point."

"One more thing I'd like to address," Chase says. "There are a lot of rumors going around that this was a hostile takeover. That couldn't be further from the truth, and you all know me better than that. I don't run my company like that. I never will. I've bought out numerous smaller companies and merged with many others. They've all had nothing bad to say about me. I have Mr. Vandenberg here today to address these rumors. I don't know who started them, but they end today." Chase steps to the side as several questions are shouted at him. He gestures to Simon and ignores the reporters.

Simon takes his place in front of the podium. "Good afternoon. I hope you're all enjoying this brisk November morning."

Gavin chuckles. "My father is so used to L.A. that anything below seventy has him bringing out his sweaters and heavy jackets."

I giggle. "I kind of agree with him, though. It really is cold today. I think it's just at forty."

Simon smiles at the chuckles in the room. "I spent a lot of time thinking about this, and it's time. We've known for a long time that my son didn't want to take over the family business. He has his own life and dreams. We're very proud of him for everything he's done and is doing to better this world, but it leaves him no time to take over his old dad's company. We've been working on a plan for years. When we were approached by Mr. Shaw, we didn't want anything to do with a big corporation. But he runs his company efficiently and cares about everyone. He's different from other firms in that it's not all about the bottom dollar to him. It's about the bottom dollar for his clients. His employees. It's something we found ourselves liking very much. The more we spoke, the more we knew Shaw Incorporated was the best option for us. The right fit. Mr. Shaw offered us a more than fair price. Because of him, we'll be able to enjoy retirement and not have to worry about our employees, who are like family, or our clients, who are also an extension of our family. A hostile takeover? Nothing of the sort." Simon nods. "I will not be entertaining questions. Please enjoy your upcoming Thanksgiving. I do hope you'll be able to spend time with loved ones. Thank you."

I watch as Simon takes some papers from the podium and follows Chase out of the large press room Gavin told me is located at Shaw Incorporated's Headquarters here in Chicago. Simon and Emily, who I've been ordered to call mom and dad now, something Gavin's previous wife never got to do, have been staying with us over the month while Gavin recovers. Simon has been flying back and forth between here and L.A. while the buyout has been worked through. Now that it's complete, Simon has visibly relaxed.

Gavin has been healing nicely. He has a small scar that's hardly visible anymore. It's inside that still causes him pain. Doctor Freeman said it's not surprising. While nothing was damaged, the bullet did cause a lot of bruising. I'm not sure I totally understand how, but I suppose when a bullet rips through a person, things are going to be painful for a while.

The entire family has pulled together for us. Alex and Josh were both really good about helping Gavin shower and move around the first few days. I love how big and muscular he is, but it means I can't take his weight the way it needed to be. He needed quite a bit of help. He was grouchy as hell about all of it, but it was necessary and far better than hiring a nurse. Which would have been male because hello? Gavin is hot. And mine.

I didn't realize how exhausted I would be helping him, so I was truly grateful that the family came by and cooked us dinner. Ryan always made sure to make enough to last us a couple of days so we could freeze it. When Josh said that they all take care of each other, I guess I never really expected the level they all go to for each other. It's so touching and heartwarming to see.

It also feels amazing to not be an outsider. We've all gotten past that, and I've been accepted wholeheartedly into this amazing family. It's something I guess I never really believed would happen to me. It's so different from everything I'm used to.

We've also hired a housekeeper. Gavin did have one that came once a week, but her services had been canceled when he'd gone to Texas. He didn't know how long he'd be gone and saw no point in having someone around when he wouldn't be. There was no point since I'd been staying with Arianna and Ryan.

With everything that had gone on, he completely forgot about rescheduling his housekeeping services. When I brought it up to him, thinking that it would help me out so my focus could be on him, he got embarrassed. It was so adorable that I laughed. The housekeeper now comes once a week again and will even if we aren't here because things get dusty whether we're around or not.

"I feel oddly content that dad can retire now."

"Me too." I look up at him. "Did we ever figure out who sent that letter to him? The threatening one?"

"Lance tracked it to Charles' dad, Gregory. He said something about the origin being from Greece." He twists a strand of my hair around his finger as he shuts the TV off. "Doesn't mean I still don't have protection on him. Not knowing Gregory's whereabouts is a huge fucking concern." He kisses my forehead.

"I hope we find him before I start school next fall," I say giddily. "I'm really excited for it."

Gavin smiles. "I've never seen anyone as excited for college as you are." He gently pulls me into his lap so that I'm straddling him.

I blush and wrap my arms over his shoulders. "It always seemed kind of unattainable to me. The fact that I actually get to go… I think out of everything you've done for me since I met you, college might be the best thing." I give him a teasing smile.

He laughs and hugs me tighter. "Huh. Even better than me clothing you and giving you a place to live when you lost everything?"

I giggle and nod. "Yep."

His hands find their way to my butt. He smiles wider. "Even better than the multiple orgasms I give you daily?"

I laugh and nod. "Even better than those."

"What about saving your life?"

"Well, am I really totally out of danger yet?"

He swats my ass and squeezes it. "Point taken. Okay. How about this? Even better than me putting a ring on your finger and giving you all of my love?"

I nibble my lip and tilt my head as if I'm thinking. "Hmm…" I tilt my head the other way.

Gavin laughs and swats me again. "Fucking brat. Adorable, but a damn rebel."

I lean in and hug him. "I don't care about anything else, including college, as long as you love me."

He hugs me to him tighter. "You'll never have to worry about that."

I giggle against his neck when I feel his length poking me. "Someone wants to be free."

He nibbles my neck. "It's not his fault. You're positioned perfectly over me, and I fucking miss you."

I run my fingers through his hair. "I know, but you have to heal. We don't want to risk injuring you more."

"You know I asked the doc about it."

"I'm just being extra careful, Gav. I…"

He tangles his fingers in my hair and tugs lightly as I take a deep breath. I know I don't need to tell him that I'm being extra careful with him because of how close we were to losing him. How close I was before I even got a real chance to show him how much I love him. I'm afraid of jostling him too much or being too rough.

Since he had been shot, Josh has made sure he's taking care of himself. That I am. He has been going to physical therapy and having regular checkups. Josh has completely taken over all things mafia. Well, the tasks that were usually done by Gavin as second in command. He has given Gavin work to keep him busy, but nothing strenuous. It drives Gavin crazy, but he understands it will take time for him to be back in top shape.

Over the past month, we've learned a lot of things about the Ruthless Warriors. Charles is the one who saw me. That was something he'd told Gavin before Josh and I got there. He showed up one night when I wasn't supposed to be working. I'd taken an extra shift. It was the night I found out about them. He became instantly enamored with me.

The guard who shot Gavin was a plant. One that Gregory was very happy to take credit for. He didn't care at all about his death. Turns out the guard knew his assignment well. Take out as many of the head guys of Lucinio Mafia as he could. He knew he'd be killed. I've never understood why people take assignments they know they won't make it out of alive. It's like our version of a suicide bomber. What kind of psych does a person have to have in order to be okay with an assignment like that?

Gregory Franklin has seemingly vanished once more. Josh has made sure he has surveillance on every single hideout we know about, but we still have no idea where his steady stream of money is coming from. Matthew Lucinio is gone. All of his accounts have been closed out, thanks to Robby and Lance. All the money laundering he was doing has been cleaned up. There's nothing coming from Matthew Lucinio's ghost. We know that Gregory was probably getting money from his brother, but with him also gone, it doesn't appear to be coming from him either.

Not to say Lance hasn't enlisted Robby's help in looking into Edward Franklin to make sure everything with him is also nicely tied up. Any accounts they knew about have been closed and deleted.

Gavin tugs my hair gently until I am looking at him. "I'm here, baby. I'm okay. Doc says I'm okay to do everything except the training I was doing. And I can't go back to actively running missions for a while. But it doesn't mean I can't start doing normal things." He grins. "You know. Things that don't involve my tongue in your pussy or your mouth around my dick."

I squeak and blush. "Gavin!"

He laughs. "I mean it. I want you. It's been a long time, and I miss that level of intimacy. Not to say blowjobs aren't great, and you know I love the taste of you, but enough is enough."

I look at him with as much concern as I can possibly muster. "Are you sure?"

He grins and locks his hands behind his head. "Yes. But if you want me to not strain myself, I wouldn't mind you just riding me."

I feel my cheeks flame red again. "You're awful."

He pushes me down against his hard cock and groans. "Put me out of my misery. I'm dying here."

He reaches down and starts undoing his belt as he watches me. He unbuttons and unzips his pants. I watch in complete fascination and probably a lot of infatuation. He is right. It has been a very long time since he's been seated deep inside me.

He reaches into his jeans and boxer briefs, his eyes never leaving mine. My mouth goes dry as he pulls out his long, thick length and starts slowly stroking it. He's already hard, but his touch only makes him harder. Bigger. I still can't believe he can fit inside me.

"Tempted?" he rumbles as he strokes.

I let out a tiny whimper as I nod and lick my lips. I stand, not taking my eyes off his dick. He doesn't take his off me. I shiver under his sexy gaze as he watches me pull off my sweater and tug down my jeans. I step out of them while he pushes his own jeans down his thighs. I reach around and release myself from my bra and drop it into my pile of clothing.

"You're still clothed…," I whisper and finally tear my eyes away from his glorious member that he still hasn't stopped slowly stroking. I look at him through my lashes. "That hardly seems fair."

"Well, you see, I got shot about a month ago." He grins with a wink that's as sexy as it is adorable. "I need a little help."

I giggle because I know he doesn't, but I oblige his request because he's so sexy that I can't help it. I pull his jeans and underwear down and put them on top of my clothes. Then I straddle him and start lifting his shirt. He grins and stops stroking himself long enough to lift his arms so I can get the shirt off.

"You always wear black shirts. You should get a girlfriend with fashion sense to help dress you more stylishly."

Gavin cracks up. "My girlfriend has a terrible fashion sense. She walks around all frumpy. Maybe you'll have to help me out. You always look like a million dollars."

I giggle. "A billion. My boyfriend is a billionaire."

"Is he? Or does he just work for a billionaire? Me on the other hand." He waggles his eyebrows. "I really am a billionaire. You can ask my financial guy. He works for Shaw Incorporated now. That Chase Shaw asshole bought out the company my guy worked for today."

I laugh as I ease myself down on Gavin's cock with a hiss. "God. You're so big. I'll never understand how I stretch that far to fit you. You're gigantic."

Gavin grins as he locks his arms around my waist. "A woman's pussy is a mysterious thing. How you can squeeze something the size of a watermelon out of something smaller than a lemon is beyond my IQ level."

I turn crimson and squeak as I get used to his size. "Gavin!" I shake my head. "That. Right there. It's the entire reason I never wanted kids."

"Well, good thing. Because I'd get a reversal on my vasectomy if you asked me to, but I hear it's painful, and I don't want any part of it. I was just fucking shot, you know." He starts moving my hips over him.

"Mmm…" My eyes roll back in my head at the feel of him. I lean back and grip his wrists as I move slowly up and down his length while he moves me over him. "So big…"

His hands move across my butt and up my back. My hands move up his arms until they reach his shoulders once more. "So tight." He grins. "And all mine."

I kiss him as I keep slowly moving up and down and thrusting my hips back and forth. Gavin's tongue slides between my lips. His fingers find their way to my hair just as our tongues begin the familiar fiery dance only they know. He tugs my hair as he pulls away, gently sucking on my tongue. He trails kisses down my chin to my throat, then to my neck.

"Oh, Gav…," I moan. I clench around him as I keep slowly moving up and down his dick. I spread my legs a little wider, taking him even deeper into my pussy as I tighten around him.

"Fuck, baby…," he moans, letting his head fall back with a low groan.

I moan softly as I rise slowly. I pause with just his head inside me. I clench purposely around his tip and twist my hips as I thrust back down, slightly harder than before. I let my head fall back as I moan and rise again, repeating the move.

"Oh, God… Yes, Gav…," I twist my hips and slide back down his length. I lean down and kiss him deeply, biting down lightly on his lip as I shift, sliding his dick deep into my pussy and start to thrust back and forth at a faster pace, but still being careful not to jostle him too much.

And oh, he feels so fucking good.

"Holy shit, baby," his eyes widen with a low moan. His hand grips my hip tightly as he helps guide the pace. I arch and moan as I feel him start to thicken inside me as he pushes lightly up into my pussy while he pulls me into his thrusts.

"Oh! Yes!" My eyes roll back and my pussy pulses erratically around his dick. My thighs start to tremble as I clench uncontrollably around him. I moan and whimper feeling every ridge of his thick length as he guides my pussy over his dick faster and harder.

"Fuck! So tight and wet for me," he rumbles with a grunt as he tugs my hair, leaning up to kiss me, deeper this time than the last. I let out a soft whimper as I meet his passionate kiss with a ferocious need of my own.

I suck on his tongue with a moan as my pussy gets tighter and tighter around him. I buck into his shallow thrusts as I teeter on the edge of falling into the pure desire he's spreading throughout my entire body. But I refuse to come yet. I won't without him.

I kiss down his jaw to his neck with quiet whimpers and moans. My pussy pulses erratically. My skin against his just like this after so long feels so amazing that I nearly lose all control and ride him hard and fast.

"Gavin, I'm so close," I whisper against his neck. My thighs tremble. I grip his shoulders tighter. "So, so close."

"Come, baby," he commands against my neck. "Let go for me." He kisses my shoulder.

So, I do.

I throw my head back with a shout. "Gavin!" My entire body feels like it quakes as my walls collapse. "Ah!" My stomach clenches as hard as my pussy, and I come, thrusting over him as uncontrollably as my pussy is pulsing.

Gavin digs his fingers into the backs of my thighs as his dick stills deep inside me just before it starts jerking. "Oh, fuck yes…," he moans as he moves me back and forth over his cock.

He fills my pussy and pulls me into him. We both tremble against each other. We hold one another tightly and pant as we both start coming down. Gavin's dick slowly stops jerking as my pussy quits pulsing, but neither of us move for a long while.

I jump at a knock on the door and groan. "Tell them to go away. I can't move."

Gavin laughs. "I'm pretty sure that's Josh. He said Lance found something, and he'd be over today."

My eyes widen and I look at him. "About Gregory?"

Gavin smiles and kisses me as he slowly pulls out. "I'm not sure. He was really secretive about it. Just said he'd be over sometime today."

The next knock is a little louder and spurs me into action. I get off Gavin gently but quickly get dressed. I help Gavin get his underwear and jeans back on and hand him his shirt when the knocking gets more insistent.

"Coming!" I yell as I hurry for the door. When I open it, Josh is standing on the other side grinning from ear to ear. I shake my head. "Don't say it. I know what you're thinking."

He laughs. "Okay. I won't say it. I'll ask it. Did he enjoy the ride?"

I swat him and laugh. "Shut up!"

Josh grins and holds up an envelope. "Lance found something I think you'll want to see. Is he decent enough for me to come in?"

I giggle. "If you don't mind seeing him shirtless. He gave me a pitiful look when I handed it to him to put on."

Josh groans teasingly. "Great. Just what I needed. Gavin strutting around like a peacock all proud of his abs and shit."

I close the door behind him and follow him, giggling. "He's just able to start doing a few things with working out. His abs are a little less defined, but he's getting them back. Be nice to him."

"I'm always nice." Josh grins as he takes a seat in a chair near the couch.

As predicted, Gavin has tossed his shirt over the back of the couch and is just turning the fireplace on. I settle next to him and pull the fleece blanket over us both. Gavin, I swear, is never cold. Even when the temperature outside is freezing. It's a good thing for me. He's like my own personal furnace.

He hugs me close, and I snuggle into him as he takes the envelope Josh gives him. "What's this?" Gavin asks. "That information you were talking about?"

"It is. I thought Harleigh would like to see it. Give her a little closure."

I tilt my head as Gavin opens the envelope. "What is it?"

"You'll see," Josh says with a smile.

"Oh shit," Gavin says as his eyes widen. He hugs me tighter and turns the document he's holding towards me.

"It took a little bit. But Lance found it. Something about finding an email address and an app. I don't know." Josh leans back as he watches me. "But he found it.

I furrow my eyebrows. "It's an email to you?" I look up at Gavin, confused and unsure if I should read it. Gavin nods and hands it to me.

I take it. Tears immediately sting my eyes when I see who it's from. "My father," I whisper over the lump in my throat.

Mr. Vandenberg,

You don't know me, but I know who you are. I know what you do. And I know who you work for. I don't care. It doesn't matter to me. You care for my little girl. Your messages to her show me that. I need your help to keep my little girl safe.

I sniffle and curl up closer to Gavin unsure where my dad is going with this.

A while ago, I was approached by the Ruthless Warriors. As I know you're aware, they were shaking down several businesses in the area my diner is located. While this was occurring, I got sick. They offered to pay off my medical bills for a greater cut of my earnings every month. But nothing I gave them was good enough. They always wanted more and more.

I was able to keep Harleigh away from their sight for a while, at least I thought I had. I put her on shifts opposite to when they would come in. One day, however, she was covering another girl's shift. I didn't know at the time, but they saw her that night. They came back with more threats. This time they didn't want money. They wanted Harleigh. They wanted me to sell my little girl to a pimple-dipped manchild, the leader's son. I refused. They left. But I knew it wouldn't be the end of it. Not for men like them.

My lower lip trembles. "I didn't know that," I whisper. " I didn't know that was the night they decided they wanted me."

Gavin hugs me tighter and runs his hand up and down my arm as I continue reading.

I couldn't risk them killing me and just taking her, so I came up with a compromise. And believe me, it made me sick to even offer it. I told them that when she was of age, I would sign a contract for her hand. But while they believed I was giving them what they wanted, I was actually searching for a way to keep her out of their hands.

After she turned eighteen, I ended up in the hospital. I begged the Ruthless Warriors for more time with her. I told them I needed her help. I was able to hold them off for a while, and they agreed to continue paying my bills, but they were running out of patience. I was running out of time. I knew it.

I put my hand over my mouth as the tears I'd been fighting so hard start to fall. "You knew," I whisper to my father. "Oh, dad…"

I see Josh move to my other side, but I barely feel him joining Gavin in hugging me. I know he says something, but I don't hear him.

And then you happened. I knew my little girl had met her one when she came in lit up like a Christmas tree. Even as I watched her ignore messages and calls because of her self-image, self-confidence, and self-worth. I knew she would never find another. I told her not to give up on you because she would regret it for the rest of her life. True love doesn't strike twice in a lifetime. I learned that with her mother. I knew you'd be the one to make her see the amazing woman she is while loving her as she deserves to be. And, selfishly, I knew you were my way out.

I had already been trying to contact Lucinio Mafia when the Ruthless Warriors came back for Harleigh. I was turned away. I couldn't even get to the Security desk of Lucinio Tech. The receptionist on the main floor refused to pass on a message for me. I have sent texts, but I fear they know about it or stopped it somehow. I found your card on her nightstand tonight while she was in the shower. As she peacefully sleeps, I find myself praying to a God that I don't really believe in that this email will reach you because I know you're my last chance. Her only chance.

The tears are fully streaming down my face now. I look up at Gavin. "How? How could they not pass on the message? Why would they do that?"

"I don't know, baby," Gavin says quietly.

I stand with the email in my hand and shake my head. I wipe my eyes. "It doesn't make sense. He was asking for help!"

"Harleigh, I have people looking into it, honey. It's not the first time we've been infiltrated by the enemy. You know that better than anyone. It's certainly not going to be the last," Josh says. I stare vacantly at him as his words, which I heard, seemingly don't sink in. "Come sit down."

I take another deep breath and sit. Except it's on the floor underneath my feet. I wipe my eyes again and continue to read.

She'll need you more than ever when I'm gone. She has no one, and I know my time is up. Please, keep my little girl safe, and tell her that I love her. Tell her I'm so very sorry I couldn't do more to protect her.

"Oh, dad," I whisper and shake my head. "I'm sorry. I'm so sorry I spent so much of this time angry with you when I should have been grieving!" I cover my face with my hands and let the tears loose.

I barely feel Josh pulling me up and settling me into Gavin, but Gavin's strong arms and masculine scent soon wrap around me. I clutch the email in my hand as I hug him and let him hold me.

I have no idea how long I cry, but when I finally pull away from Gavin's chest, Josh isn't in the room with us any longer. Arianna and the rest of the girls have arrived and are all surrounding the two of us. Raleigh gently rubs my back as Arianna hugs me as tightly as Gavin is.

I don't say anything. I don't need to. I've come to learn rather quickly that when something happens in this family, no matter how big or small, everyone comes together. I don't need to look outside to know all the guys are out there helping Josh grill something delicious. It's just how everyone here works.

I stay curled into Gavin, still not saying anything because I simply have no words for the gratitude I feel for everyone, and finish reading the email.

Above all else, make sure that you give her all of the love that I never did. I was never the perfect father, but I have always only wanted what's best for my little girl. Please make sure she knows I'll be looking in on her from time to time. And my love for her will not pass with me. That it will surround her forever.

Presumptuously your future father-in-law
Jake Harlow

I fold the letter carefully and put it back in its envelope. I clutch it to my chest knowing that this is something that I will cherish forever.

Dad, I don't know if you can hear me or not. I take a breath and look up towards the ceiling. I smile softly. *But I love you. Thank you for this. I'm sorry I was so confused and doubted your intentions. I hope you'll forgive me.* My heart feels lighter and lighter the more I let myself talk to him. The more I feel him around me. *Thank you for doing all you could to protect me. But mostly, thank you for being the best father you knew how to be. And for leading me to Gavin. I know that was you. He's my forever. You knew that before me.* I close my eyes. I swear I feel his arms around me. *I love you,* I whisper to him. *Always.*

As if everyone has felt the weight I've carried lift off my shoulders, the confusion I've felt over my father's actions dissipate, I feel the mood in the room shift from somber to something else. Something… something I need.

Happy.

Joyous.

At peace…

The End

Next In The Lucinio Family Series

The devilishly dark and alluring Lucinio Family Series continues with ***Encrypting My Heart***.

My entire life, I knew I was gay. The problem was, I didn't want to admit it to myself. So, I didn't. I dated women. A lot of them. I was even in a long term relationship with one. But I could never get off unless I was thinking about a guy. Well, let's be honest here.

One guy. One. My best friend, Lance.

We've worked together in the Lucinio Mafia for years. We're close. He's out, and he's proud of it. It's something I've always admired and secretly loved about him.

Just when I start to feel comfortable with myself and we're ready to reveal our relationship, though, chaos in the form of a sixteen-year-old girl whirls into our life, turning it upside down and backwards. She needs our help. We need her light.

But with her comes a Texas sized tornado of mayhem and a lot of questions that beg to be answered. I'm just not convinced we'll get those answers before the twister licking at our heels swallows us all whole…

Order ***Encrypting My Heart*** Today!

The Lucinio Family Series

Available on Amazon

Rising From The Ashes
The Player's Rebel
Encrypting My Heart

Other Books By Melony Ann
The Beautiful Dream Series

Available Now

Loving You
My Love, My Heart
Softening Lyric
Undercover Temptations
Captain Charming
Breaking Boundaries
Crashing Into You
Tactical Inferno
Ravishing Our Queen
Cherished By The Texan
Unveiling Our Passions

Box Sets Available

The Beautiful Dream Series: Box Set: Part 1
The Beautiful Dream Series: Box Set: Part 2

The Crane Family Series

Available Now

The Reluctant Mafia King
Sweet Lies
Billion Dollar Love Story
Be Mine
Protecting Her
Dangerously Forbidden Love
His Heart
Love In The Dark

Box Sets Available

The Crane Family Series

The Deimos Trilogy

Available Now

Connor's Legacy
Aryan's Alpha
Kade's Redemption

Box Sets Available

The Deimos Trilogy

The Forbidden Temptation Series

Available Now

The Detective's Forbidden Temptation
The Running Back's Forbidden Temptation

Multi Author Series
Piper Falls: Firehouse 49

Available Now

Ignite My Fire by Melony Ann
Regain My Fire by Kindra White
Playing With My Fire by D.L. Howe
Fight My Fire by Darley Collins
Against My Fire by Anneke Boshoff
Relight My Fire by Louise Murchie
Harness My Fire by Ayana Lisbet
Quench My Fire by Havana Wilder

Let's Be Friends

Follow me on

Bookbub

Facebook

Goodreads

Instagram

Tik Tok

Visit my website
www.melonyannauthor.com

Subscribe to my newsletter and get a FREE never-seen-before NOVELLA
just for subscribers!
https://www.melonyannauthor.com/exclusive-content

Join my Facebook Reader Group!
Jason's and Melony's Sizzling Book Nook

The official Lucinio Family Series Playlist on YouTube
https://youtube.com/playlist?list=PLGEiD5wbQmDdjFYhMKrFsomQOTr
RK7x9Y

Dedication

To the rebels of our hearts and the fire that guides our souls.

Acknowledgements

Brad - It gets so hard sometimes to put into words how grateful I am to you. I just love you.

Laura - My pretty angel. I love you to the edges of the universe and back.

Jay - I love you so much it hurts sometimes.

Ayana - I can't fathom what my world would be like without you in it. Thank you for always being on my side.

Anneke - One day our virtual hugs will become real. Until then, thank you so much for always being willing to send me one. Even when I don't really know I need it.

Jason - As I sit here doing all of these reformats, I can't help thinking that I really wouldn't be doing this without you. Thank you for all of your invaluable support.

To the Bookstagram Community.

To my family.

To all of those who believe in me and support me.

To all of those who don't.

Cover by: Carter Cover Designs

Edited by: Alyssa Skaggs

About Melony Ann

Melony Ann began writing short stories and poetry as a child. She continued honing her craft over the years until she took the plunge and began publishing her work, despite having severe anxiety.

Melony writes contemporary romance stories that are full of suspense and a lot of steam.

When she isn't writing, she is loving her family and working to make her life something she deserves.

Melony believes that if her writing can inspire just one person, then all of her hard work is worth it.

Her hope is that her writing allows each and every one of her readers to escape for a little while. To dive into a different world one book at a time.

www.ingramcontent.com/pod-product-compliance
Lightning Source LLC
Chambersburg PA
CBHW060548260626
47161CB00003B/1105